Parrot Talk

David B. Seaburn

The final approval for this literary material is granted by the author.

First printing

This is a work of fiction. Names, characters, businesses, places, events and incidents are either the products of the author's imagination or used in a fictitious manner. Any resemblance to actual persons, living or dead, or actual events is purely coincidental.

ISBN: 978-1-61296-855-1
PUBLISHED BY BLACK ROSE WRITING
www.blackrosewriting.com

Printed in the United States of America
Suggested retail price $17.95

Parrot Talk is printed in Adobe Garamond Pro

For Bonnie, with all my love

Parrot Talk

1

Millie watched as Janice pinned a slip of rolling paper to the table with her thumb and struggled to open the Ziploc baggie with her other hand.

"You okay?" said Millie as she rubbed her own temples with her fingertips.

"It's this damn arthritis." Janice leaned an elbow on the receipt and pulled on the baggie haphazardly with her gnarled fingers. With a deep sigh, she turned to Millie. "Here, can you open it?" Millie, the skin on her hands shrink-wrapped across brittle bones, studied the bag.

"Lucky they put this plastic nub on here." Millie gripped the nub between her thumb and forefinger, then slid it across the top of the bag. "There you go," she said, handing it back to Janice.

"There you go, there you go," said Paul.

"That's right, Paul," said Millie.

"Thank you, thank you."

Janice sprinkled weed across the paper and started to roll it.

"Doggone it," said Janice when most of the marijuana blew off the paper and fluttered through the balcony railing, disappearing long before it reached the street below.

"Do you have any more?"

"Jesus, yes," said Janice.

"Jesus, lover of my soul," said Paul.

Janice picked more weed from the baggie and spread it across the paper again.

"That's the spirit, Paul," said Janice.

"That's the spirit," said Paul. "Going in now. See Judge Judy."

"Why don't you just wait a bit longer?" Millie stroked the back of Paul's head.

Parrot Talk

Janice, hunched over the table, continued to grapple with the paper. "Goddammit, where did I put my good pair of hands?"

Millie winked at Paul and patted him again.

"We'll go back inside in a few minutes. Janice is getting my medicine ready."

"Yes, Dr. Janice is hard at work." Janice slid her tongue across the paper's edge and ran her dampened finger along the length of the joint to seal it.

"There," she said. "Do you have any matches?"

Millie reached down to the floor and picked up a long Bic lighter. She held it up and they both studied the metal wand with its red handle.

"Where'd you get that thing?"

"It was in the bag when the church deacons brought my groceries."

"Why the hell'd they give you something like that?"

"I can't make it work," said Millie. "Gotta press the one do-hickey forward and then kind of pull back on the trigger thingy."

Millie handed the lighter to Janice. Janice handed Millie the joint.

"Hmm." Janice turned the lighter over in her hands several times. She pressed here and pulled there. "Dammit."

"Go back in," said Paul.

"Don't worry, Paul, just a few more minutes."

Millie glanced across the Monongahela at the PPG tower, its cathedral-like spires glistening in the late afternoon sun.

"This ain't workin'," said Janice, dropping the lighter on the table.

"Huh?" said Millie, still taking in the view.

"Jesus," said Janice, pounding the lighter with her fist.

"Lemme look in the kitchen. Maybe I got some matches." Millie leaned forward in her chair and reached for her walker, her face wincing as she steadied her legs, her house dress falling straight as a potato sack.

"No you don't. You just sit yourself back down there, Millie Ingersoll." Janice got up and walked into the apartment, disappearing around the corner and into the galley kitchen.

Millie leaned back in her chair, her hand shading her eyes as she spied the great fountain at the confluence of the lazy rivers. A white river boat, its massive paddle churning, turned slowly and headed back up the Allegheny as a barge passed it going the other way. Across the Allegheny, sprawling on the shore was the arena, asleep for now, where her Steel City gladiators performed their mighty deeds. Just beyond it, laid the little brother, home of the emerging Bucs.

8

Cars and trucks sped across the slender bridges carrying the city's life blood to and fro. Millie's face settled, relaxed.

"Hit the jackpot," said Janice, clutching a box of matches and a bag of Doritos as she returned to the balcony.

"Seems like a lot of trouble," said Millie.

"No trouble at all."

"I probably shouldn't even be doing…"

"Now don't you start that again. You know it always makes you feel good."

"Against the law, you know."

"Law? What law? What happens in the privacy of your own place ain't no one else's business."

"What would God say about an old woman—"

"He'd say, 'Mind if I pull up a chair and have a toke?'"

Millie curled the corners of her mouth and shook her head.

Janice lit the joint and drew on it long. She held her breath, her face tight as a drum, like she was waiting for the smoke to reach her toes. Then she exhaled. "Oh my, that's good." She held it out to Millie, who frowned and then took it between her thumb and pointer. She studied it for a moment.

"I don't know why I ever let you talk me into this, Janice Beechem."

"Cause you know I love you and would do anything for you, old woman."

"Old woman for sure. Smokin' reefer." Millie inched the joint toward her lips.

"Reefer madness," said Paul.

Millie chuckled as she drew on the joint. She coughed hard. "My goodness me." She drew again and handed it back to Janice. "Enough."

"What's 'at?" said Janice.

"My legs are sticks of butter on my best day. I don't need them to melt completely."

"Come on," said Janice, drawing again.

Millie took a handful of Doritos. "Look at that sunset."

Janice leaned against the balcony and shook her head.

"Makes those muddy rivers look mighty pretty."

"Mighty pretty," said Paul.

"You got that right," said Millie, smiling at Paul.

A man stepped onto the neighboring balcony and glared around the corner at them.

"Am I smellin' what I think I'm smellin'?"

Parrot Talk

"If you don't like it, Frank, go back in your goddam apartment," said Janice.

"I shouldn't have to stay inside just because of you two old druggies. My God, put yinz together and yinz must be a hundred and fifty, if you're a day."

"And proud of it. Just hush up," said Janice.

"I oughta call the cops on yinz two, you know that?" Millie grinned and waved. "Gosh darn it, what are you doin' to her, Janice?"

"Tend your own business, Frank, or I'll tell Ellie why you're always stopping by 108."

"Tend your business, Frank," said Paul.

"That's right," said Janice. "You tell 'im."

Frank turned away, waving his hand limp-wristedly as he went back into his apartment.

"Such a nice man," said Millie, her smile fixed, her eyelids at half-mast. "Who was that nice man?"

Millie reached again for the Doritos.

"So, Millie, wha'd the doctor say this time?"

Millie tipped her head to one side and put a hand to her ear as if she couldn't hear.

"The doctor. What did he say?"

Millie raised her eyebrows and chomped on her chips. Janice waited for her to swallow. Millie reached for the chips again.

"Wait a minute, Mill," said Janice.

"Wait a minute, wait a minute, wait a minute—"

"Shut up for once, Paul," said Janice.

"You shut up," said Paul.

"Listen to me; don't take another bite," she said, her hand up like a stop sign. "What did the doctor say?"

"The same thing he always says."

Millie was into the Doritos again.

"My God, woman, I'm glad you *didn't* smoke more." Millie's mouth was full.

"Why dontcha just put the bag over your head?"

"What'd you say?" said Millie. She put the bag down and wiggled her feet into her slippers.

"The doctor. What'd the doctor say about your chest pain?"

Millie shielded her eyes with one hand and looked at the sunset, layered in pink and purple and grey.

"Millie?" Janice leaned forward and tapped her friend's arm.

"Huh?"

"The doctor?"

Millie sighed and shifted her weight. She turned to Paul, but he had drifted away. She looked at Janice from the corner of one eye.

"I'm an old woman, so it don't matter anyway."

"Don't give me that old woman crap. Eighty ain't old no more. You just got a worn out heap of a body."

Millie reached for another Dorito, then dropped it into her lap. She looked at Janice defiantly, her eyes popping wide under wedged brows.

"I didn't go to the doctor's."

"You didn't go?"

Millie waved for Paul to come close.

"Millie. For God's sake, why didn't you go? You been talking 'bout this chest thing for months."

"Don't feel bad at all right now," she said, pumping her fists up and down slowly, the waddle of her upper arms shaking like two half-filled water balloons.

"I'm sure it don't. Nothin' feels bad right now." Janice stood and leaned over the balcony, looking at the parking lot below, then turned again to Millie. "Look, Millie, this ain't right. Your heart can't take nothin' more. You know that. You don't want a repeat of last year, do you?"

Millie shrugged. "I can't hardly remember yesterday, let alone last year."

"Something's going on and you know it," said Janice. Millie smiled and took another handful of Doritos. "At least go back and hear what he's got to say."

"I know what he's gonna say—'Get some tests.' That's all he ever says."

"Maybe that's what you gotta do."

Millie took a single Dorito, turned it this way and that, stared at Janice, and then chomped off one corner truculently.

"Get tests, Millie; get tests," said Paul.

"Now he's making sense," said Janice, nodding to Paul. "Think of him if you ain't gonna think of yourself."

"Paul, you stay out of this, hear me?" said Millie.

"I mean, last week you couldn't hardly breathe, remember? You called me all panicky-like. 'What am I gonna do?' you said. 'Go to the doctor,' I said."

"Breathing fine now." Millie inhaled as deeply as she could before she started hacking.

"Yeah, right. A week ago, your arms were aching and you were throwin' up for no reason whatsoever. And that's just stuff you told me. Who knows what else goes on when I'm not around?"

Millie dropped the Dorito back into the bag.

"He wants me to get some test. It's called, I don't know, some letters. They stick you in a tube no wider than your shoulders. Bangs real loud the whole time is what he said." Millie straightened her back and jutted her jaw. "No reason to put myself through that."

Janice sat down again, her hands open, resting on her knees. "Don't you wanna know what's goin' on?"

Millie's eyes narrowed. "No. I don't."

"My God, you're damnable stubborn," said Janice.

"I'm the stubborn one?"

Janice placed a hand on Millie's knee. "Look, I'm not tryin' to be no bother. Just worried, that's all. Don't want nothing to happen to you."

Millie reached for the taped handles of her walker, pulling it near as she scooted forward in her chair. She rocked back and forth to gather some momentum.

"Here, lemme help you," said Janice, standing now.

"No, that's okay." Janice's arms fell to her side. Millie labored on, huffing and puffing until she was on her feet, grey curls stuck to her forehead. "Look at me. Smoked a joint. Ate a bag of Doritos. Now I feel like ten bucks." She caught Janice's eye. "If you were listening, you should be laughing."

Push, shuffle, push, shuffle, push, shuffle. Millie turned and backed up to the davenport. She let out a triumphant sigh as she tumbled into her spot opposite the TV. Janice stood by the bookshelf examining the salt and pepper shakers, puppies, kittens, cows, giraffes, taxi cabs, dice, Empire State buildings, roses. "Jesus," said Janice. "How long'd it take you to get all these."

"Long enough," said Millie. "God bless that Lillian Vernon lady."

"Ever use 'em?"

"Not for using."

Janice picked up a photograph from the top shelf and read the inscription: "*Wishing you many more Super Bowls, Franco Harris, #32.*"

"Franco, Franco!" said Paul.

"The man himself," said Millie.

"Yes, indeed."

Janice put the photo back in its spot, adjusting it so that it was angled just right. Then she picked up another photograph, this one older, cracked at the corners, yellowed. She held it close to her face and studied the two boys. One was a head taller than the other. They both had summer crew cuts and held fishing poles in their hands. They had squinty-eyed smiles, their heads cocked as if to avoid the sunlight flooding in from behind the photographer. The smaller one held his hand up. The bigger one's left hand was perched on his younger brother's head. There was a picnic table to one side and a lake in the background. Janice placed the photo gently back on the shelf, hoping not to make any noise.

"You're terrible quiet back there." Millie turned to see what Janice was doing.

"Just lookin' at all your stuff," said Janice. "Too bad it's the only picture you got." Millie turned back, silent. She reached for the remote and pointed it at the TV just in time to see Judge Judy read someone the riot act. "What was the younger one's name again?" Millie stared at the Judge.

"Oh, now I remember. Grinder." Janice waited. "And the other one was?"

Nothing.

"Lucas, that's right."

Millie snorted. "Why are you pretended you don't know anything?"

"This ain't my business, I suppose, but don't you think they oughta know what's going on with you?"

"You're right. None of your business," said Millie.

Janice sat down beside Millie. She reached for her hand.

"Look, Mill, we known each other for, well, forever, it seems. You know I'm not one to pry." Millie raised her eyebrows and chuckled. "Well, not usually, and never when it comes to them boys. But look at us. Life's gettin' short."

Millie squeezed Janice's hand and then let it go. "Janice, honey, you are the best friend I got in the world. But this ain't open for discussion."

"Between friends, everything's open for discussion," said Janice.

Millie's eyes widened. "Janice, Janice. If they came to my door, I wouldn't even recognize them. What could I possibly say to them after all these years?"

"Everything."

"And why should they listen?"

"Why shouldn't they?" said Janice.

Millie pursed her lips and turned back to the judge.

Parrot Talk

"Here comes the judge, here comes the judge," said Paul.

Janice folded her arms and watched Millie pat Paul's back.

"This here's my only boy now," said Millie. "My sweetie pie."

"What kind of pie?" said Paul.

"Don't you start now," said Millie, waving a hand at Paul and shifting her weight off her left hip.

"Okay, Okay," said Janice. "Knew I shouldn't have bothered."

"You are a good friend."

"You, too." Janice leaned nearer to Millie and hugged her.

"Always been a hugger, haven't you?" said Millie.

"Yes, I have." Janice kissed her cheek. "Better get back. Ronald's probably starvin' and I didn't leave him nothing to eat. Man worked in a steel mill for his whole life, but can he make himself a sandwich?"

"Your cross to bear."

"Yeah, well, that's a whole other conversation."

Janice gathered up her paraphernalia. Millie stared at the TV. Paul gawked at both of them.

"Okay, then. You let me know if you need anything, or if you feel sickly at all. Billy'll be by with another bag tomorrow. I'll save some back for you."

"You're one of the good ones, Janice."

"I try. That's about all you can do in this life." Janice waited but the conversation was over. "Okay." Millie wagged a hand at her.

When the door closed, Millie studied Paul for a long while. Paul pressed his head against Millie's shoulder.

"You're a good boy."

She rolled her neck to one side and then the other. She reached for her temple, then let her arms drop. "Jesus Christ," she whispered. "Got a damn thumper."

"A thumper," said Paul.

"Oughta just lop this head of mine right off," said Millie.

"Lop it off, Millie!"

"You foolish thing."

Millie leaned her head against the cushion and settled into *Judge Judy*, the evening news, *Wheel of Fortune* and, last but not least *Jeopardy*, although she couldn't answer a single question. "G'night, Alex," she said and clicked off the TV. Paul looked at her. "Okay, better get on with things. Gotta eat something. At least that's what they keep tellin' me."

Millie clutched the corner of her walker and hoisted herself out of the davenport. She reached for the floor lamp, turned on the light, and then stopped at the bookshelves to take down the picture.

"The boys," said Paul.

"Yep, Paul, the boys." She tried to put the photo back on the top shelf, but it slipped from her tingling hand and fell to the floor. She looked at it for a moment. She tried to bend over, then thought better of it.

"They'll have to stay there for now," she said, Paul looking on.

Millie shuttled into the kitchen, cane in hand this time, and took a can of Ensure from the stack on the counter. Paul watched as she removed a plate of leftover Kraft Macaroni and Cheese from the refrigerator, slid it into the microwave, set the time and pressed the button.

Millie sat at the kitchen table, leaning on her elbows to catch her breath.

"Oh my."

Millie laid her head on the table and closed her eyes. When she opened them, she balled her fists into her stomach and groaned. She stood but the room whirled, like she was on a merry-go-round. She flailed her arms, reaching fruitlessly for the molded plastic kitchen chair. She hit the linoleum floor with a thud. Millie rolled over, her arms falling limp at her side, and closed her eyes again.

The kitchen was quiet, except for the grinding whir of the microwave. The timer went off...*Ding!* But Millie didn't move.

"Millie, mac and cheese!" said Paul. "Mac and cheese!"

2

Grinder opened the truck door, his lanky legs almost reaching the pavement before he slid off the driver's seat. He stood for a moment, looking both ways, his work shirt hanging off him like a flag waving in the breeze. He wiped his nose on his sleeve and pulled his Buffalo Bills cap even with his eyebrows. He closed the truck door, snatched his work gloves and a bucket from the truck bed, then crossed to the middle of the street where a woman wearing a terry-cloth robe and slippers stood.

"What is that thing, anyway? It's not a rat, is it? I mean, I never seen a rat that big around here." She retreated to the curb and yelled at her two small sons who were watching from the front stoop. "Get back in the apartment, you hear me?"

Grinder waved several cars around the dead animal. He motioned for the woman to stay put. She stepped back up on the curb. Grinder knelt, his knees crackling; he put his gloves on and studied what was left of the animal. Back broken. Blood on the street. Intestines exposed. Beady eyes still open. Longish snout and thick tail.

"Just weren't quick enough," he whispered. Grinder ran his gloved hand across the animal's stiff grey fur.

"What the hell is that thing? Is it poisonous? Got rabies or something?"

"Never knew what hit you, huh?" said Grinder to the motionless critter. "Maybe that's good."

Grinder picked up the animal by its tail. The woman gasped and covered her mouth with her hands. "It's a 'possum," said Grinder.

"A what?"

"An o-possum," he said precisely, holding it out to the side like a prized catch.

"What the hell is a thing like that doing in the city? Ain't they supposed to be on a farm or something?"

"You'd be surprised," said Grinder. "The city's got just about everything. Deer, fox, coyotes even." The animal made a dull thud when he dropped it into his bucket.

"My God," said the woman. "And you gotta go around and pick them up?"

"Yes ma'am."

"What an awful job."

Grinder's eyes twinkled. "I guess so."

"Do I owe you anything?"

"No, ma'am, the city takes care of that."

"What do you do with them?"

"Eat 'em." Grinder squinted as a grin crossed his face.

"Oh," she said, her eyes wide, her face white.

"Actually, I keep them in a dumpster. Guy comes around and hauls them off to a factory." He pulled an apple from his pocket and took a bite.

"Well, I guess someone's gotta do this."

"This is true."

He raised his apple to her, as if tipping his hat, and crossed the street to his truck. He dropped the bucket in the truck bed and covered it with a plastic lid. He hoisted himself into the cab and stretched his back. The cell phone on the dashboard began to chirp *Sweet Home Alabama*. He looked at the number and rolled his eyes.

"Yeah."

"Where are you?" said Lucas.

"I'm right here." Grinder turned the key and the engine roared to life.

"Wherever the hell 'here' is, it's not where you're supposed to be. My phone's been ringing like crazy. People trying to get into the lot, but it's closed. No one's there. You're not there, Grinder."

"Had a pick up." Grinder looked in his side mirror and then pulled into traffic.

"Couldn't it wait? I mean it's a goddam dead animal. It's not going anywhere. I got people trying to get to work on time. They gotta park their cars, you know what I mean?" Lucas slammed his water glass on the counter.

"Lukie, you sound upset. Martha got you by the you-know-whats?"

"Don't call me Lukie. And don't talk to me about that woman."

"That woman? You mean your wife."

"She's not my wife." Lucas threw his head back and glared at the cell phone

17

in his hands.

"Living in your house?"

"What does that matter?"

"Mother of your child?"

"It's complicated and you know it."

"Sleeping together?"

"Not as often since the divorce. Hold on." There was a muffled argument going on in the background. Something crashed to the floor. "I'll clean it up. I'll clean it up, I said. Just leave me alone." Static followed. "Okay, I'm back."

"I'm on St. Paul, passing the Genesee Brewery," said Grinder. "Should be at the lot in a minute or two. It's only 6:45. Take a Xanax."

"She's going to drive me crazy. I'm telling you." Lucas pressed the phone to his chest. "Shut the fuck up, will you!"

"Don't cry to me. I told you she was a bad news right off the bat. Remember? You brought her around to meet me after a Red Wings game? She didn't like my apartment? Said it smelled?"

"It did smell."

"Not the point. It took three whole minutes before the two of you were fighting about some damn thing; oh yeah, whether to go to Nick's for a garbage plate or try out some high end café on Park Ave. that you couldn't afford."

"Yeah, yeah."

"She punched you. Remember?"

Lucas fell silent. "Okay, okay. It is what it is."

"Look"

"Don't 'look' me. I'm telling you, I'm gonna explode. I got Martha. I got the city breathing down my neck about taxes on that damn slab of concrete. I got a laundromat that's taking me to the cleaner. And I got you."

"Don't need to worry about me."

"Right."

"Like I said—"

"Don't 'like I said' me, Grinder. I wake up every morning and wonder whether you're gonna show up at the lot or not. Every day."

"Look, brother of mine, have I ever let you down?"

"Yes. You have. Remember college? Remember job after job? Do I have to go through the whole list?"

"That's ancient history. I'm talking about the parking lot. Have I ever not been there when it counted?"

Lucas didn't answer, but Grinder could hear the whistle in his nose.

"Calm down, Lukie."

"Don't call me that."

"Just chill. I got it. I'm pulling into the lot now. No problem. Everything's cool. Got to go." Grinder rolled into a spot beside his booth.

"Hey, wait a minute," said Lucas.

"What?" He was out of the car now and waving to cars lined up on the street.

"I gotta come by later to talk. Something's come up."

"Something's come up?" Grinder cupped his hand over one ear so he could hear.

"Yeah. I'm afraid so." Lucas's eyes were dull; his neck looked flushed.

"What is it?"

"Got a call last night. From Pittsburgh."

"Yeah. So."

"I been getting calls from an area code I didn't recognize so I just ignored them. You know what I mean? Must have been ten calls. I don't know."

"Okay. And?" Grinder walked across the lot, taking cash and sticking tickets under wipers.

"Area code was Pittsburgh."

"Uh huh."

Lucas stood up from the kitchen chair. He ran the palm of his hand across his bald head. His mouth was tacked up in one corner. "Well, when I saw the number again last night, I decided to answer. Don't ask me why. And this lady, Janice, I think it was, must have been in her late sixties somewhere by the sound of her, well she asks me if I'm Lucas Ingersoll. And I says, 'Yes, I am.' About now I'm ready to hang up, figuring she's gonna try to sell me something. But she says, 'Millie's son?'"

Grinder pulled the sliding door to his booth shut and slumped onto his stool. He looked out the window at a driver and waved her in. "She said what?"

Lucas leaned one hand on the kitchen counter.

"She asked if I was Millie Ingersoll's son."

Grinder opened the door to his booth and stepped outside again. He squinted into the morning sun and pulled his ball cap down a little further over his eyes.

"Grinder, you still there?"

"How did she find you? Was she IRS or something?"

"No, nothing like that. She was a friend, I guess." Lucas stood up and rubbed the back of his neck. He crossed the kitchen and went into the living room. He turned on the reading lamp over his lounger and took a seat. He wiped his face with a handkerchief and loosened his belt a notch.

"A friend?"

"I guess so," said Lucas.

"Lives in Pittsburgh."

"Who knew?"

"Did Pop ever say anything about Pittsburgh?"

"Pop never said anything about anything." Luca huffed.

"Pittsburgh." Grinder went back into the booth and turned the space heater on. Then off again. His jaw was clenched as he swallowed hard. "What did this woman want? What's her name?"

"Janice something." Lucas cleared his throat. He chewed the inside of his right cheek.

"A friend of Ma's. So Ma in trouble or something?"

"No. She's not in trouble. Janice says Ma died." Lucas got up from his lounger, a sweat stain up the back of his shirt. "So I guess she's dead."

Grinder pressed the cell phone to his chest as he waved angrily at two teenagers who were standing on the hood of a car parked in the far corner of the lot.

"Grinder? Are you there?"

Grinder took a rock from the box at his feet and threw it at them. The rock skipped harmlessly across the pavement and into traffic.

"Gregory? Did you hear me?"

Grinder pulled his shirt tail out of his pants and wiped sweat from his upper lip.

"Yeah. I heard you. She's dead. That's what you wanted to talk to me about?"

"Yeah."

"Didn't know she was alive. Now she's dead."

"Yeah." Lucas walked back into the kitchen, took a glass from the cupboard and pressed the button on the refrigerator for some crushed ice, then water.

"Did this Janice woman say anything? Is there gonna be a funeral or something?"

"Been dead a month, I guess," said Lucas.

"Huh. A month."

"She said it took that long to find one of us."

"So that's that," said Grinder.

"Well."

"Well, what?"

"That's not quite that."

"What do you mean? She's dead."

"I guess she left a bunch of stuff behind."

"Stuff? What kind of stuff?"

"I don't know exactly; pictures, clothes, I'm not sure; just a bunch of stuff."

Lucas gulped the water as he paced back and forth between the kitchen and living room. He waited for Grinder to respond. Nothing. "Look. I wanna come down there to talk to you about this. Martha can cover the laundromat."

"What's she want us to do with Ma's stuff?" Grinder dug his heel against the wall of the booth. The corner of his mouth was screwed up tight.

"I don't know. Look, it's not just her stuff. This Beechem woman said something about somebody called Paul." Lucas shook his head and shrugged.

"Paul?"

"Let me come down there."

"Who the fuck is Paul?"

3

"I told you not to buy that damn place. Who goes to the laundromat anymore? You're just throwing your money away." Martha shimmied on her spanks, then her jogging pants, and finally her PINK hoody. "If I didn't know better, I'd swear you bought it just to take a loss; just so you wouldn't have to pay me what I deserve." She ran a brush through her platinum hair, frowned into the mirror and sprayed her do, leaving a cloud of sticky mist in her wake. "But you're not smart enough to figure that angle. At least that's what my lawyer says." She turned to Lucas. "How do I look?"

"Like you always look."

"And people wonder why it didn't last."

"Look Martha, it'll just be for a little while." Lucas lay back on the bed, his arms outstretched.

"I don't care," said Martha, her nose in the air.

"I gotta go see Grinder."

"Again, I don't care."

"C'mon." Lucas propped himself up on his elbows.

"Why do you have to talk to him? What's that loser done now?"

"Nothing. We need to talk about something. No big deal."

Martha brushed past Lucas in search of her Sketchers. Lucas studied her broad bottom.

Martha glanced over her shoulder. "Still gets to you, huh?" she said.

"Grinder?" Lucas shrugged.

"No, my ass."

"Oh. Yes. Your ass still gets to me. Oh boy. Oh baby."

"Smart-aleck," said Martha, as she bent over to tie her sneaks. Struggling to breathe, she sat back on the bed and crossed one leg over the other. "We'll see how you are when my ass is strictly off limits."

"And when exactly will that be? I need to plan ahead. Whatever will I do?"

"Shut up!" Martha, her face beet red, stood up and pulled the waistband of her hoody down around her hips. "So?" she said, making a slow turn.

"You look fine."

"Thank you." Martha pinched Lucas's cheeks together with one hand and kissed his lips. "Why do you treat me like shit, Lucas? What did I ever do to you?" she whispered, her warm breath on his face.

"You married me," said Lucas.

"You know I would never have done that if you hadn't asked me."

"Then I guess I brought this all on myself."

"I guess you did," said Martha, pressing her palms against his chest and gently pushing him back on the bed. "So what's this 'no big deal' that you have to talk to Grinder about? His dumpster full of dead crap again? Neighbors complaining about the stink?"

"No, nothing like that," said Lucas, sitting up again.

"I'm telling you, he's nuts. Selling, like, dead animals," she sputtered. "Who the hell wants to buy a bunch of rotten smelling rats and dogs and God knows what else?"

Lucas reached for a tissue and blew his nose. He balled the paper and tossed it toward the waste basket in the bathroom. It bounced off the wall. He went into the bathroom, picked up the wad and dropped it into the toilet. Martha stood in the doorway, weight on one leg, hand on hip, a frown in the corner of her mouth, her penciled eyebrows raised in an inverted 'V'.

"What?" said Lucas.

"What's up, Lucas? You never just go talk to your brother unless there's a reason and usually the reason involves trouble."

"Look. I'm telling you there's no trouble. Alright?"

Martha sighed, shook her head, and relaxed her formidable eyebrows. "You know, Lucas, if you'd've just learned to talk to me, we might have stayed together."

"Might have stayed together?" he said, his fleshy arms outstretched. "This is about as together as two people can get. Is that your stuff in the medicine chest?"

"Lucas, you know what I mean."

"Is that your underwear in the dresser over there?"

"Lucas—"

"Is that you standing right smack dab in the middle of the bathroom? I mean, really, have we ever been more together?"

"I guess you're going to be a fuck today," said Martha. "But, you know what? I'm not going to be a fuck. I refuse to play your game. Where are the damn keys for the laundromat? I'll look after that dump for you, alright? Even though I wouldn't be caught dead in there. And you know why I'm going? I'll tell you why. Because somewhere up there, someone's keeping track of all this shit and in the end you're gonna pay, Lucas, you're gonna…" Lucas's face was buried in a Kleenex as he blew his nose again and again, folding and refolding the tissue, studying the results of his efforts. "Why say anything to you?" she said, stomping toward the bedroom door. "I'm outta here."

"Wait," said Lucas, his sausage hands hanging at his side now, empty.

Martha stopped in the hallway, but didn't turn.

"Look. It's my mother."

"Your mother?" Martha turned, her head cocked. "Mildred?"

"Yeah."

"Are you kiddin' me?"

"No, I'm not kidding you."

"Geez. Your mother."

"Yeah, Ma."

"What the hell does she want? I mean, after all this time. What's it been? Thirty-something years, I'll bet. The bitch never even came to our wedding."

"We didn't invite her. We didn't even know where she was."

"Doesn't matter. She should have been there. How'd she find you? You were a kid and now she wants something. I hope you told her to take a hike."

Lucas told her about Janice what's her name and the phone call and what had happened.

"She's dead? Your mother's dead? How is that possible?"

Lucas put his hands in his pockets and shrugged.

"It happens. Anyway, that's why I have to talk with Grinder."

"My God. Where is she?"

"Pittsburgh."

"Pittsburgh for chrissakes. All these years and that's where she was?"

"Yeah, I guess." Lucas's eyes rested on the space between him and Martha, his clenched jaw struggling to support his doubled chin.

"Well. Good riddance," said Martha. "She was no kind of mother. You deserved better. Grinder, not so much, but you, yes."

"So, you can watch the laundromat for a while?" Lucas dug into his pocket for the keys, then handed them to her. "Thank you."

"You're not gonna have to pay for a funeral, are you? I'm telling you, we can't afford it. It's highway robbery anyway and she doesn't deserve—"

"No, that's over and done."

"Okay. So, what's left?"

"Just some odds and ends, that's all."

"Are these 'odds and ends' going to cost you? 'cause my lawyer says—"

"Shit, Martha." Lucas wiped a bead of sweat from his reddened forehead. "You and the damn money. You know, I gotta say this: Fuck your lawyer. This isn't about you. It isn't about us. It's about my goddam mother."

"Okay, okay," said Martha, losing her balance as Lucas passed.

"I'll call you later."

"Lucas? Honey?"

Traffic on 490 was slow as he neared his exit. The light standards were dark, and the parking lot was empty at Frontier Field. The once great pinnacle of Kodak Office cowered in the background, tiles missing from its roof. Lucas took the Inner Loop, crossing the brown Genesee, and exiting onto St. Paul. Downtown was quiet, empty, even on a work day. He could see Grinder in the distance, his long, wiry body, posture like a praying mantis, Bills cap turned around on his head. Lucas honked his horn. Grinder turned. Lucas waved. Grinder nodded. As Lucas surveyed the quarter block of city property that was his lot, he felt like J.R. Ewing pulling into South Fork.

"What's all that junk?" said Lucas, pointing to some beer bottles and boxes and hefty bags in the corner of the lot. "It's a damn mess. I told you the city doesn't like eyesores."

"Morning," said Grinder, picking his teeth with a stir stick.

"Just clean it up, okay?"

"Yessir," said Grinder, saluting indignantly. A car pulled into the lot. Grinder pointed the driver to an open space, tore the ticket in half, sticking one part under the windshield wiper and keeping the other. "Have a good day, man."

"Almost full," said Lucas.

"Been pretty good today," said Grinder, stuffing cash in his pocket.

"Why don't you put it in the cashbox?"

"Don't want to."

"Getting mugged wasn't enough."

"Guess I'm not as smart as I look."

Lucas rubbed his face with his left hand, his lips tightening.

After a long moment, Grinder walked back to the booth. He opened the cashbox and deposited the money, then locked it again and dropped the box in the desk drawer, locking it, as well. He reached for his cup of coffee and returned to the lot.

"So, what's this all about?"

"She's dead. That's about all I know."

"So you said." Grinder squinted into the morning sun. "How'd she die?"

"Don't know."

"Don't know?"

"Didn't ask."

"Uh huh."

"I don't know. I didn't ask. What can I say?"

"Doesn't matter."

Lucas strode over to the boxes, crushed them with his foot and then stacked them against the neighboring building. He kicked several Genny beer bottles behind the pile of boxes.

"Don't want this place to look like a goddam slum."

"It *is* a goddam slum."

"Well, it doesn't have to look like one, does it?"

Grinder kicked an empty milk carton and a Gatorade bottle toward the pile of boxes.

"So, why did this person, whatever her name is…"

"Janice something," said Lucas.

"…Janice something, call us?"

"Well, she's our mother. I mean, she was," said Lucas, shrugging his shoulders.

Grinder poured his cold coffee on the cement, crushed the cup and tossed it in a long arc toward the trash barrel beside the booth.

"Two points," said Lucas.

"Three." Grinder crushed some newspaper and tossed it, as well. Then some more.

Lucas frowned at Grinder, took a deep breath, holding it for an extra beat before letting it out in increments. He tilted his head to one side, then the other, listening for a crack in his neck.

"Look, Grinder, about Ma."

Grinder turned his cap around, pulling the brim down, his eyes barely visible.

"This Janice something woman said Ma left some stuff behind and she didn't want to be the one—"

"Sure Janice something is for real?"

"Yes, I'm…Why would some woman call me out of the blue from Pittsburgh and tell me our mother died if it wasn't for real?"

"She was living in an apartment in Pittsburgh all this time." Grinder's light grey eyes went dark under the awning of his cap.

"Yeah." Lucas leaned against the booth.

"Who's Paul? Why can't he take care of it?"

"Beats the hell out of me. I asked her and she got all twitchy, like she was hiding something. She said, 'You'll understand when you get here.' I figure maybe he's retarded, or what do they call it now, developmentally messed up or something."

"Great." Grinder turned to his brother, leaning over him like a willow. "I don't think we need to do this."

"C'mon."

"Really?"

"Look, we'll drive down together. I'll pay for a motel room. We'll meet Janice something. We'll figure things out. We'll have dinner together. Y'know? You and me." Lucas reached for Grinder's forearm. "Okay?"

Grinder leaned against the booth and folded his arms. "Remember what she said? 'I'll be back, boys; I'll be back in an hour or so.'"

"Don't do this," said Lucas.

"'Where you going, Ma?' 'Just going to the mall, honey.'"

"Grinder."

"'Can you get me some sweat socks, Ma? I need them for gym.' 'Sure, I can. I'll be right near Sears.'"

"C'mon, man."

Another car pulled into the lot. Grinder grinned and gave her a ticket. "Let's see. I was eleven. So you must have been, what?"

Lucas crossed his arms, resting them on his belly.

"Fifteen?" Grinder leaned forward and stood up, slipping his hands into his pockets. The sun slid behind a building and the air went chill.

"Yeah," said Lucas, his doughy chin resting on his chest.

The brothers watched as an ambulance sped through the intersection, an old man barely making it to the curb. "Look, Grinder. I'm going to do this. I'm going to Pittsburgh." Lucas pulled his trousers up at the hips. "And I'd like you to come with me."

Grinder bent over to tie his left shoe. The lace broke.

"Jesus, why don't you buy a new pair of shoes?"

"Just need new laces. I'm not a rich fat-cat like you."

"And you never will be," said Lucas.

"Another one in the win column for you," said Grinder, licking the tip of his finger and slicing the air with it.

"So?" said Lucas.

"Who's going to mind the store?"

"We'll just double Archie's shifts. He won't care."

"I don't know," said Grinder.

"C'mon."

Grinder tipped his head toward his brother, deep creases around his mouth, his eyebrows bushy over his lids.

"You know this is ridiculous, don't you?" said Grinder.

"Yeah, but look at it this way," said Lucas. "Maybe we'll find those sweat socks you've been waiting for."

4

"Hey Carl, how's it going?" called Grinder, as he stood at the end of his driveway, a massive, blue trash receptacle on four wheels beside him.

"Good, my friend." Carl slid out of the cab of his 1999 Chevy C/K 3500, which was outfitted with a haul-all garbage body and a hydraulic lift. Red, white and blue signage on either side read *Acme Rendering, Inc.* Stenciled on the *Inc.*, like it was a chew toy, was a dog, a cat, a raccoon and a squirrel. Standing behind the lettering, as if proudly holding up the whole shebang, was a statuesque buck, as distant and implacable as Bambi's old man.

"How you doin'?" said Carl, pulling his work gloves from his back pocket.

"Can't complain." Grinder reached for Carl's hand.

Carl peeked around Grinder, admiring his new purchase.

"Jesus, looky here. This ain't no garbage can, it's an actual dumpster. Three cubic yards?"

"Yep."

"That's what I call an upgrade. What the hell are you planning to do? You got some neighbors you wanna get rid of?" Carl's laugh was more of a growl.

"No, they want to get rid of me." Grinder grinned and raised his eyebrows.

"Ha! I hear you, brother."

"Always complaining about the smell."

"Yeah, well, it ain't pretty, that's for sure. Most people don't like dead things just lying around. Makes them nervous, I think."

"Had a deer a while back, y'know."

"Uh huh."

"Didn't have enough room for it in the old bin, so I stuck it under a tarp beside the garage. So, someone called the cops on me. Thought I killed a neighbor and hid him back there."

Carl shook his head and spit. "My God, some people are dumb. As if you'd leave a dead body right out in the open where anyone could find it."

"Well, won't have to worry about that anymore."

"You sure won't," said Carl with a shake of his head.

"Still stinks like hell, though." Grinder removed his ball cap and rubbed his forehead.

"Well, I guess that falls under *tough shit* in the way of things, don't it." Carl poked Grinder in the ribs. "So, whadaya got for me?"

"Pretty much the usual."

Carl lifted the bonnet on the receptacle.

"You sure do get your share of squirrels. My goodness. Is that a 'possum?"

"Yep. First in a while."

"Don't see them in the city much. 'Course we got 'em all over the place down where I come from. You can hardly drive your car at night without killing at least one. Sometimes a whole damn family of 'em." Carl shook his head for the shame of it. "See you got a pooch," he said, his voice almost a whisper.

"Yeah," said Grinder, head bowed, nodding slowly.

"Hate to see dogs in the dumpster." Carl tipped his head to one side. "The way of all things, I suppose," said Carl, matter-of-factness in his voice.

Grinder turned when he heard a nose being blown. He waved to Lucas, who was gingerly navigating the space between Carl's truck and Grinder's house.

"Hey, want you to meet my brother," said Grinder, his arm out as if welcoming the next celebrity on the red carpet.

"My God," said Lucas, his handkerchief over his mouth and nose.

"This is Carl. Carl, this is my brother."

Carl reached out with his leathery hand, but Lucas didn't seem to notice.

"For chrissakes, Grinder, how do you stand this?"

"What?" Grinder glanced at Carl and winked.

"It smells like death, only worse, like death rolled in a pile of crap and then threw up on itself."

"It's all very natural, uh…" Carl leaned forward, his hand still out.

"Lucas," he said, hesitantly taking Carl's hand.

"It's all very natural, Lucas."

"A garbage bin full of road kill in the middle of the city is not natural," said Lucas. The smell was making his eyes water.

"Folks can get all girlish about this sort of thing, I know." Carl drew his chest up in a deep breath, like a teacher getting ready to explain shoe tying to a first grader. "There's no doubt about it. Death has a certain smell. And it ain't pretty. Not meant to be. This is how we'd all smell if undertakers didn't get us first, pump us full of formaldehyde, spray us all over with perfume, dress us up and put us on display like we was part of some department store window display." Carl took another deep breath, his chest swelling to twice its size. "Talk about unnatural," he said, spitting on the grass again.

"Thank you, Carl, but I prefer the display." Lucas leaned over the bin, pinching his nostrils with his handkerchief. "Oh my God, what the hell."

"They are the forgotten casualties of urban living," said Grinder, nudging his brother in the ribs.

"Exactly," said Carl.

"It's just a bunch of chipmunks and squirrels. Is that a 'possum?" said Lucas, now more curious.

"Genocide by any other name," said Carl, striking a dour note.

Lucas studied Carl's face, expecting him to break into laughter, but, instead, Carl didn't flinch. Lucas turned his back to Carl and raised his eyebrows at Grinder.

"Is Carl here serious?" he mouthed.

"Very," said Grinder, eyes wide.

Lucas turned back to Carl and slapped him playfully on the shoulder.

"So, Carl, what's going to happen to all these dearly departed?"

"Process 'em and make 'em into other stuff." Carl put his work gloves on again.

"Yeah, that gorgeous red lipstick Martha slathers on her face every morning is probably made of these animals," said Grinder. "Maybe even the soap you used this morning. Even the concrete on your precious parking lot comes from, what's the official name, Carl?"

"Rendered byproducts," said Carl, his back straight, his head raised in pride.

"Rendered byproducts. Candles, medicines, polish, wax, lard, pet foods," said Grinder.

"Toothpaste, mouthwash, nail polish, toys, anti-freeze."

"Glue, crayons—"

"I get the picture," said Lucas, folding his handkerchief to double its thickness.

"So the next time you give your wife a big wet kiss on her ruby red lips, think of these animals and the sacrifice they made." Grinder smiled.

"Sure," said Lucas. "Look, Grinder, I hate to break this up, but we got a trip ahead of us." Lucas took Grinder by the arm and steered him away from Carl. He turned to Carl and stuck out his hand. "A sincere sensation meeting you, Carl." Carl stuck out a fist. "Oh, okay, fist bumps, of course. There you go," said Lucas, closing his hand into a doughy fist and tapping Carl's boney, cracked knuckles. "Okay, then."

"Big brother's in a hurry, Carl. Can you weigh them," he said, nodding to the trash receptacle. "We'll settle up when I get back?"

"Sure, boss. Where you headed?" said Carl.

"Pittsburgh."

"Pittsburgh?"

"Yeah."

"Pittsburgh. Why you going there?"

"Mother died."

Carl scratched his head and stared at the trash receptacle. "Hey?"

"What?" said Grinder, looking over his shoulder.

"If you get a chance, stop at a place called Primanti's for a beer and a sandwich."

"Okay."

"Strip District. Not the suburban ones."

"Will do."

Carl shook his head slowly. "Your mother, huh?"

"Yeah."

Carl caught Grinder eye-to-eye in the somber silence that followed, the weight of loss hanging there between them. Carl opened his mouth, then closed it again. Grinder waited as his friend struggled to find the right words.

"About that place, I think it's spelled P-r-i-m-a-n-t-i-s," said Carl. "Can't spell for shit, but I'm pretty sure that's it."

"Oh. Well… yeah, thanks."

Lucas hustled quickly to the car as Grinder sauntered along behind, stopping to check his mail, tossing it onto the front porch. Lucas slammed the car door and leaned out the window,

"C'mon!"

"I'm coming, for God's sake." Grinder crouched into the passenger side, folding his legs in gingerly.

Lucas drummed the steering wheel hard.

"What?" said Grinder.

"Where the hell do you find them?"

"Find what?"

"People like Carl."

"What's wrong with Carl?"

"If I have to tell you, then there's no point…"

"You didn't like Carl?"

"I don't know him well enough not to like him. It's just…"

"Just what?"

"Never mind." Lucas jammed the car into gear.

"No, really."

"You're still bringing home strays," said Lucas, squinting into the rearview mirror and pulling into traffic. "Remember after Ma left, for a while you brought home a stray dog every other day. Pop would take them to the shelter and then you'd bring home another one."

"Here we go." Grinder turned his head and looked out the passenger side window.

"Carl's another stray dog. Can't you make friends with normal people? 'Animal genocide', for God's sake."

"Carl's normal enough for me," said Grinder, turning back to his brother.

"Why settle for 'normal enough'?"

"Why not? He's a good guy. Who cares if he's a little…"

"Crazy?"

"A little off kilter. I like him." Grinder studied his hands, balled them into fists, then opened them again.

"I've been telling you all your life that the people you associate with make all the difference. If you spend your time with crazies, everyone's gonna think you're…" Lucas twirled a finger around his ear, stuck his tongue out like a hound dog and crossed his eyes.

"That's very nice," said Grinder, lowering the passenger side window a few inches for air.

"Look at me," said Lucas, palm on his chest. "Seriously. Years ago I made a point of being careful who I associated with. It matters, I'm telling you. Why do you think I joined the Chamber of Commerce and the Rotary? Do you think it's because I like those people?"

"Yes?"

"No. They're a bunch of assholes. But being around them makes me more legit in the eyes of the community. When I walk down the street, people take notice. They think, 'Hey, there goes a businessman, a pillar of the community.'

That feels good, you know what I mean? Don't you want to be more legit?"

Grinder frowned at his brother. "Lucas, you run a laundromat in a town about the size of a thumbnail."

"And a parking lot in a major city."

"Largest city between Syracuse and Buffalo," said Grinder, a scoff in his voice.

"And I'm damn proud of it. I'm making something out of my life. It's the American Dream. Don't you want something more out of life than sitting in the lot all day and night or scraping dead animals off the street? I mean, c'mon, you were the smart one, for chrissakes."

With that, Lucas squirted nasal spray into both nostrils and pulled into Dunkin' Donuts for two large black coffees. Allergies contained, sinuses clear, he guided his Chevy Cruze onto 490 heading west, the sun over his shoulder. Both men settled into the whir of the road beneath them, the city receding in the rearview mirror, suburb after suburb coming and going, town and country, too.

"I packed some things there," said Lucas, pointing over his shoulder to the Styrofoam cooler in the back seat. "You hungry?"

"I guess."

"Take what you want."

"I will." Grinder lifted the cap off his cup.

"Be careful. I don't want a big brown spot on the upholstery."

Grinder glanced at his brother, but didn't speak. He pressed the lid flap back, a few drops hitting the seat. He slid his leg back and forth, absorbing as much as he could while his brother watched a car load of college types whiz by.

"Joined a chat room," said Grinder.

"What?"

"A chat room, you know, one of those online things."

"Yeah? Why's that?"

"Meet some people, I guess."

"Good, that's good," said Lucas, a long, crooked grin spreading across his face. He sat up straighter and put both hands on the wheel. "That's great. See what I mean? Meet some people other than Carl. Good for you."

"Uh huh."

"So, does this thing have a name, or something? Is it like a dating thing?"

"No, nothing like that."

"But it's called something, right?"

"Yeah."

"So?"

"It's called the Octagon Room," said Grinder, glancing over his shoulder at the cooler. He leaned back in his seat and sipped the coffee.

"The Octagon Room?"

"Yeah." Grinder glimpsed his brother without turning his head.

"Like the shape?" said Lucas, scanning back and forth between the road and Grinder, smiling, nodding.

"Yeah."

"So. Octagon. Why octagon?" Lucas drew up the right side of his face like he might have had a mild stroke.

"I don't know for sure."

"Well, there must be some reason. They wouldn't have just picked a name like that out of thin air."

Grinder raised both hands as he struggled to explain. "I guess it's because, you know—an octagon, it's an odd shape. It doesn't fit in anywhere easily."

"Uh huh. I still don't get it."

Grinder's hands dropped into his lap. He took a deep breath and spoke hesitantly. "It's like, you know, square pegs don't exactly fit into round holes, so imagine what it's like if you're an octagon trying to fit into a round hole."

Lucas grimaced. "I still don't get it. A square peg in a round hole, I get that, but an octagon. Why make it more complicated than it has to be?"

"Look, I didn't make up the goddam name. It was there when I joined."

"Uh huh. Might want to suggest to the group that they change—"

"Look, the group is the Octagon Room, okay? Case closed."

"Okay, okay. You don't have to get your drawers in a knot."

Miles of highway passed below them in the lull that followed. Eventually, Grinder turned and knelt on the front seat, reached for the cooler and removed the Styrofoam lid. He snatched two Hostess cupcakes. "Here," he said, handing one to Lucas. "This should be real easy for you. It's round. Should fit perfectly into your pie hole."

"God, I love these," said Lucas, tearing the wrapper off with his teeth. "You and me and Hostess, right?" He put half the cupcake in his mouth. "Man, they used to be so much bigger, y'know?"

"We were just smaller," said Grinder, nibbling the squiggle off the top of his cupcake.

"God, these are good. And they were gonna stop making them. I wrote a dozen letters."

"Always fighting the good fight," said Grinder, his teeth blackened with chocolate.

An eighteen-wheeler swept by. Lucas clutched the steering wheel, coffee between his legs, as the car shuddered. On the horizon, an armada of grey clouds gradually enveloped the blue sky.

"So, the Octagon Room. Meet anyone?"

"Not face to face. You just talk back and forth."

"But isn't the point to meet someone? To get to know someone?" Lucas took his coffee cup in his right hand and steered with his left hand which rested in his lap. "I mean, aren't you trying to find an octagonal hole?"

"No such thing as an octagonal *hole.*"

"You know what I mean. An octagonal *shape* or whatever you want to call it. Don't you want to find some kind of fit?"

"Not that easy."

"What do you mean, 'not that easy'? If you've got all these people in the room, there's got to be someone you can fit with. Maybe some divorced woman or someone who's all alone for some reason, has an illness or something, crippled, maybe kinda mental; you know, anyone."

Grinder popped the rest of the cupcake into his mouth. He wiped his chin on his sleeve and took another sip of his coffee. "You know, I always thought Ma was the one who put the Hostess cupcakes in my lunch bag every day. But when she left, they kept showing up. I knew it wasn't Pop. He coulda cared less. For a while, I thought maybe she snuck home at night just to put a cupcake in my lunch bag. Then one day I saw you packing the lunches and all of a sudden I knew."

"You were just a kid."

Grinder reached for the cooler and pulled out two more Hostess cupcakes. He tore one open and gave it to his brother.

"You know, I've always been an octagon, Lukie. I think I always will be."

5

The skyline of Buffalo huddled meekly on the western horizon as they turned south on 90. Grinder pointed east at the light standards of Ralph Wilson Stadium.

"What can you say about our Bills?" said Lucas.

"Wide right," said Grinder.

"And there you have it."

Both brothers squinted into the sun and then tilted their visors down. Grinder lowered his window a few more inches.

"Remember the time Pop took us to see them play the Pats? Back in the Joe Ferguson era? Remember?"

"We were sitting so far up we could see the white caps on Lake Erie. Froze our asses off," said Grinder.

"Yeah, we were about three rows from the top of the stadium. There must have been fifty thousand empty seats. And would he let us move down to where we could see the damn game? No."

"'We didn't pay for *those* damn seats,' he said, 'We paid for *these* damn seats.'"

"We were supposed to tailgate before the game, remember? Wasn't until we got to the lot that he realized that all he brought was a case of beer," said Lucas.

"So we sat in a freezing car listening to the pregame on the radio while Pop drank Genny after Genny."

"Loved his Genny."

"Yeah, you could smell it on him, even when he didn't have a can in his hand."

Lucas leaned his head on the steering wheel and laughed, the car veering across the rumble strips. "Whoa." Grinder white knuckled the arm rest and held his breath. Lucas swerved back onto the road, a delivery truck driver leaning on his horn.

"Sorry man," said Lucas. "I'm tellin' you, that was funny. You're right. The old man always smelled like a beer truck."

"Yes, he did," said Grinder, looking out the window, letting go of the arm rest. "He was a laugh riot, wasn't he?"

"Well, you have to admit he was a funny drunk some of the time. Remember he'd tell us how stupid we were, how we weren't learning anything in school, and then he'd stand in the middle of the living room and try to recite all the continents and all the oceans without looking at the globe. Sometimes he would stand on the coffee table. God. And he could never remember Australia. And you'd say, 'Australia, Pop' and he'd argue with you. 'Australia's a damn country; it can't be a continent.' And you'd say, 'It's both.' And he'd say, 'Can't be. That'd be against the rules,' and you'd say, 'What rules?' and he'd say, 'The rules, the rules!' About then you'd get the World Book and look it up and he'd turn red as hell, like he was absolutely going to explode. God, he would get pissed." Lucas pounded the steering wheel with his fists, almost in tears. "I nearly died. Every time."

"So did I."

"C'mon, you gotta admit the sight of Pop standing on the coffee table, wobbling like crazy, was funny."

"Hilarious." Lucas was still chuckling. Grinder's face was deadpanned serious. "You never spoke up."

"I wasn't an idiot. You always said something. You never learned." Lucas glanced at Grinder. "You never learned."

Grinder turned in his seat, his face drawn.

"Do you remember the rest?"

"What?"

"Do you remember the rest of what happened?"

Lucas clenched the steering wheel.

"Pop would get two volumes of the World Book, right?"

Lucas stared at the merging traffic.

"And this was the best part. He'd make me hold 'em out at arm's length, one book in each hand."

"Okay…"

"I was what? Nine, ten maybe?"

"Pop didn't mean to—"

"Ma would say, 'Stop!' and Pop would shake a fist at her."

Lucas slumped in the driver's seat.

"Then she'd take her pack of cigarettes to the porch and smoke." Grinder leaned over to Lucas, shoulder to shoulder. "Remember?"

"Look, half the time Pop didn't know what he was doing."

"By then I was crying and he'd say, 'You little crybaby. You're not my son. No son of mine would cry like a little girl.'"

"He always apologized. I mean—"

Grinder reached over and smacked Lucas hard on the thigh.

"Time for a pit stop. Gotta pee."

Lucas opened his mouth, then closed it, air rushing out his nostrils. He put the turn signal on. "Okay, we'll stop at Angola."

They crossed the covered walking bridge that linked the parking lot to a mini-mall of restaurants, gifts shops and restrooms. Two young boys stood at the window pumping their arms up and down as each eighteen-wheeler passed beneath them. They gave each other high fives if a driver blew his horn. Grinder and Lucas stopped to watch.

"You know," said Lucas, "Pop cried too, but you never saw that. By then you and Ma were in your bedroom, door locked. But Pop would feel awful. He'd say how sorry he was and how he was a bad father and how he didn't deserve to have us as his sons. He'd lay there on the couch moaning and blubbering."

Grinder watched the boys. "Hey, you two, here comes another one."

"Thanks mister!" they said, pumping their arms as hard as they could.

"He wasn't always mean."

"Not to you, he wasn't. He liked you." Grinder pumped his arm along with the boys.

"I don't know about that. I don't know if you could say he liked anyone. Maybe when he was starting to get a buzz on, you know, after four or five beers; he was nicer for a while then."

"Nicer to you."

Grinder and Lucas went to the men's room and then stood outside MacDonald's listening to the theme from *Star Wars* on a player grand piano. In the gift shop, Grinder bought a bag of yogurt covered raisins and a peach Snapple; Lucas bought Skittles and a Coke Zero. They sat together on a bench near the exit.

"So, did you call him?"

"Pop?"

"Yeah," said Grinder.

"Yeah."

"What did he say?"

"He was surprised it had happened so recently."

"Why?"

"Thought she died long ago, after Grady left her. Don't know what made him think that. Told him she'd been living in Pittsburgh with some guy name Paul."

"That was it?"

"He got all quiet, covered the phone, started talking to Lucille. I don't know, he sounded upset."

"Uh huh, right."

"He asked how old she was and I told him I wasn't sure. Then he got all quiet again. Finally, he said he had to go and that was about it."

Grinder stared at Lucas, his eyes blank.

"What did you expect? I mean, Ma was three wives ago."

"Was he drunk?"

"No, still sober."

"Been a while."

"Yeah, a lot of years."

"Did he say he was sorry for our goddam loss?"

"Grinder, I don't even know if *we're* sorry for our goddam loss."

"She was our mother."

"I suppose that's true."

Once back on the road, Grinder let his seat back as far as it would go, then turned on his side, hoping to fall sleep. He listened to the steady whir of the road. Lucas closed his Skittles bag, took a long sip of his Coke Zero and then put it back in the holder. He looked at his brother, trying to measure his breathing.

"Grinder?" he called in a whisper. "Grinder? Are you awake? Mind if I turn on the radio?" He waited for what seemed like a reasonable time and when Grinder didn't answer, Lucas turned it on, searching for Rush Limbaugh.

Grinder lay still as could be, eyes wide open, the car door vibrating against his forehead.

6

They passed acre after acre of grapevines along 90. A long blue ribbon of lake separated the steel grey sky from the brown shoreline. Erie gathered shape in the distance. Lucas put on his turn signal and slowed down for the exit.

"What are you doing?" said Grinder.

"Want you to see something."

A few minutes later he pulled into the Lake Erie Racetrack and Casino parking lot as a bus load of grey-haired ladies and a few slow-moving men shuffled happily toward the entrance.

"Why are we stopping here?" said Grinder, his voice flat, his eyes blank.

Lucas opened the door, ready to go.

"C'mon. Where's the harm?"

"A casino."

"Racino."

"I don't do these."

"Just because you've never done one, doesn't mean you can't. It's fun. You'll see."

"It's money down a rat hole," said Grinder.

Lucas turned on his hip, his jaw clamped. "Look, you sonofabitch, this is our road trip; we're going to play some slots, take a piss and then leave. And you will have fun." Lucas got out of the car and slammed the door.

Grinder opened the car door and stepped onto the pavement. He rubbed his lower back as he tried to straighten up. He put one hand on the side mirror to steady himself.

"You should have come on that bus." Lucas pointed at another herd of senior citizens ambling toward the entrance.

Lucas and Grinder stopped at the valet parking lane and studied the pyramid-shaped skylight of multi-colored Plexiglas rising above them. Strobe lights played off the panes while techno music pounded the air. Lucas nudged Grinder.

"It's not Vegas, but pretty cool. I mean everything in Vegas is so massive. It's like a whole other world. But this, this is good, too. It's like a mini-mini-Vegas. It's Erie."

"I wonder if you can still set fire to the lake."

A young man greeted them at the door. He wore an ill-fitting charcoal grey bellman's uniform with gold buttons and piping, topped off with a pillbox hat adorned with a billowy pink feather. "Welcome to The Lake Erie, gentleman." He opened the door and stared across the parking lot at nothing in particular. "Everyone's a winner at The Lake," the young man mumbled as he bowed half-heartedly.

Lucas smiled broadly as they walked up the stairs past the fountain and into a massive room full of slot machines. The ceiling glistened with dazzling silver stars against giant turquoise paisley water droplets. The carpeting was a dizzying conflagration of mint green and teal geometric and amoeba-like shapes that appeared to consume each other. The air was blue with cigarette smoke. Bells rang, whistles blew, lights flashed, and music blared. "Wheel…Of…Foorrtuuune!!" Old women wearing practical shoes sat in front of their favorite machines, motionless except for their thumbs.

An elderly gentleman approached them. A cigarette dangled from the corner of his mouth. He pulled a tank of oxygen on roller wheels, the plastic tubing disappearing into his nose.

"Didn't they card you when you came in, fellas?"

"What?" said Lucas.

"No one under seventy allowed," he said, laughing and then choking. His face turned red. Grinder took a step forward, but the man raised his hand as his hacking continued. Finally he took a deep breath and then a drink from the water bottle that was conveniently attached to his white leather belt. "Welcome!" he said, flinging one arm into the air. "We can always use new blood. Especially from kids like you. What are you, thirties, forties, I'll bet. Think of The Lake as a senior center on steroids. Watch out for the ladies. They may look decrepit, but you'd be surprised what they will do when the lights go out." He raised his eyebrows twice.

"Well, that certainly is a warning we'll take to heart," said Lucas as he tried to walk by.

The old man pulled his arm. "Hey, don't go in that room. The slots are tighter than a goddam drum." He pointed in the opposite direction. "Try them. Loose as my bowels after a bowl of chili."

Lucas's face pinched. Grinder grinned.

"Hey, you want to join us?" said Grinder. "I don't know anything about gambling."

"Well, I've lost more money than I can remember, so I'm an expert at this. Name's Oscar, but you can call me Butch." He stuck out his hand, which Grinder shook eagerly.

"My name's Grinder and this here's my brother, Lukie."

"Pleased to meet you, Lukie." Butch started to cough again, this time dropping his cigarette on the floor. "Sorry about that. Could you, uh…?" he said, pointing with his chin at the cigarette. Grinder picked it up and put it back between Butch's thumb and forefinger. "Thanks. Let's try again." He pushed his glasses up his nose and held out his hand. "Lukie, you said?"

"Lucas, the name is Lucas."

"Very nice to meet you boys. Let's get it on." Butch adjusted his tubing, took a deep gurgling breath, and then shuffled across the floor toward the Boca Room.

"Need any help?" said Grinder. Butch breathed heavily, stopped, and then kept on going without a word.

"There, there, that's the one. Sure fire. Basket of Riches," said Butch, his oxygen tank clanging at his heels. "Best of the penny slots. Sit!"

Grinder and Lucas slid into the swivel chairs in front of gleaming machines that were bedecked with scantily clad vixens holding baskets of gold, their ample, perky bosoms beckoning. The keys lit up randomly; letters, numbers, baskets of gold filled the screen.

"This is it, boys."

"So, you've won big on this machine?" said Lucas.

"That very one," said Butch, wincing as he lifted himself onto the adjacent chair while holding the tubing to his nose. "Last week I won twenty-five dollars on that baby."

"Wow," said Lucas, laughing. "How much did you spend to win that basket of riches?"

Butch waved his hand at Lucas. "Don't matter. I won. Money in my pocket instead of theirs." He laughed until he coughed and then choked again; this time he pulled a handkerchief from his pocket to wipe his mouth.

"Are you sure you're okay? Should we get someone?" said Grinder.

Parrot Talk

"Nobody to get." Butch's chest heaved as he caught his breath.

"I mean…" said Grinder, raising his eyebrows at a group of Hawaiian shirted and pin cushion coiffed older adults advancing on the buffet. "Are you with them?"

"I don't hang with old people."

"Should have guessed."

"How old are you?" said Grinder.

"That's a pretty personal question." Butch leaned back in his seat and lifted his feet onto the rest. "Eighty-seven, last I checked."

"So, how'd you get here?" said Grinder.

"Same way as you boys, I suppose. I drove."

Without moving their heads, Grinder and Lucas raised their eyebrows at each other.

"So, do you two wanna get rich or do you want to stand here yacking all day about how old I am and how I need a keeper?"

"I think I'll pass actually," said Lucas, standing. "Grinder, maybe we should hit the road."

"What do you mean, Lukie? We're on the road. Having fun, right?" He turned to Butch. "I'm all in. Let's get ourselves filthy rich," said Grinder.

"'Atta boy," said Butch.

Butch hoisted up his seersucker trousers, belted, as they were, just below his chest, to accommodate a protruding abdominal hernia. He had wisps of grey hair on his temples, bushy, unkempt eyebrows that flowed over the frames of his glasses and gauzy blue eyes, magnified to twice their size by his thick lenses.

"You got some money?" said Butch. Lucas pulled out his wallet and produced a crisp, clean twenty. "That's good for a start." Butch stuck the bill into the machine.

"Now what?" said Grinder.

"Now you don't got any money anymore; you got credits, which is the same thing, only by changing it to credits they think you'll forget what it is and spend more. See those buttons? Pick how many credits you want to spend." Grinder pushed the five button. "Okay, now push that one." Grinder pushed the button and watched the screen as everything whirled by. The machine stopped abruptly.

"What happened?" said Grinder.

"You lost. Push it again."

Lucas leaned in, his interest piqued. "Here, let me push that thing."

"Hey, hey, you'll jinx it. Get your own machine," said Butch. Lucas scowled and then sat down at another Basket of Riches and slipped in a twenty.

"You from around here?" said Grinder as he pushed the button again.

"Erie, yeah. All my life. Had a shoe store for years and years."

Pushed again.

"Yeah?"

"Uh huh. It was different back then. We sat down with our customers, measured their feet, made sure they got what they wanted. Every style. Loafers and wingtips and wedges and pumps. You name it. We talked to them. Made friends with our customers, y'know? Talked about everything, birthdays, vacations, anniversaries. Not like today. You go to a shoe store and there's no one around. Just some kids standing at the cash register staring at their damn phones. Ask 'em a question and they just look at you. You have to do everything yourself. What is that? What happened to service?"

Pushed again.

"I hear you," said Grinder. "Things sure have changed."

"And not for the better, I might add. Hey, look, you just won thirty credits. Go again."

Grinder pushed the button as he studied his companion.

"Married?"

"What's that?"

"Married? Got a wife?"

"I got nothing over here." Lucas moved to another slot.

"Had a bunch of 'em. First wife, she died thirty years ago. Only one I ever loved. What's a man supposed to do, though? Didn't like being alone, you know. So I got married again. Then she up and died. Went for the hat trick and that one only lasted a year. After that, I thought, 'I can't afford the funerals. They're killing me!'" Butch was breathing easily now, the perspiration fading from his brow. He pointed toward the button. Grinder pushed again. "There you go; one hundred credits. You've almost got your twenty back."

"Got any family around?"

"Nope. Son died about ten years ago. Cancer. What an awful mess that was." He waved his hand like he was swatting a fly. "Then his wife died. My daughter's retired. She and her husband live in one of those retirement villages. Arizona. Always complaining about the 'illegals.' I don't know. They don't seem to mind them mowing their lawn. Live and let live."

"See them?"

Parrot Talk

Butch pulled out his handkerchief again and mopped his upper lip.

"Naw. They've got their own life. Golf and whatnot. They want me to be a, what do you call it, Facebook. Not for me. Miss her, but what can you do?"

"I'm done." Lucas slid back into the seat beside his brother.

"Goes fast if you don't know what you're doing," said Butch.

"What's to know? The house always wins."

"Can't be greedy. If you're patient and smart and get to know these machines, make friends with them kinda, you can almost always walk away even or a little ahead. That's the most you can hope for in this life, boys." Butch pointed to the button and Grinder pushed yet again. Nothing. Again. Nothing.

"Okay, I can see we need a new strategy here. Open it up. Go for broke. Try one hundred credits a bet," said Butch.

"I'm going from a penny to a dollar, y'know," said Grinder.

"Yeah, well, sometimes you gotta push the throttle to the floor."

"Do what the man tells you," said Lucas, nudging Grinder.

"Okay, here goes." Grinder pushed the button and they waited, eyes unblinking, the lights flashing off their faces.

"Oh my God!" cried Butch.

"What?" said Grinder.

"Oh my God." Butch stood up, his arms over his head.

"Are you okay, Butch?" said Lucas.

"Looky here, looky here."

"What?" said Grinder.

"You got a hundred free spins."

"Uh huh. And that means what?"

"Just shut up and watch this thing go."

The three men sat motionless in front of the slot machine for fifteen minutes, watching and listening as it robotically played over and over again, racking up credits as it went.

"Sweet Jesus," whispered Butch. "You may have killed the darn thing."

When it stopped, Butch couldn't speak. He looked at Grinder and Lucas, tears in his eyes. Then he pointed at the credit score.

"What happened?" said Grinder.

"Cash out, cash out!" said Butch. "Cash out before it lures you back in."

Lucas reached for the button to cash out. When he looked at the receipt, he'd won six hundred and fifty-six dollars.

"For real?" said Grinder. "I mean, this is for real?"

"This is as real as it gets," said Butch. He reached for Grinder's hand and shook it hard. "You've won big, son. Way to go."

"But I didn't do anything."

"Doesn't matter, the gambling gods took a liking to you." Butch adjusted the tubing in his nose. He stood up as straight as he could and pointed at the brothers. "It sure is something, isn't it? I could sit here all day dumping pennies into that machine and walk away penniless. Then the next guy sits down and he's a winner. The following day, the opposite could happen. That's why you play; 'cause you never know what will happen. That's why you do anything." Butch leaned against the machine, suppressing a cough. "Win, lose. The important thing is to play. That's life, boys, put a penny in the slot and take your chances."

Lucas and Grinder strolled across the parking lot, smiling like Cheshire cats, swagger in their hips. Lucas patted Grinder on the back.

"Nice of you to give Butch a hundred."

"Nothing, really," said Grinder.

"Five hundred and fifty-six smackers. And you didn't even want to stop here."

"I guess Butch was right; you gotta drop a penny in the slot."

"What are you going to do with all that dough?"

Grinder took the wad of money from his pocket. "I'm going to roll it up like this, put a rubber band around it and shove it back in my pocket."

"And?"

"See what comes."

7

"Two, please," said Lucas.

"Seat yourself," said the waitress, a soiled white apron wrapped around her waist.

Lucas and Grinder walked sideways through the crowded room to an empty table in the corner. Swarthy, bearded men wearing Steelers shirts and caps sat at the bar, foamy glasses of Iron City in front of them. The walls were covered with colorful, cartoonish murals of Pittsburgh's heroes, Bill Mazeroski, Myron Cope, Franco Harris, Roberto Clemente, Mean Joe Greene.

A waitress swiped the table with a wet cloth and slapped down two menus. "I'll be back," she said without looking at them.

"Sure this is the place?"

"Yeah. Said Primanti's out front."

"I know, but…"

"But what?"

"It's, well, I don't know."

"Good eats. Local color," said Grinder, glancing at the menu. "Hungry?"

"Well," said Lucas.

"Come on."

Grinder nodded 'hello' to a gangly man with a long grey ponytail who was sitting with a squinty-eyed woman in torn jeans and a Bucs T-shirt. The man raised his index finger to the brim of his Steelers cap and nodded. Lucas studied the menu.

"I assume you're from around here," said Grinder, pointing to their shirts and caps.

"Yessir, lived in the Burgh all my life. Wife, too."

Grinder looked at the woman. "How long you two been married?"

"I ain't never been married," she said.

"Oh."

The man stretched his long skinny arm around her and raised his eyebrows. "She's my woman."

"And he's my man." She rose and kissed his cheek.

Grinder opened his mouth but then only nodded.

"I guess you'd call it an 'arrangement,'" said the man. With that, both of them started to giggle like middle school girls.

"Alrighty then," said Lucas as he reached into his pocket for a tissue.

"What can I get for yinz guys?" said the waitress, neither pencil nor pad in hand.

"What are they having?" said Grinder, pointing at another couple sitting across the way, mounds of food on their plates. "Looks interesting." The waitress turned and leaned over their shoulders.

"Sandwiches and beers," she said.

"Oh," said Lucas.

"Tell me about this sandwich," said Grinder, pointing at the menu. "Says it's the second best seller."

"House specialty. Your choice of meat. Bologna, Turkey. Roast beef. Whatever. Top it with spicy coleslaw. Then French fries. All on homemade Italian bread."

"What's your number one seller?" said Grinder.

"Beer," she said.

"Okay then. I'll take your number one and number two with, uh, roast beef. You?" he said, nodding to Lucas.

"Okay, yeah, same thing."

"Two cows!" called the waitress over her shoulder as she walked away.

The pony-tailed man leaned over, hand outstretched. "Name's Jack."

"Grinder, Jack, and this is my brother Lukie." Lucas glared at Grinder and didn't bother to reach across the table to shake hands with Jack.

"Yo," said Jack anyway. "I didn't want yinz guys to get the wrong idea. I love my wife. But Brenda, well, Brenda's Brenda, y'know."

The waitress returned with glasses of Iron City.

"Cheers," said Grinder, lifting his glass to Lucas, Jack and Brenda. "God bless."

"Thanks man," said Jack. He slapped Grinder on the back as Brenda headed to the bar. Jack toddled after her. "Hey, babe, where you goin'?"

"God bless America," said Lucas, clinking rims with Grinder. He raised his glass higher. "Here's to the American marriage. Long may she wave." They clinked again.

"Hey, don't be so harsh. There's about one degree of separation between you and Martha and those two."

"I was never that unfaithful."

Grinder sat his beer down on the table and looked at Lucas with his don't-bullshit-me face on.

"Maybe once. Twice, I guess. There was other messing around stuff, but I don't even think that counts. For sure, I didn't go around like Jack, showing it off everywhere. I was better than that."

"Uh huh."

"Go to hell." Lucas blew his nose again. Took a bite of his sandwich. "Hey, at least I gave it a try. More than you did." Grinder took a bite of his sandwich and then gulped his beer. He chewed in silence. Lucas rolled his tissue and put it in his pocket. "Look, what do you expect? Ma and Pop weren't exactly…hell, it was like watching a car crash in slow motion for ten years. How was I supposed to do any better?" Lucas looked at Grinder, who took another bite but didn't speak. "Say something for chrissakes."

"What do you want me to say?"

"I don't know." Lucas looked at his sandwich and then put it back on the plate. "Anyway, Pop was never unfaithful. As far as I know. Ma was the one."

Grinder took another bite of his sandwich, his eyes on the table. He gulped some beer to wash it down and looked at his brother while wiping his mouth. He bit hard on the sandwich again.

Lucas leaned back in his chair and put his napkin on the table. He studied his brother and cleared his throat. "I never asked you. Did you suspect anything between Ma and Mr. Hopkins?"

Grinder was mid-chew and didn't speak.

"I guess you were still young enough not to notice things," said Lucas. "All those teacher conferences to 'address your learning needs.' For chrissakes, you were an 'A' student."

Grinder swallowed and glared at his brother. "If it wasn't for Pop, she wouldn't have—"

"Pop didn't make her screw your English teacher."

"If *I* had been married to Pop, *I* would have screwed my English teacher, too."

"Look, blame Pop all you want, but Ma was the one who walked." Lucas swallowed a belch and rubbed his belly. Grinder ran his finger around the rim of his glass.

"And there you were thinking Ma was taking a real interest in your goddam education. You remember that? She was never interested in anything but herself," said Lucas, all snarly.

Both men sat with their heads down, chewing and clutching their glasses of beer.

Grinder took a deep breath and let it out slowly. He looked at his brother. "She was reading me *To Kill A Mockingbird*."

"What?"

"We were assigned *To Kill a Mockingbird* in English class. She loved that book and wanted to read it with me, to help me understand the 'different levels of the plot,' as she liked to say."

"You're kidding me."

"She asked Mr. Hopkins if she could borrow a copy so we could both have one at home. That's how they met, I think. She came to school. I saw them. They were smiling." Grinder raised his beer again. "After she left us, I kept reading the story every night. Fewer and fewer pages at a time, trying to slow it down, stretch it out, thinking she'd come back before I finished. But she never did." He put the glass to his lips. "I finished the book. It was good. I see why she loved it."

"You never told me that."

"At the time, what did it matter?"

Lucas wiped his nose on a napkin and stuck it under the corner of his plate. He put both elbows on the table and interlaced his fingers. He cleared his throat so Grinder would look. "You were always the smart one. I was the grunt, just plodding along. You were the one with potential. *I* could even see it. Then you totally blew college. I mean, you had the future in your hands. I never got what happened."

Grinder tossed his napkin onto his plate and wiped his hands on his jeans. He put one hand on the table and leaned on his other elbow. "I don't know. Something stopped." Grinder shrugged.

Lucas took another drink, wiped his mouth with the back of his hand, and set the glass down with a crack. "I wish things coulda gone the other way." Both men shuffled their feet as if they were about to stand, then sat there another minute or so. At last, Lucas looked at his watch and then slapped Grinder on the forearm to break the spell. "C'mon, brother, let's get out of here. We got a date with Janice what's-her-face."

8

"What's it say?" asked Lucas.

"'The Monongahela incline is the longest continuously operated funicular,' whatever that is, 'in the United States. It has been running since 1870.'"

Grinder and Lucas stood at the base of Mt. Washington, the Monongahela River at their backs, watching two tiny, red train cars, windows trimmed in gold, scuttling up and down the side of the steep hill; both being raised and lowered by a single cable.

"Looks like something you might put under a Christmas tree," said Grinder.

"I'm not riding that thing."

"How else are we going to get up there?"

"Look at that. Must be a ninety-degree angle."

"Plaque says seventy-eight."

"Wonder how many people have died riding it?" said Lucas.

"Let me see," said Grinder, bending close to the plaque. "Approximately three dozen people perish annually while commuting on the nation's most venerable incline."

"What the hell?"

"Nothing. It'll be fine. Part of the Pittsburgh experience."

They bought tickets and boarded the incline, the bucket shaped, leather seats hugging them tightly. Lurching out of the station, the incline rose steadily above the skyline which was grey in the overcast morn. The hefty Smithfield Bridge receded below them, looking no more significant than a tinker toy. Once at the top, Grinder and Lucas leaned into a stiff wind and stood at the overlook admiring the towering glass and steel on display before them, the brown river far below, seeming motionless.

"Hard to believe that Ma would live here," said Grinder.

"Why's that?" Lucas snorted repeatedly, the wind playing havoc with his sinuses.

"She was afraid of heights."

"Things change in thirty-five years."

"Yeah, I guess." Grinder gripped the railing and leaned over, studying the tiny figures scurrying around Station Square below.

"So, where are we heading?"

Grinder pulled directions from his back pocket. "Looks like we cross the street down there, go another block, turn left, then right and keep going for a few blocks and the building should be on the right—2601 Fitzgerald St., apartment 680."

It turned out to be a twenty-minute walk through a hilly neighborhood. Lucas and Grinder were breathing hard when they arrived at The Haven, a 1950s-era apartment building with concrete columns guarding its modest entrance. There were intricate panes of leaded, beveled glass on either side of the front door, the final vestige of what its builders must have thought would be a lasting treasure high above the smoke-filled metropolis of old Pittsburgh. The smoke and flames and the steel that once produced them, were long gone. And The Haven, newspapers strewn on the sidewalk and overgrown shrubbery clutching its brick exterior, had outlived its promise, yet hung on gamely as a 'low income housing site.'

"This is it, I guess." Lucas looked up the side of the building at the sixth floor.

They entered the front door and Grinder pressed the button for 680. There was no response, so he pressed it again. On the verge of pressing it a third time, the door buzzed and the brothers entered the lobby. They pushed the button for the elevator and waited.

"This is weird," said Grinder.

"Weird how?"

"I mean, our mother used to ride this thing."

"And?"

"We're probably breathing the same air she breathed."

Lucas shook his head and chuckled. "Where do you get this stuff?"

"It's true. Her molecules are still here."

"Honest to God…"

"I'm not kidding. It's a proven fact. Physics." Grinder tucked his hands into his pockets. "Nothing is lost."

Parrot Talk

"Except *your* mind." Lucas leaned back against the mirrored wall.

The elevator jerked to a stop. They slid the gate back, pulled open the door and walked down the narrow hall. Lucas and Grinder stood in front of 680 studying the welcome sign: "Knock…if you dare."

Grinder crinkled his nose. "Okay, then."

"Let me do the talking," said Lucas. He knocked. There was loud whispering and shuffling on the other side. When the door opened, a short, stout woman with a round face stood before them, her grey-brown hair pulled up in a bun, a long hair pin jabbed through it. She cleared her throat and held out her arm as if welcoming them into a palace.

"You must be Lucas and Gregory," she said. "Please come in." She stepped back, her arm still extended. "Welcome to our home." Beyond her, sitting in a red lounge chair, legs up, remote in hand, was a man wearing a T-shirt and work pants that were open at the waist to allow for his considerable girth. His eyes never left the TV. "Ronald, these are Millie's boys." Ronald was unmoved by this news. "Ronald! Say something! They came all the way from Rochester, New York."

Ronald turned his head slowly.

"Want a beer?"

"No thanks." Lucas was already reaching into his pocket for a tissue.

"Get 'em some beers," said Ronald, waving a hand at Janice.

"They don't want no beers," said Janice. "Didn't you hear the man?"

"They ain't gonna say, 'Hey, gimme a beer.' Too polite for that. So just get the beer, for once."

"Goddammit, Ronald. Don't you get it? Some people don't start the day with a six pack of IC, for God's sake."

"We're fine, really," said Lucas.

"Get the goddam beer, Janice." Ronald shifted in his chair as if he might get up.

"If you want a beer, get it yourself."

"Get the beer, Janice."

"I'm not getting no beer." Janice's jaw was set, her fists clenched.

"Get the beer, Janice. You're making our guests uncomfortable."

"Read my lips, old man. No beer!"

"Janice, I don't want to have to get up out of this chair…"

"Ha! You couldn't if you wanted to." A triumphant smile crossed Janice's face, as if, for once, she had won a round.

"For chrissakes," mumbled Lucas.

Grinder took a step into the living room and held his hands up.

"Excuse me, excuse me. Please. We want to thank you for your hospitality." Janice and Ronald stared, unblinking, at Grinder. "And my brother and I also want to thank you for looking after our mother for, well, how long did you know her?"

"Twenty-five, almost thirty years," said Janice. Ronald blinked, then shook his head in agreement.

"Well, we want to thank you, that's all." Grinder bowed slightly.

Ronald smiled. "You're welcome. Why don't you two have a seat?" He settled back and pointed to the couch. "Can I get you a beer?"

"No, but thanks for offering," said Grinder as both brothers sat on the afghan-covered sofa. Janice scurried away, returning with glasses of water.

"Thank you," said Lucas.

"Don't drink beer?" said Ronald. Janice kicked the side of his Barcalounger.

"Maybe they'd prefer some weed, Janice. That's your—"

"Hush!"

In the silence that followed, they all shifted in their seats, each then choosing a wall to contemplate.

"Your mother was a real sweetheart," said Janice. "Everyone here loved Millie."

"Is that so?" said Lucas, edgy.

"She had a good heart, but not a very healthy one."

"Oh." Grinder leaned forward.

"That's what finally got her."

"She had a heart attack?" said Grinder, his eyebrows lowered. "Is that what happened?"

"They think so. I mean there wasn't no autopsy or nothing, but she'd had problems for years, so we just guessed that that was what it was. Found her in the kitchen, on the floor, actually." Janice grimaced apologetically. "She looked kinda peaceful, I suppose." Janice smoothed her dress and crossed her legs. "She had bad arthritis, too, poor thing. Very hard to move around. Used a walker, even though she hated the thing. She never gave up."

"Might say she was a hard ass. No disrespect," said Ronald, hacking as he spoke.

"Well, I dunno 'bout that. She was spirited, that's what she was."

"We wouldn't know," said Lucas, his tone clipped, impatient. "Haven't seen or heard from her in years."

"Not since we were kids," said Grinder, softness in his voice.

"Yes, I knew that," said Janice, her face blanching. "Such a sad thing."

"How did you get to know her?"

"Well, when I first met her, she was a waitress at the Triangle Café, down near the point. She'd been there, geez, I don't know how long. She took me under her wing and showed me the ropes." Janice's face got a faraway look. "Good waitress. Terrific, actually. Customers loved her."

Lucas looked out the window to the balcony. Grinder, elbows on his knees, leaned his chin on his clasped hands.

"She was seeing this guy at the time. What was his name?"
Ronald shrugged.

"No matter. Didn't last long. She didn't have much luck with men."

"Did she marry?" asked Grinder.

"No. She swore she'd never make that mistake again."

"Did she have any children?"

"No. Except, of course…" Janice gestured towards Lucas and Grinder, then stood, brushed the front of her dress again and smoothed her hair with one hand. "Can I get you boys some more water? Would you like a cup of coffee?" They both declined and she sat down again. "I know this must be kinda hard for yinz two. I mean, coming here and all."

Lucas looked at his watch.

"She loved you both very much."

"Why would you say that?" said Grinder.

"Well, she talked about you often. She told me that when you was little, Gregory, that you used to grind your teeth when you were sleeping, so your brother started callin' you Grinder. You'd cry like the dickens when he said it, but your mother'd tell you it was good to be a 'grinder,' it meant you never gave up." Janice smiled and then laughed. She tilted her head toward Lucas, who was looking out the window. "And she told me you was always a 'little man,' even when you were just a bitty thing, no more than two; always makin' plans and startin' projects." Lucas looked at her, opened his mouth but didn't speak. "Here, let me show you this." Janice got up and reached for a box behind Ronald. She took out a framed picture. "Do you remember this?"

Grinder took the picture from her. Lucas slid over beside him and together they studied the two figures under the glass.

"Jesus. I remember this." Grinder pointed. "That's Charlotte pier behind us. We were going fishing. Ma used to take us. Remember? When Pop was...unable to, let's say."

Lucas stood without answering. "You asked us to come here because there was some unfinished business you thought we needed to take care of. So we came; but I'm not sure we can help you with it."

"I know this is—"

"I'm not sure I even want to."

"Yes, I know she up and left your father—"

"She left *us*. Just ran off." Lucas wiped perspiration from his forehead with his wrist. "My brother was only eleven."

"She told me about your father—"

"Never mind Pop. At least he stayed."

Grinder laid the picture on the coffee table, then stood beside his brother. He put one hand on Lucas's shoulder. Ronald wobbled in his chair, trying to get up, but then thought better of it and leaned back again.

"Yinz shoulda had that beer," said Ronald.

"I think what my brother is saying is we don't know why we're here. There was something about someone named Paul, who lived with Ma. You wanted us to do something. I don't know what that's about. We don't know any Paul." Grinder took a deep breath and let his shoulders relax. "Look, we want to thank you for letting us know about our mother dying and all, but—"

"But it doesn't matter to us," said Lucas. "Come on Grinder. Let's get out of here."

Grinder nodded to Ronald as both men turned for the door.

"Could you at least meet Paul?" said Janice. "It might not mean nothing to you, but it woulda meant a lot to your mother."

"We really should get—"

"When will he get here?" asked Grinder.

"He's already here." She motioned them to follow her to the bedroom at the end of the hall. Janice opened the door and, just as she had done when they entered the apartment, extended a welcoming arm. Lucas and Grinder walked into the room. They looked around, but no one was there.

"I don't understand," said Lucas. "Where is he?"

"He's there," said Janice.

"Where?"

"Right there."

"That's Paul?"

"Yes, that's Paul."

Janice gestured to a bird on a perch near the window, its head buried under one wing. Beside him, in the corner, was a large cage made of chicken wire. Inside the cage was another perch. Attached to the cage was a plastic box full of wood shavings.

"I don't get it," said Grinder. "As far as I can tell, that's a bird."

"An African grey parrot, actually." Janice straightened her back with pride.

"You're kidding, right?" said Lucas. "Tell me I haven't driven the whole way from Rochester, New York to meet a goddam bird."

"African greys ain't just birds; they're one of the smartest animals in the world," said Janice. "And Paul's about as remarkable as they get."

"Unless he can stand on his head and spit nickels while reciting the Gettysburg Address, I don't care," said Lucas. He started to back out of the room.

The bird lifted his head from under his wing, whistled loudly once and then spoke. "Four score and seven years ago."

Grinder crossed the room to Paul. He was little more than a foot long from his black beak to his cherry-red tail feathers. He had a white mask and cropped grey feathers on his head that flowed down across his back. There were empty patches along his legs, under his wings and on his belly. He looked like he had been in a fight and had lost badly. His yellow eyes, speckled black in the middle, shifted with each step Grinder took.

"So this is Paul; Paul is not some guy who lived with my mother, our mother; he's like, Polly-want-a-cracker," said Grinder.

"He doesn't like to be called Polly."

"My apologies."

"Thank you," said Paul, as he ducked his head under his left wing, preening vigorously.

"Poor fella," said Janice.

"Poor fella?" said Lucas.

"Look at him. He's just about falling apart."

"How can you tell? It's a damn bird."

"Damn bird, damn bird," said Paul.

"Look at them feathers. They're all dull and thinned out terrible. He's been pickin' at 'em day and night. He barely sleeps."

"He barely sleeps." Lucas scratched the back of his neck. "Okay. Grinder, let's get out of here. This is ridiculous and I don't have time—"

"He loved your mother very much. And she loved him back."

"Well, that's wonderful. We haven't seen or heard from her in, what has it been, Grinder?"

"About thirty-five years." Grinder's eyes never left Paul.

"Yeah, and all the while she has been shacked up with a bird."

"That's an awful damn thing to say." Janice's jaw was jutting now.

Grinder came forward and tried to touch Paul's head with his finger. Paul leaned back and then lunged, pecking his hand. Grinder pulled back, but there was delight in his eyes.

"They were together for over twenty years," said Janice. "I know it's gotta be hard for you to hear, but Paul was, well, he was the light of her life. I mean, she and I was close friends, but Paul, he was different. He was everything to her."

Grinder reached again for Paul. When he didn't peck him, Grinder rubbed Paul's head gently. Paul pressed against Grinder's finger.

"Look at this," said Grinder.

"C'mon, really?" said Lucas.

Ronald appeared in the doorway. "Something, ain't he? Watch this." Ronald took a heaving breath and bellowed: "Go Steelers!"

"Go Steelers! Go Steelers!" said Paul, flaring his wings.

"Little fella loves his Steelers."

"Little fella loves his Steelers," said Lucas, shaking his head. "Well, that's very special, but I don't see what this has to do with us."

Grinder held out his arm and Paul put one foot, then the other on Grinder's hand. He whistled loudly again and chortled while bobbing his head vigorously. Grinder laughed.

"Seriously, Lucas, look at this."

"He's already takin' a liking to you," said Janice.

"What's wrong with him?" Grinder stroked Paul's head with his pointer.

"Do we actually care what's wrong with him?" said Lucas.

"Ain't sure, exactly. He don't want to eat. He picks at those poor feathers all the time. They're everywhere. Always been a big talker, but lately he don't have hardly nothin' to say."

"Been to a vet?"

"We can't afford no vet," said Ronald. "We're living off social security mostly, as it is. We make a little off the pot, but not much."

"Shush!" said Janice, swatting at Ronald with an open hand. "Don't pay no attention to him."

"You deal drugs?" said Lucas.

Janice and Ronald looked at each other and chuckled.

"No, I ain't no drug dealer. I just sell a little bit to some folks here in the building," said Janice.

"I could be wrong, but I think that's the definition of 'drug dealing.'"

"Absolutely not. We ain't like those scummy people they show on the TV, sellin' drugs to children, sleepin' in the gutter. My God, they should put them all in jail and throw the damn key away. My nephew gives me some from time to time, an ounce or so, and I sell it cheap to people who, you know, need it for pain or whatever. I provide a service. Like a nurse."

Lucas rubbed his forehead with the tips of his fingers.

"It's just weed," said Janice with a shrug.

"Did our mother use your service?"

"I never sold Millie any weed."

"Good." The folds in Lucas's forehead began to relax.

"I give it to her for free. She was my friend. She had arthritis so bad, you wouldn't believe." Janice's eyes got moist as her mouth turned down at the corners. "We used to sit on the balcony, just the two of us. I'd roll a joint. We'd toke back and forth. Millie'd always get the munchies, so we kept a bag or two of Doritos on hand, and we'd sit and talk and watch the sun go down and solve the problems of the world." Janice sniffed and wiped her eyes. "Made her all mellow."

Lucas looked at Grinder, his mouth hanging open. "Our mother was a drug addict."

"Don't you dare say that!" Janice lurched toward Lucas, her jaw jutting again, her fists clenched. "Don't you dare. Millie mighta been a shitty mother, I don't know, but she was a good woman."

"Shitty mother good woman," said Paul.

Grinder smiled broadly and rubbed Paul's beak. "I don't know. Ma sitting on the balcony smoking a joint while the sun goes down. I like it." Paul jumped from Grinder's hand to his perch. He spread his wings and then started pecking at the downy feathers on his legs.

"Janice, I think *you* are a good woman, too."

"I'm sure you do," said Lucas.

"Hey, watch it," said Ronald.

"But I don't know what you expect from us," said Grinder.

"Millie, your mother, was the best friend I ever had. And Paul is the only thing left of her. It would kill me to think of him dying or somethin' just 'cause I got no money. Know what I mean?" Janice's face looked like a topographical map of the world.

"Not really," said Lucas.

"You want us to take him to a vet?" asked Grinder.

"That would be wonderful." Janice's face smoothed into a broad grin.

"And pay for it, too," groused Lucas.

Janice focused on Grinder and tried to ignore Lucas. She put her hand on Grinder's arm and squeezed. "I think you must like your mom, some."

Before Grinder could say a word, Janice had left the room, returning with a smaller cage, a bag of mixed nuts and a Ziploc baggie.

"There's a vet on the North Side, he's expert on these exotic birds. I already called him and set up a time for tomorrow."

"What the—" groaned Lucas.

"Just 'cause I hoped that you'd be the good people I knew you'd be; that you'd do this one thing for your mother. We're so sorry we can't do nothin' more for Paul."

She handed everything to Grinder. His face opened wide as pie plate. "You want us to take Paul now?"

"The appointment's at 8 and he's way across the river. Just thought it'd save you time to have Paul with you. He's used to the little cage. You can let him out in the motel room. He won't do nothin', won't go nowhere. Look at him."

Paul was staring out the window now, a small pile of feathers on the floor beside him.

"You've gotta be kidding with this," said Lucas. He pulled Grinder away from Janice, but Grinder wouldn't make eye contact. "Are you serious about doing this?"

"I deal with dead animals all the time. I scoop 'em up off the street when you can hardly tell what they are. I trash them and sell them. Never saved a single one." He shrugged and glanced over his shoulder at Janice. "Yes, we will do this one thing."

"Bless you, bless you, bless you!" Janice hugged Grinder and planted a kiss on his cheek. "I'm thanking you from your mother." She turned to hug Lucas but quickly reconsidered.

She motioned Grinder to come closer. She handed him a Ziploc baggie. It had two shriveled marijuana buds in it, both about the size of Grinder's thumb, and several small papers. Grinder shook his head and chuckled.

"Just a little something for your trouble."

As they headed for the door, Ronald called out, "Wanna beer for the road?"

9

Lucas and Grinder crossed Clemente Bridge, its golden girders brilliant in the morning sun. They craned their necks to get a glimpse of PNC Park nestled on the Allegheny shore. Paul whistled, clucked and squawked in the back seat.

"Goddam feathers everywhere," said Lucas.

Grinder turned in his seat and reached for Paul. "How you doin' big guy?"

"How you doin'? How you doin'? How you doin'? How you doin'?"

"Enough already," said Lucas. He barely got his handkerchief out of his pocket before sneezing explosively.

Paul scuttled back and forth on his perch. "Lukie."

"Did you hear that? He said your name. Say it again, Paul. C'mon, boy." Grinder reached for some nuts and inched his hand toward the cage. "Here, boy." Paul looked out the window. Grinder spoke again, this time in a high-pitched squeal. "C'mon, Paul, one more time. Say it. Say Lukie. Say Lukie."

"For chrissakes, it's bad enough having one goddam bird…"

"Say Lukie, Lukie."

Paul head-bobbed back and forth as he watched Grinder's performance. "Lukie, my boy," said Paul. His voice, an octave lower now, quaked and quavered as he said the words again, this time slowly. "Lukie…my boy."

Grinder gasped and looked at Lucas who stared straight ahead as if nothing had happened. Grinder turned back around in his seat and fell silent.

"Lukie, my boy," said Paul, low and tender.

"Did you teach him that?"

"No."

"Last night when I was trying to go to sleep. You were in the bathroom for a long time with that bird."

"I didn't teach him anything, I swear."

"Cause I'm telling you…"

"I didn't." Grinder looked at his hands, like putty in his lap. He glanced out the window at nothing at all. Lucas huffed and blew his nose again.

"Must have gotten it from Ma." Grinder turned his head and gazed at Paul, who was chomping on the bars of his cage.

"Must have gotten it from Ma, my ass."

Paul reached for the seatbelt strap and began to twist and chew it.

"Where else?" said Grinder. "When we were growing up, that's what she said every time you came into the room, 'Lukie, my boy.'"

Lucas slammed on the breaks and leaned on the horn as a car suddenly stopped in front of him.

"You idiot!" he yelled at a driver. "What's the matter with you?" Once the idiot moved on, Lucas turned the car sharply, barely avoiding an oncoming bus. "Okay, this is the street, right?"

Grinder, catching his breath, didn't answer at first, but then checked MapQuest. "Yeah."

Two more blocks and they arrived. Lucas pulled into the tiny parking lot beside an American Foursquare house that had been converted into a veterinary hospital. Its waiting area jutted out from the side of the building like a massive goiter. The sign on the door said, "All human beings must be accompanied by a cat or a dog."

In the waiting room, Paul buried his head under one wing.

"Is this Paul?" said the lady at the desk.

"Yes," said Grinder.

"He doesn't look very happy today. What's wrong?"

"Don't know. That's why we're here."

"How long have you had Paul?"

"A day," said Lucas.

"Oh my, you're beginners. What made you decide to get an African grey?" The woman, her smock covered with kittens, smiled brightly.

"We didn't decide. It was our mother's," said Grinder.

"Oh, I see. She can no longer take care of him?"

"Not since she died, no," said Lucas.

"Oh." The lady shuffled nervously through a stack of manila folders until she found the right one. Then she quickly typed a form, printed it out and clipped it to the folder. "Well, I am so sorry. I am sure Paul is in good hands. Doctor will be with you in a few minutes."

A black and white cat eyed Paul. "Don't worry," said the woman with the carrier on her lap. "He's just bluffing. Wouldn't know what to do with a bird if it landed in his mouth." She leaned forward and wiggled her finger at the cat, which bit her. "Goddammit." The woman sucked on her injured finger, then, once the pain had subsided, studied the wound for a long while, looking for teeth marks. Finding none, she turned to her cat again. "C'mon Bootsy, be a good boy."

Paul paced back and forth on his perch, bobbing his head and clucking loudly. "Oh my, Oh my."

"Wow, he can talk," said the woman.

Grinder grinned and nodded. "He's a genius."

Lucas rolled his eyes and blew his nose again. "I'm telling you, that bird is driving my nose crazy." Sniff, sniff.

"I've been allergic to Ivan ever since I got him eleven years ago," said the man sitting across from Lucas and Grinder. He cupped a balled handkerchief in his hand. On the chair beside him sat a basset hound, his eyelids drooping, his paws gnarled. "Isn't that right, Ivan?" The man patted Ivan briskly and the dog wagged his tail ponderously. "But I'd rather deal with the allergies than get rid of my buddy here." Ivan gagged, coughed up a ball of thick phlegm and then deposited it onto his master's lap.

Lucas blew his nose again.

A balding man in a white coat opened the door and entered the waiting area. "You must be Paul," he said politely, leaning over the cage, his eyes wide with welcome. "And the two of you must be Paul's humans. I'm Dr. Vettman, and no, that's not a made up name. Come on in."

The exam room smelled like wet dog fur bathed in disinfectant. Lucas sneezed three times. "Oh my," said Dr. Vettman. "I'm so sorry."

Lucas waved his hand dismissively.

"Okay." Dr. Vettman leaned forward and spoke to Paul. "What seems to be the trouble, fella?" Lucas and Grinder looked at each other and then at Paul. Dr. Vettman stuck a finger in the cage and Paul pecked him. "Hey!" said Dr. Vettman, lurching back and grabbing his finger tightly with his other hand. "Is he always this aggressive?" He looked at his finger and shook it hard, as if the scratch might fall off onto the floor.

"Well, yes, he likes to peck," said Grinder.

"I guess he does." Vettman tried to laugh but only coughed.

"He hasn't been himself lately."

"Sick, you mean?"

"Yeah, he's not eating. Doesn't play with his stuff. Plucks his feathers all the time."

Dr. Vettman leaned forward again, his face near the cage. "His skin is bare in places. The tips of his wings are a bit of a shambles. His legs look like toothpicks. Poor guy." Dr. Vettman tried to reach for Paul again, but Paul lunged at his hand. "When did all this start?"

"When our mother died."

"Oh, I'm very sorry."

"It's okay. We hardly knew her," said Lucas. He folded his handkerchief and shoved it back in his pocket.

"Millie!" Paul flared his wings and cawed.

"What's he saying," asked Dr. Vettman.

"Nothing. He's just pretending to say stuff." Lucas hit the cage with his hand.

"Pretending to say stuff?" Grinder sighed and shook his head. He shifted in his chair so his back was turned to his brother as he spoke to the vet. "He's saying Millie."

"Millie," said Vettman.

"That was our mother's name."

"Millie need a joint! Millie need a joint!" Paul squawked loudly and banged the side of the cage.

"What's was that?"

"Who knows?"

"Sounds like, 'Millie needs a joint' to me."

"Yes, yes," bawled Paul.

"No, no, I think he's saying, 'Millie, what's the point?'"

"Ah. What's the point, indeed." Dr. Vettman put his face against the side of the cage, as if examining a bug under a microscope. "A little existential jokester, huh?" He suddenly leaned back in his chair and crossed his arms over his chest. "Doesn't surprise me one bit. You know, these African greys are smart cookies. They can develop quite a vocabulary. And they know how to use words properly." He chuckled at this, the creases around his eyes forming double parentheses. Paul hit the side of the cage again. Dr. Vettman didn't seem to notice.

"*Too* smart if you ask me," said Lucas. "Look, Doc, could he be, like, faking that he's sick?"

Grinder turned in his chair, stretched his legs out, crossed them at the ankles and listened to his brother's new theory.

"Faking?" Dr. Vettman placed one hand on his chin, scratching his cheek with his index finger. "Hmm."

"I mean, I've seen him go to his food and take some in his mouth. But when he sees me at the door, he spits it out again and starts messing with his feathers."

"You've given this a lot of thought," said Grinder.

Lucas glowered at his brother. "Shut up."

Vettman was staring at the ceiling now, deep in thought. "And why would Paul do that?"

"I think he's trying to piss us off."

Grinder snorted.

"You think your mother's parrot is trying to piss you off by not eating and by plucking out his feathers," said Dr. Vettman. "And he wants to piss you off, because?"

"How am I supposed to know? That's your job. You said they're smart, right?"

"Yeah, they're smart. But not sinister."

"I don't know. I'm telling you he looks at us strange."

Grinder laid a hand on his brother's shoulder. "Are you okay?" Lucas shrugged his hand away.

"Strange?"

"Look, Doc, I don't think my brother—"

"Look at him. Right now he looks just fine, doesn't he?" said Lucas.

Both men looked at Paul, who stared at them, dead eyed.

"Yeah." Dr. Vettman rolled up the sleeves of his lab coat.

"If you weren't here, though, he would be, I don't know, kind of squinting at us, at me, actually."

"Lucas?" Grinder tapped his brother on the shoulder.

"Squinting? Not blinking?" Dr. Vettman glanced sideways at Paul again. Paul whistled, his eyes big as saucers.

"Yeah, squinting."

"And you think his squinting means what?"

"I think it means he hates our guts."

"Lucas, people usually gotta know us more than two days before they start hating us. I'm sure it's the same with birds," said Grinder.

"Uh huh." Dr. Vettman was standing now, his enthusiasm for this topic clearly on the wane. "Well, I don't know anything about African greys that squint or what it might mean." With that, he abruptly reached into the cage and scratched Paul's head. Paul did not object.

"I'm telling you, doc, that's what he's doing. Nothing but hostility in his eyes, like he wants to peck us to death or something."

"Ok. I don't know about that either. Tell you what, though. I do know someone who might be helpful." Vettman opened the top drawer to his desk and pulled out a business card. He handed it to Grinder. "Someone who works with this sort of thing."

"What's that supposed to mean?" Lucas's left eye lid began to twitch. Paul whistled again loudly and leaned forward at Lucas, hissing.

"He's a psychologist…"

"Oh my God," said Lucas, his eyes in a continuous roll.

"…that specializes in people and pets."

"Does he have a little tiny couch?"

"Stop it." Grinder took the card from Dr. Vettman.

"Gentleman, do as you please." Dr. Vettman reached for the door again, then stopped and bent down to Paul. "Good luck."

Back at the motel, Grinder waited for Lucas to take a shower before calling Dr. Goldbloom. Shortly Lucas returned, enveloped in a heavy mist. He held a towel around his waist with one hand while using a face towel to rub his wet scalp with the other.

"Oh my God, that felt good."

Grinder was sitting on the bed holding a phone to his ear, Paul in a cage beside him.

"What are you doing?"

"Thank you very much," said Grinder. "No, we can make it. Okay, see you then."

"See who what?"

Grinder held up the business card that Vettman had given them.

"Dr. Sidney Goldbloom. When I told him about our case—"

"Our case? When did we become a case?" Lucas threw a towel onto the bathroom floor.

"Case the joint, case the joint," said Paul, who was tugging on a piece of the curtain draw that Grinder had cut off and put in his cage.

"'Case the joint', isn't that hilarious?" Grinder grinned from ear to ear.

"Grinder, what are you thinking? I don't have time for this crap. I gotta check out of this place; Martha's going to kill me." Lucas's whole body was red. Made worse by a sneezing attack that bent him over the desk.

"God bless you, God bless you, God bless you." Paul was weaving and bobbing now.

"Shut up…bird!"

"Lucas, sit down, take a breath for God's sake. The world's not coming to an end. I spoke to the desk and we have the room for two more days, longer if we need it." Grinder took the pot from the Mr. Coffee on the dresser and poured some into a Styrofoam cup. "Want some?"

"What?" Lucas tore off his bottom towel and stood naked in front of the window.

"Nakey, nakey, nakey, nakey," cawed Paul, his defoliated wings flapping.

"Do you want some coffee?"

"No, I don't want any goddam coffee." Vertical lines, like goal posts, rose between Lucas's eyes as he glared at Paul. "You can't be serious about this shrink thing."

Grinder nuzzled the cage with his nose. Paul whistled and poked him softly with his beak. "Grinder, my baby; Grinder, my baby," said Paul, low and gentle, just like Ma. Grinder sat bolt upright. Then he pressed his face to the cage and listened but Paul didn't speak again.

"Did you hear that?"

"What?"

"What he said to me."

"No. Why?"

Grinder's eyes welled.

"What the hell is wrong with you?"

"Nothin'. Forget it."

Lucas rolled another tissue and tossed it into the wastebasket under the desk. Grinder wiped his eyes with the back of his hand and stood over Paul's cage as Paul tight-rope walked back and forth along the perch. Paul gripped the bars with his beak and shook them. He then gave four sharp chirps, cocked his head and opened his mouth, wagging his black tongue.

Lucas watched. "Grinder?"

Grinder sat down on the bed beside the cage. His face had stupor written all over it. Lucas stared at him and frowned.

"Hellooo-o! Is anybody home?"

"What?" Grinder's eyes were locked onto Paul's.

"Are you okay?" asked Lucas.

"Fine." Grinder turned to face his brother. "Look, I think we should do this. Where's the harm?"

"Where's the harm? It's ridiculous. It's a waste of time and money. Animal shrinks probably charge up the wazoo 'cause they know that if you're there to begin with, you're crazy enough to pay anything. I'm telling you, I may be screwed up, but I'm not that screwed up."

"I got the money from the casino. We'll use some of that."

Lucas huffed and frowned and sneezed.

"My money. My call. Let's drop another penny in the slot."

Dr. Goldbloom's office was in a strip mall. With its vaulted glass exterior and shuttered drive-up window, it looked like it had been the branch office of a long defunct bank. The sign at the door said, *University of Pittsburgh Medical Center, Division of Animal Behavior, Sidney Goldbloom, DVM, PhD.*

Grinder nudged Lucas in the ribs. "Look at that."

"Can't be for real."

"Looks pretty real to me."

Dr. Goldbloom, or Sid, as he preferred to be called, had bushy grey hair that ringed his head and neck like a lion's mane. He had glasses perched on top of his head and reading glasses balanced on the tip of his nose. He nodded with interest and shook his head slowly no matter what they said. He appeared to be either pondering everything in depth or falling asleep.

"So, Dr. Goldbloom…"

"Sid. Please."

"Okay. Sid."

Dr. Goldbloom wiggled a finger at Paul and then looked back at Grinder.

"My brother and I are not exactly sure why we are here."

"Ah," said Sid, rocking back in his swivel chair.

"The other guy, Vettman…"

"Excellent vet, Vettman." Sid leaned forward now, his eyes steady.

"He's the one that said we should see you," said Grinder. "He thought there were issues."

"Which I think, just to be honest, is a load of crap. No offense," said Lucas.

"Hm." Sid leaned his elbows on his desk. "And yet you came?" Sid tilted his head slightly as his left eyebrow crinkled. Lucas took a tissue from his pocket and blew his nose. Grinder laid his hand on top of Paul's cage.

"And yet you came," said Paul, sticking his tongue out and bobbing his head.

"I like him very much already," said Sid, his hands now clasped behind his head. "He's sharp, isn't he?" Sid got up from his chair and plopped down on the floor beside Paul's cage. Paul extended his wings and hissed. Sid sat quietly and studied Paul, saying nothing. In the long silence that followed, Lucas nudged Grinder and jerked his head for them to leave. Grinder shook his head vigorously yet almost invisibly, as if he were having a seizure.

"They do not know what to do with you, do they?" said Sid, his eyebrows drooping. "Mommy would know what to do, wouldn't she?" Lucas dropped his tissue into his lap. Grinder leaned back in his chair. "Do you miss your mother?" asked Dr. Goldbloom.

Grinder and Lucas sat stone still. Grinder inhaled. "We didn't really know our—"

"I was asking Paul."

"Oh."

"Dr. Vettman emailed me some information." Sid inched closer to the cage. "Do you miss Millie?" Grinder leaned forward, elbows on his knees. Lucas didn't move. Paul side-stepped across his perch and plucked at the cage with his beak. He opened his wings wide again. His thinning grey feathers clung to partially exposed quills. Dr. Sid reached into the cage with one finger. Paul looked at it, then took Sid's finger in his mouth, but didn't bite. He massaged it with his tongue and then let go. He whistled and then chortled.

"Yes, I understand," said Sid.

"Is he serious with this?" whispered Lucas.

"Shh." Grinder, his face red, wouldn't look at his brother.

"But is he serious? I mean, really?"

Sid rubbed Paul's head with his finger and scratched his belly. He picked up the cage and sat it on his desk.

"You know, it doesn't take a veterinarian with a degree in psychology to tell what's wrong with Paul. Have you ever seen someone who is depressed?" Grinder and Lucas stared. "They look kind of disheveled; haven't groomed themselves in a while; maybe lost some weight; got no energy." Sid pointed at Paul. "Look." Paul was still now, a few random feathers sticking out at odd angles, bare spots here and there. Even when he cawed and chirped, his voice sounded raspy, worn.

"Paul is unhappy. Simple as that. You've got a sad little guy on your hands."

"Is there any chance that you are just a tiny bit nutty yourself? Sid?" asked

Lucas.

Sid fell into his chair snorting with laughter, then stopped as quickly as he started. "No. Not a chance. Like I said, African greys are very smart. They are attuned to their surroundings and to the people that love them. Or don't love them. When something goes wrong, they know. Think about it. One day she's here and the next day she's not."

The exam room was quiet except for the click, click, click of Paul tapping the cage. Perspiration beaded Lucas's upper lip. Grinder stood and placed his hand on top of the cage.

"Look at his feathers. They're a mess. His eyes look vacant," said Goldbloom.

Lucas wiped his lip with a tissue and Grinder looked out the window.

"Even birds having feelings."

"C'mon." Lucas scowled.

"When you look at someone, you can tell a lot by their expression, posture, tone of voice, change in habits. There are a million ways you can tell that someone is depressed. The same is true for other animals, even birds."

"I'm tellin' you, I'm looking at Paul here and all I'm seeing is a bird with buggy eyes, and claws that can rip your face off if you aren't careful," said Lucas.

Grinder reached into the cage again, trying to scratch Paul.

"Family is often part of the problem. And can be part of the solution."

"Look, Doc."

"Sid."

"Whatever. We aren't his family. In case you hadn't noticed, we aren't birds; we aren't flying around your office and shitting on your head."

Grinder gripped his brother's arm. "What Lucas means is that we don't know Paul. At all. We hadn't seen our mother in, well, let's just say a very long time. We didn't even know she was dead, let alone that she had a bird."

"How long did your mother have Paul?"

"It was a long time." Grinder turned and took a long look at Paul. "Longer than she lived with us."

"Okay. And now she's gone," said Sid.

"Dead, yeah," grumbled Lucas, his head tilted back, face about to explode as he waited for another sneeze, but it never came.

"And it was just the two of them?"

"As far as we know, yes."

"Hm," said Sid. He rolled the sleeves down on his lab coat.

"What?" said Lucas.

"Well, Paul's unhappiness, his grief, makes sense." He reached into the cage again. This time Paul walked along the perch and then leaned his head against Sid's hand. "He must have been very attached to your mother. And she must have loved him very much. Not unusual for people to form very close bonds with their pets, like they were children or spouses. Often when a pet dies, the owner will experience deep sadness and grief." Sid leaned over and looked into Paul's eyes as Paul trilled. "In this case, the pet has outlived the owner. He is all alone. Probably knows it at some level. And is sad."

"We're still talking about a bird, right?" said Lucas, his arms folded across his chest.

Grinder wiped the corner of one eye, then the other. "Doc, are you saying that he's not eating because he misses our mother?" Sid raised his eyebrows and tipped his head as if to say, "Of course."

"How long's it going to take for him to snap out of it? I mean, he's a damn bird," said Lucas.

"Well, that's hard to say. Most animals make the transition fairly smoothly. If they have someone who cares for them, loves them." Sid glanced up from the cage and gave Lucas the stink eye. "But some don't. Some need help."

"So, can you do anything about this, Doc? I mean, we have just arrived on the scene. We don't know anything." Grinder stuck his finger into the cage, but Paul hid his head under his wing.

"Am I the only one here who can tell that he's just a goddam bird," said Lucas.

"That is probably not helpful. He may feel your hostility." Sid took the glasses off the top of his head and tossed them on his desk.

Grinder stepped between Sid and Lucas. "Come on, Lucas. He's the expert."

"Have you gone crazy? This is a bird with a brain the size of my thumbnail. Do you think all of this psycho-crap is for real?"

"I don't know. Do you have a better explanation?"

"Yes, he's just a bird who hates our guts."

"He can hate, but he can't feel sad?" said Grinder.

"Listen to yourself. You have totally drunk the Kool-Aid," said Lucas.

"What's that supposed to mean?"

"Gentleman, please, there are people and, more importantly, their pets in the waiting room." Sid's face was pinched, like he had tasted something sour.

Parrot Talk

"Look, Doc, I'm sorry," said Grinder. "We aren't bad people. It's just that we don't know what to do."

Paul clung to the side of the cage, his beak closed tightly around the metal. From his throat came a gnawing sound, low and painful. Sid pointed at Paul.

"Look."

Grinder turned, but Lucas didn't. Sid's dark eyebrows met in the middle. He nodded for Lucas to pay attention.

"Alright, alright," said Lucas.

Paul leaped from one side of the cage to the other, clenching the metal mesh again in his beak.

"You think *you're* confused. African greys can be fearful, even phobic, when their world is turned upside down. They come undone when everything is in flux. They are like newborns, completely dependent." Sid's mouth was pulled up to one side as he paused. "Dependent on you two, unfortunately. You two have to be his nest, for lack of a better way of putting it."

"I didn't sign on for this bullshit," said Lucas.

"Do any of us sign on for the bullshit in our lives?" said Sid. "Face it, he is your inheritance. Your mother didn't leave you a million bucks or a nice big trust fund. Instead, she left you Paul."

Grinder looked at Sid and smiled apologetically.

10

Lucas pushed the speaker button on his phone, tossed it onto the pillow and collapsed on the bed. "Martha—"

"Don't Martha me. I'm sick of you and your half-wit brother traipsing all over hell's half acre, while I'm stuck watching these nasty people wash their nasty clothes."

"But—"

"You know what I found last night?"

"No, what?"

"Guess, just guess, I dare you. I found a pile of crap in the corner by one of the dryers. A pile of crap, for God's sake. Who the hell are these people? They come to wash their clothes and they can't control themselves?"

"It was a dog."

"What?"

"Guy comes in every week and his dog craps in the corner. I warned him about it but—"

"But what? What?"

"He's a regular."

"What the hell does that mean?"

"It's hard enough to keep business going without chasing people away."

"So, if I took a crap at Grandpa Sam's Restaurant, like right there in front of God and everybody, are they supposed to say, 'Oh well, she's a regular, heat up the marinara.'"

Grinder watched as Lucas's powder blue shirt turned navy from perspiration.

"Lucas?"

Lucas sat up in bed, took off his sweaty shirt and threw it on the floor.

"Lucas! Don't do this. Don't pretend you're not there. I'm not that stupid."

Lucas took the phone in both hands, put it in his mouth and bit down hard.

"Lucas!"

"What, what, what! What in the world do you want from me? My goddam mother's dead and now we have a goddam bird and we're here in a goddam motel in goddam Pittsburgh. What do you want from me?"

"Why did you let Grinder talk you into keeping that thing? What were you thinking? The man trolls for dead animals. For chrissakes, he's an idiot and now you're an idiot."

Grinder leaned close to his brother's phone. "Hi Martha. Sorry about the whole Grandpa Sam thing. Just doesn't sound like you."

"You go straight to hell, you hear me, you, you, you dead animal lover!"

Lucas scowled at Grinder and waved for him to leave the room. "Martha, why the hell did you call me anyway?"

Grinder went into the bathroom and closed the door. He sat on the toilet seat. He looked at Paul, his cage balanced precariously in the bathtub. "Hey, buddy, how you doin'?" Grinder ran hot water into the sink. He got out his razor and some Gillette foamy. Lathered up and ran the blade across his cheeks and under his chin. He let the water out and wiped off before turning to Paul, who was watching him with great interest.

"So, how do I look?"

Paul clicked and yowled. He swayed forward and back, then moon-walked sideways along his perch. He yacked loudly several times before Grinder looked again.

"Hey, what's up?"

"Thank you, Grinder," said Paul. "Thank you. Thank you. Eeeeeck-ooooo-aaaww."

Grinder's face went puzzly. He knelt on the bath mat beside the tub. He stared into Paul's eyes and waited. "What did you say?"

"Thank you. Thank you." Paul coughed like he was clearing his throat. "You are good boy. Always good boy, aaaaawck! Will always be good boy."

Grinder got up and leaned back against the sink. "Paul?" he said, tentatively. "Paul?" But Paul was busy trying to untie a knotted piece of rope. He squawked and trilled as he held it down with his claws.

Lucas pounded on the door, startling Grinder, who fell back into the corner by the sink, unable to move. "Grinder, what the hell are you doing in there?" Grinder's mouth dropped open as he continued to scrutinize Paul, who now was shelling a peanut. "Grinder, come out here. We gotta talk." Grinder hesitated to respond, but when nothing else came from the beak of the feathered oracle, Grinder decided to open the door.

"My God, you look like you saw a ghost. Are you sick or something?"

Grinder closed the door behind him and then slumped into the easy chair by the window.

"Paul."

"What about him?"

"He talked to me."

"You just noticed this? He's been yammering nonstop ever since we got him." Lucas, hands on hips, waited for Grinder to say something. Grinder turned his head, but then looked back out the window at the Gulf Building. "So? What?"

"Nothing." Grinder got out of the chair and opened the mini-bar.

"Hey, hey, that costs money." But Grinder had already opened a bag of cashews and a bottle of Iron City. Lucas shook his head and huffed, then took a bottle for himself. "Look, I gotta talk to you."

"Wha'd she want?" asked Grinder, his face still chalk white.

"It's about Pop."

"Don't tell me he's dead, too."

"Worse."

"What worse?"

"He's coming to Pittsburgh."

"What?"

"Martha said he called, looking for me. He was all upset and wasn't making any sense. He kept talking about wanting to get things right. I don't know if it's 'cause Ma died or what."

Grinder opened the bathroom door and peeked in at Paul.

"Are you listening to me?" said Lucas.

"Yeah. Pop's usual bullshit."

Lucas dropped his empty bottle into the wastebasket and checked the mini-bar for another. Finding none, he opened a Mountain Dew. "I don't know. Martha said he sounded crazy as usual, but sincere, like he meant it."

"Drunk?"

"No, sober as a judge." The flood gates let loose on Lucas's sinuses; he started sneezing and couldn't stop. Grinder picked up the box of tissue by the bed and tossed it to him. He blew as hard as he could while Paul honked in the bathroom like a Canada goose. "Is that damn bird making fun of me?"

Grinder shrugged. Lucas regained his composure, crunched the tissues and dropped them in the wastebasket.

"Martha said he left yesterday. Driving straight through from Jupiter."

"He what?"

"You heard me."

"He's on his way?"

"That's the story."

Grinder went to the mini-bar for a Toblerone. He pointed it at Lucas, who said, "Yeah." He tore the wrapper apart and broke off a piece for his brother. He lay on the bed, studying the stain pattern on the ceiling. "What the heck is going on?" he said.

Lucas sighed through his muffled nose. He scratched his head and then sat on the bed beside his brother. "Well, Martha said something about religion."

"What about it?"

"Pop's got it."

"Religion." Grinder reached into his mouth to loosen a chunk of Toblerone that was stuck on his molars.

"Yeah. Martha said he had some kind of religious experience while carving the turkey last Thanksgiving and he hasn't been the same since."

"Carving the turkey."

"Yeah, I don't know, he saw something in the turkey or the turkey did something, it's all unclear to me. Martha said that even Lucille thought it was a little more wacky than usual, but she went along with it 'cause Pop was so ecstatic about the whole thing. She was just happy he wasn't sitting on the front porch counting cars all day long. Instead of counting cars, he started talking about his conversion to anybody who'd listen, and even to some who wouldn't listen."

Grinder bit off another piece of Toblerone and held the remainder of the candy bar out for his brother to take.

"No thanks. Took to preaching about it at the mall, but the mall manager asked him not to do it because it was upsetting customers and made them worry that the end of the world was coming."

"Because of a turkey?"

"Not sure exactly. But the mall guy was pretty insistent 'cause they were just starting their annual 'Be a Santa' mall-wide sale. Martha said Pop was pretty insistent himself and started talking about his God given freedoms. I guess he even tossed in gun freedom for good measure."

"We're still talking about the turkey?" Grinder struggled with a wad of Toblerone and spit some of it into the wastebasket.

"Yeah. Anyway, Pop finally settled down and they came to a compromise."

"Uh huh," Grinder twisted his tongue sideways to nudge one final piece that was stuck between his gums and cheek. He pulled it out with his finger, looked at it and then popped it back into his mouth.

"So, Pop's allowed to preach in front of the mall all he wants, just so he isn't within fifty feet of the entrance."

"God bless America."

"Yep." Lucas looked into the wastebasket at the remaining Toblerone, but thought better of it. "So, it sounds like he's got it bad and he's not giving up on it."

"All 'cause of a turkey."

"I guess."

"Martha sure talked to Pop for a long time."

"She sure did."

"What does she think?"

"She doesn't know. She said he was awful convincing. Guess he's going to a church or tent place or something and everyone there thinks he's all kinds of inspiring. What was it they said?" Lucas closed his eyes tight in heavy thought. "That he had a 'revelation,' that's what it was. They all thought he'd had a divine revelation and now was speaking God's truth."

"That's never good." Grinder began to laugh but then started coughing and couldn't catch his breath. Lucas wacked him once on the back.

"This isn't funny."

"I beg to differ. This is as funny as it gets."

Lucas walked across the room, rubbing his face and forehead. He pulled a T-shirt from his suitcase, put it on and then turned to his brother. "Look, I don't care about Pop and his turkey and his religion. I just want to get rid of that damn bird…"

"What?" Grinder stopped trying to pick the Toblerone from his teeth.

"…and go home. That's all I want. Lose the bird and go home."

Grinder was standing now, too, both men looking like they were facing off for a duel. "What are you talking about? Sell Paul?"

"Have you looked at it lately? Who the hell would buy that thing? I figured we'd give it to the vet or a shelter or something. Anything. You didn't think for a minute that we were gonna keep it."

Grinder chewed the corner of his mouth. "What made you think this was your call? I'm not sure we should get rid of Paul at all. He's sick."

"You're as crazy as Pop."

Grinder's eyes narrowed. "Look, Lucas, it ain't right to dump Paul off like he's just, just…"

"A bird?"

"No, like he's just nothing."

"I'm not saying it's nothing. I'm saying it's nothing we have to deal with. Look, Ma died and flipped us the bird, literally. What in the world makes you feel like we got some responsibility for it?"

"*Him*."

"*It, him*, whatever. He's not our problem."

Grinder sat up, his arms raised for emphasis. "He's a living creature."

"Since when did you give a good crap about 'living creatures'?"

Lucas crossed the room, pulled back the curtain and sat on the sill. He stared out the window at nothing at all. Grinder turned his back on his brother, then headed for the lounge chair across the room. Like two boxers in their respective corners, both men rested and waited. Finally, the silence allowed for a change of subject. Lucas looked over his shoulder at his brother.

"We're not going out again, are we?" he said.

Grinder nodded. Lucas stepped away from the window, dropped his drawers and kicked them onto the love seat. He sat on the end of the bed and started clicking through the channels, settling on *Entertainment Tonight*. Grinder took off his pants, too, and hung them in the closet. He pulled the red sweatshirt over his head and smelled it before tossing it on the closet floor. He took off his black T-shirt, rolled it in a ball and tossed it on the floor beside the sweatshirt. He stood for a moment in near-nakedness, wiggling his toes, and then sat down again in the lounge chair.

"When's Pop gonna get here?" said Grinder.

"How should I know?"

They fell silent until the next commercial. Grinder examined his brother. He had never noticed the ring of extra flesh that gathered in a fold around his neck.

"Hey?"

"Uh huh," said Lucas.

Grinder paused, thinking.

"What is it?" Lucas turned and looked at his brother from the corner of one eye.

Grinder scratched his belly. "We're not getting rid of Paul."

"You think?" said Lucas calmly, but with an edge.

Their eyes locked briefly. Grinder got up, opened the bathroom door and went in.

"There's my good boy," said Paul.

11

"Is anybody in there?" The door rumbled and shook. "Wake up you lazy good-for-nothings!" *Bam! Pow! Pop!* "I'm tellin' you, open the goddam door!"

Lucas snorted, rolled over and looked at his phone. Grinder rolled the other direction, closed his eyes and pulled the sheet over his head.

"Lucas! Lucas! Lucas!"

Lucas, foot tangled in his sheet, fell onto the floor. "I'm coming goddammit!" He stubbed his toe on the way to the door and was holding his foot in his hand when Martha barged in.

"What's wrong with your foot? You can't take care of yourself for ten minutes without me." The barometric pressure in the room crashed as Martha blustered past Lucas. "What a dump? Why couldn't you go to a Marriott or Wyndham? What is this? What's wrong with you?"

Lucas hopped to the bed where he nursed his swelling toe while wiping his running nose. His face was beet red, his blood pressure ramping up to meet the challenge of the engulfing storm.

"Where's that stupid brother of yours?" Grinder lifted one arm into the air and then let it fall dead at his side. "Why are you doing this to my husband?"

"Ex," said Lucas.

"Whatever. I'm talking to you, Grinder. What are you doing with your mother's bird? A mother, who, may I remind you, never gave two shits about you boys. What's with the bird? What are you trying to do? Drive my poor Lucas half out of his skull?"

Grinder sat up, made bug eyes at Martha, then lay back down again.

"What is that?"

Lucas wiped perspiration from his brow. "Why did you come here?"

"What?"

"Why are you here, Martha?"

"What, no 'Hi, honey, how are you?' 'Happy to see you, darling.' Is this what it's come to?"

"Yes, this's exactly what it has goddam come to. What in the world are you doing standing in my motel room three hundred miles away from the laundromat?"

"I gave my best years to you."

"The laundromat?"

"And this is the thanks I get."

"For chrissakes, the laundromat."

"I shut it down."

"What?" Lucas struggled to his foot, dancing to and fro to keep his balance. "Whada you mean?" Clouds gathered around his eyes. "You did what?"

Martha's face sobered. The pain in Lucas's foot didn't matter anymore as he walked toward her, double-chin jutting. "Tell me you didn't close the laundromat. Tell me you didn't. Please. I need to hear you say that you didn't do such a colossally stupid thing."

"Okay, I didn't close the laundromat." Lucas straightened his back and stretched his arms. His jaw loosened and he blinked for the first time. "Not permanently. I put a sign on the door. It said 'closed due to family catastrophe; back soon.' Smiley face." She held her arms out as if to say, 'Ta-da!' Lucas reached for his T-shirt and wiped sweat from his neck.

"Are you okay?" asked Martha. She put her hands on his shoulders and examined his face.

Lucas opened his eyes wide and said in a whisper, "My God. My God. What were you thinking, Martha?"

"C'mon, bubby, you only keep that place open so you can take a loss. Really. I'm no dope. Your tax man'll be happy."

Lucas tried to wipe the defeat off his face with the bedsheet. "Why the effing eff are you here?"

Martha pulled him closer, pinched his cheeks, kissed him hard on the mouth, then erased the lipstick with her thumb and rubbed it on his T-shirt. "Honey, really. Somebody has to look after you." She glared at Grinder. "It sure isn't gonna be that guy." Grinder rolled over on his side, got up and tumbled onto the easy chair. Wrapped in a sheet, his face in expressionless repose, he looked like an addled Buddhist monk. "Look at him."

"I'm telling you, you didn't have to do this. We have things under control," said Lucas.

"Oh you do, do you? What are you going to do with that bird?"

"Get rid of him." Grinder shook his head vigorously in disagreement. "Maybe."

"What are you going to do when your old man comes?"

"Who knows?"

"When are you coming home?"

Lucas shrugged.

"You're right," said Martha. "Everything's under control, just like always."

"Don't start with me." Lucas pulled away from Martha and toppled back into bed.

"Don't start with you? If it wasn't for me..."

"What? If it wasn't for you, what exactly? I would be a happy man?"

"Happy, my ass. Happy is overrated. Trust me. So don't gimme any of that 'you ruined my happiness' crap."

Lucas turned his head to the window. The air conditioner hummed into action. Muffled laughter filtered into the room from the neighbors next door. Grinder lifted his head and smiled at Martha. A frown crawled into the corner of Martha's mouth. "What?" she said.

"Would you like to meet Paul?"

"Paul? Who's Paul."

"The bird."

"The bird? You call him by, like, a real name?"

"Yeah, that's his name. Just like your name is Martha, instead of—human being."

"I should just smack you."

Martha took two steps toward Grinder before Lucas corralled her. "C'mon, for God's sake."

"I'm tellin' you, Grinder." Martha shook a fist in his direction.

"Do you wanna meet Paul?" said Grinder with annoying calm. He opened the bathroom door. Paul was motionless on his perch, as if ready for inspection. Martha took a cautious step into the room.

"Jesus, it stinks in here," said Martha. She leaned forward and squinted at

Paul. "My God, he's big for a parakeet." Martha shuffled forward on her heels. "Coo-coo! Coo-coo!" Paul didn't move, didn't blink. "What's the matter with him? Isn't he supposed to be super smart? Doesn't seem so smart to me. Hey! Coo-coo! Squawk! Squawk!" Martha flapped her arms. Paul tilted his head. Martha was on her knees now beside the bathtub. "What's wrong with his feathers?" Martha pressed her face nearer the cage. "Hi, Polly." Paul leaned forward, almost parallel to the bottom of the cage. "Does Polly want a cracker?" Martha snorted and looked back over her shoulder at Grinder. "Do you ever give him a cracker?" Martha put a finger through the cage. "Hey, you?"

Paul leaped from his perch, his wings flared, his eyes dark and fierce, and snagged Martha's finger in his beak.

"Oh my God! He's killing me to death!" Martha was on her back now.

"What the hell's going on?" said Lucas as he lunged into the room. Grinder sat on the toilet seat, legs crossed, arms folded on his lap. "Do something!"

Grinder shrugged as Lucas captured Martha around the waist and pulled her away from the cage.

"Grinder, for chrissakes! This isn't funny. He coulda hurt her."

"Coulda? Whadaya mean coulda? Look at that finger. My God, look at that nail, the polish, my God, I just paid eighty bucks for a mani and look at it now."

"What are you doing spending that kinda money on your damn finger nails?"

"I'm gonna sue that little bastard! Did you see what he did to me?" The tip of her finger was bleeding. Lucas grabbed her wrist, stuck her hand in the sink and turned on the cold water. Grinder took a handful of popcorn and dried bananas from a bag beside the toilet and dropped them into the cage. Paul made siren sounds—"Woop, woop, woop!"—pecked at the popcorn, took a banana slice in his beak and returned to his perch, where he shuffled and bobbed, whistled and cawed.

"Look at him, he's laughing at me," said Martha as she clutched her damaged finger, now wrapped in layer upon layer of toilet paper.

"Goddammit, Grinder," said Lucas. He took Martha by her good arm and escorted her from the bathroom, slamming the door behind him.

Grinder turned off the water and sat again on the toilet seat, his hands behind his head as he leaned back against the wall. He gave Paul a sideways glance. Paul tap danced across the perch, whistling and dinging like a doorbell. Grinder watched him, puzzled. He got off the toilet and knelt on the floor. Paul stopped as Grinder rested his arms on the side of the tub.

Grinder shook his head at Paul and smiled. Paul leaped again to the side of the cage, his head between the bars, his pale yellow eyes steady. Grinder reached out with one finger and scratched the top of Paul's head. Paul seemed to clear his throat.

"You got something to say?" said Grinder.

"Millie love Grinder, eeeeeck."

"What?"

12

The Fort Pitt tunnel spewed traffic into downtown Pittsburgh and the sun glistened off the two-hundred-thirty-one glass spires adorning PPG Place. The rivers were quiet in the windless morn. The fountain at the point spread a ghostly mist across the entrance to the Ohio. Confused by the events of the previous night, Grinder, nevertheless, was calmed by the view. Behind him, Martha and Lucas battled wordlessly over what little territory remained of their Queen-sized bed. He hadn't yet removed the towel that covered Paul's cage, although he thought he heard him rustling. The coffee maker gurgled in the background.

"Do you mind?" Martha sat up and held the sheet tight to her bosom.

"Not at all."

"You're naked."

"I know that," said Grinder, about to turn around.

"No! Don't move. Honest to God, are you gonna be twelve forever?" Martha studied her thumb. Then she pulled on a robe and got out of bed. She hid her eyes with the palms of her hands. "Look, I wanna take a shower. Can you take that damn bird out of the bathtub?"

Grinder slipped on a pair of jeans and retrieved Paul from the tub. "You are good to go."

"Just keep him away from me," said Martha, her eyes still shielded. "Are you still naked?"

"As can be."

"What is wrong with you?" she said, one arm stretched out in front of her as she gingerly crossed the floor. "Ouch!"

"That was the door."

"Go to hell."

Martha disappeared into the bathroom and immediately turned on the shower. Grinder lifted the towel off the cage. "Good morning, big guy." He paused, giving Paul time to reply, but instead, Paul bobbed and weaved side-to-side and yowled. Grinder poured seed into Paul's feeder, tossed a handful of nuts and dried fruits into the cage. "How's that?" Grinder said expectantly, but Paul was busy shelling and munching his breakfast. Grinder was glad that he was eating.

Lucas struggled to sit up. "Is she gone?"

"Nope."

Lucas shook his head vigorously and blew his nose with such ardor that Grinder thought his brother might turn himself inside out. Then, like always, he checked his tissue, for what, Grinder was unsure. Lucas lay back on the bed and sighed.

"Tough day already?"

"Don't be a smart ass."

"Smart ass, smart ass," said Paul.

"Isn't there an off button on that thing?" Lucas sat up again, tucked two pillows behind him and then leaned back. "I've got you and that yapping bird, and now, Martha; all in this one room. She in there?" Lucas nodded toward the bathroom.

Grinder gave him a thumbs up. Lucas closed his eyes. Grinder took the plastic cover off the Styrofoam cup and poured some coffee. He leaned over his brother, holding the coffee near his nose. Lucas opened one eye and, seeing the coffee, sat up. "Thanks." Lucas sipped, then gulped. "My God, that's awful. Why can't these coffee machines make coffee that's actually hot?" Lucas finished his cup.

"Want some more?"

"Yeah." Grinder took his cup. Paul snorted and crackled and whistled. He reached with his beak for the curtain draws, pulling one into his cage. "Gotcha, gotcha. Paul gotcha."

"My God," said Lucas. He sat up as Grinder handed him another cup of coffee, but before taking it, he covered his face with a tissue and sneezed. Grinder pulled the cup away.

"God bless you, Lukie," said Paul, but Lucas couldn't hear him over the trumpeting sound of his own nose.

Lucas took the coffee from his brother. "Thanks. Look at that bird. Preening his butt off. We've got a mentally ill bird." He raised his cup. "Thanks Ma."

Lucas threw off his blanket and sat on the edge of the bed. He gulped his coffee and raised his cup to Grinder who filled it with dark tan lukewarm liquid once more. Paul jumped onto the side of the cage, then back onto his perch, then to the side again. Grinder leaned over and unlatched the cage door. "What the hell are you doing?" said Lucas.

At first Paul didn't notice, but then he hopped to the edge of the door where he squatted for a moment as he looked out at the room, his head bobbing wildly. He raised his thinning wings for balance and jumped onto the arm of the chair. "Eeeeeeeeee!"

"He better not be coming for my eyes."

Grinder scratched Paul's head— "Atta boy"—and then turned to his brother. "I was thinking."

Lucas blew his nose again, wadded the tissue and stuck it under the mattress. "Thinking what?"

"Had an idea."

"An idea, great."

"I want to go to the cemetery."

"The cemetery?"

"Yeah." Grinder sat on the chair beside Paul. Paul trilled and rubbed his head against Grinder.

"What for? I mean it's been a million years." Lucas turned so he could look at his brother square. "It's not like she's even there."

The muscles in Grinder's jaws rippled. His eyes narrowed.

"What?"

"I don't know; it's just something I want to do. You're staying until Pop gets here, right?" Lucas shrugged one shoulder. "So we got the time."

The bathroom door burst open and out came Martha. She was wearing purple yoga pants and a pink shell; her hair was wrapped in a towel. "Why is that thing out of its cage?" She waved her hand at Paul. Paul's head bobbed slowly back and forth as if he were measuring his opponent. "Go 'way." Paul flared his wings, opened his mouth and stuck out his tongue. Martha went to the other side of the bed.

"Look Grinder, it's not gonna bring her back. I mean she's gone for absolute good now."

"What are you boys talking about?"

"Nothing," said, Lucas.

Grinder raised his arm, encouraging Paul to get on, but he was picking at the fabric in the corner of the chair and glaring at Martha.

"Sure sounds like something."

"It's only going to get you all stirred up."

"Stirred up about what?" said Martha.

Grinder ran his pointer finger down the center of the bird's back. Lucas got up but fell back when Paul hissed. "I don't want you to get all messed up over this. It's been too many years for that. What's done is done."

Grinder crinkled the corner of his mouth and waggled his head. "'What's done is done.' I don't even know what that means."

"It's case closed."

"What's 'case closed'?" said Martha.

"For chrissakes, this is between my brother and me. Can't you stay out of it?"

"Excuse me for giving a shit." Martha took a bag of cashews from the mini-bar and tore it open. She sat with a thump on the easy chair and crossed her arms and legs. Lucas rolled his neck, listening for each crackle.

"Look, Grinder wants to go to the cemetery, that's all." Martha turned her head away.

Lucas raised his eyebrows at his brother. He leaned over and reached with his hand to pat Grinder's arm, but with Paul scowling and lunging, he couldn't get close enough and patted the arm of the chair instead.

"Lucas, I'm telling you, nothing's ever been finished. I mean, one day she walks out the door and as far as I'm concerned, that door never closed."

"C'mon, you don't want to do this." There was pleading in Lucas's voice, as if he were begging his brother not to cross the street against the light. Grinder's face was cold, his eyes dark. Lucas waited for a moment, then shrugged. "Well, you know what my vote is." Then he disappeared into the bathroom.

Paul cawed and ding-donged and gnawed on Lucas's watch strap. Grinder scratched Paul's head. Martha shifted in her chair and unfolded her arms. She looked sideways at Grinder and cleared her throat. Grinder focused on Paul. Martha cleared her throat again and huffed once.

"You know what I think?" said Martha. Grinder looked up but before he could open his mouth, Martha went on. "It's no secret that I have always thought you were kind of a loser, Grinder. Please take no offense. It's just an objective assessment. I mean, you are like, forty or something, right, and you work in a parking lot, and in your spare time you work for the city scraping dead animals off the street." She raised one eyebrow, crimped the corners of her mouth and tilted her head as if no further proof were needed.

"Well—"

"Shut up. I'm not finished." She got up and tiptoed past Paul and then sat on the bed closer to Grinder. "I don't think being a loser is all your fault. I mean some of it is your fault; the whole dropping out of college thing almost drove your brother bat-shit crazy, so, there's that. But, on the other hand, you never had much to go on, you know what I mean? Your father? My God. Lucas puts your old man on some kind of pedestal, even though Lucas mostly can't stand the man, but as far as I can see, Pop wasn't a father at all. He was just a guy who drank like a fish and happened to be living in your house."

Martha paused, not waiting for Grinder to speak, but to gather her thoughts for the next volley. Grinder sat back in the desk chair, his face expressionless, but focused and intent.

"I didn't know your old lady, at least not directly, but I heard all the stories. You know I did. The battles with your old man; all the times she holed-up for hours, even days, in her bedroom, door locked, the whole nine yards; how she hung onto you and wouldn't let go, although, in the end, she did. Jesus. She sure didn't do you any favors. Then she was like, 'Oh my, I'm so depressed, I must go away with my son's teacher and never come back.' What the hell kind of mother would do that?"

"Well, she—"

Martha held up a hand. "I'm still talking." Paul was now roosting on Grinder's knee. "Now, since Lucas was always closer to your dad, he's been able to make some strange peace with him; probably because he never has to see him; only talks to him a few minutes a year. Hi, bye."

Grinder didn't dare open his mouth, though Martha's face appeared to invite a response.

"Ok? Ok. And you were closer to your mother, but y'know, she up and disappeared—pffft! —just like that, and you never got a chance to even things up with her. Right? Of course, I'm right." Paul hopped onto the bed a few feet from Martha, but she was on a roll and didn't notice. He was cooing now, like a mourning dove.

"So, that's the deal, huh?"

"Yeah. As a matter of fact, that is *absolutely* the deal." Martha double took a glance at Paul. "You gonna sick him on me?" Martha stacked two pillows between her and Paul.

"Why are you telling me this?" said Grinder.

"Because I think you're right."

"What?"

"I said, I think you're right."

"About?"

"About the whole cemetery thing. If going to the cemetery helps you stop pissing your life away, then, by all means, do it. You were your momma's boy. I know it hurt you more than anyone when she left." She stopped again, as if waiting for Grinder to say thanks or give her a great big hug. When it didn't come, she went on. "That's not the only reason why you, well…why you didn't *blossom*, shall we say. But it was a big factor. I know. I'm a mother. What do you think would have happened to Mandy if I'd left her?"

"You did leave her."

"For six months. And I came back."

"But then you left again."

"Three months. That's not the point. The point is I came back. I didn't walk away for the rest of her life and just die."

Grinder stood and stretched his arm out to Paul, who hopped on.

"You've made a friend." Martha held up her forearm for protection. "I mean he's just a bird, but a friend is a friend, I guess."

"A friend is a friend. A mother is a mother. You get what you get."

"Wow, deep." Martha stood and unraveled the towel from atop her head, her hair falling around her face like damp straw. "So, I guess what I'm saying is I'm on your side this time."

"Thank you, I think."

"You're welcome, I think." Martha squinted and one corner of her mouth rose into her cheek. "Anyway, your old man should never have done what he did."

Paul poked Grinder's shoulder with his head. Grinder turned, his face glazed. "What?"

"What what?" Martha swallowed hard.

"What did you say?"

"What did *I* say?"

"Yeah, about Pop, what shouldn't he have done?"

Martha forced a laugh and started drying the ends of her hair. "There's so many things, I wouldn't know where to begin."

Grinder was on it now, like stink on a skunk. "Why don't we start with what you meant when you said, 'Your old man should never have done what he did'? Maybe we start with that."

The bathroom door flew open and out stepped Lucas looking like a beef steak tomato wearing an apron.

"Oh my God, that felt great. Hot water to spare. Should run some of it through that coffee machine." Lucas wrapped a towel tightly around his ample belly. Martha and Grinder stared at him, zombie-like. "Who died?" Martha glanced at Grinder. "What the hell is going on?" Lucas reached into his suitcase for a pair of jeans and a Buffalo Bills T-shirt.

"Nothing. Your brother and me, we were just talking. I told him I think he should go to the cemetery, if it'll make some kind of difference."

"That's interesting. I didn't know you had a vote in this. Why do you care?"

"Well, Grinder's had it hard and maybe this will help. It couldn't hurt. So why not do it?"

Lucas approached Martha and waved his hand in front of her eyes. "You under some spell or something?" He turned to his brother. "What have you been feeding her?"

"Nothing. Actually she was about to tell me a story about Pop, something that has to do with Ma. Go ahead, Martha." Grinder sat on the bed again and crossed his legs.

"What are you talking about?" Lucas laughed, but the room was quiet. Even Paul was still. "What?"

"You were saying that Pop should never've done what?"

Martha had pasted a smile on her face that was now all a quiver. She started panting and fanning her face with both hands.

Lucas pulled on his pants and turned to her. "Martha?"

"Maybe I can help," said Grinder. "We were talking about when Ma left and Martha said, 'Your old man shoulda never done what he did.' And I said, 'What?' and she said 'What what?' and then you came out of the bathroom singing the praises of hot water."

Lucas took a hand towel from the rack and started mopping his head and neck. "Dammit Martha."

"I didn't mean anything."

"So, let me see; you know what happened and you know what happened. I don't seem to know what happened." Grinder's jaw was set, his head forward in head-butting mode.

"Look Grinder, it's forever old, water over the bridge."

"Under the bridge."

"Yeah, that, too."

"Over under over under." Paul was clucking and tossing the wood chips onto the floor. He gnawed on his left wing.

"Why don't you tell me about this 'water'?"

Lucas rubbed his face with one hand and shook his head slowly.

"You're gonna take this all wrong, I know it—"

"Lucas."

Martha sat with a pillow on her lap and picked at her eyebrows. Lucas did a quick analysis of his brother's face, which looked a little volcanic.

"You know after Ma left, Pop really started hittin' it hard. I mean he was a bigger mess than ever before. Drunk, didn't care about work, yellin' all the time. He was totally, like, out of his mind." He stopped, hoping for acknowledgement from Grinder, but none came. "So, anyway. I guess maybe you didn't know that Ma called Pop and wanted to meet."

"She what?"

"She called him. Like a month after she hit the road."

"You knew this?"

"Look, Pop thought it would be better if you didn't know because you were still so squirrely about the whole thing and he was afraid you'd go off the deep end."

"But he told *you*."

"Yeah. Older brother, first child thing, I guess."

"And you didn't tell me."

"What was I supposed to do? I was just a kid, too, y'know."

"You were my fucking brother."

"I'm sorry, what can I say."

Martha decided it was her turn. "Look, Grinder, your brother was doing the best he could. You should thank…" Martha relinquished her turn when she saw that the vein on the side of Grinder's neck was about burst like a water balloon.

Grinder stood and went to the window. It was raining now and traffic on the Fort Pitt was stalled. He leaned his head against the cool glass.

"C'mon," said Lucas. "I meant to tell you, but, you know, I thought it woulda, I don't know, I just didn't think it woulda been good for you. And then, like, ten, twenty years passed and it didn't seem to matter."

"What did she want?"

"I don't remember exactly. I mean Pop was tanked and wasn't making much sense."

"Lucas." Grinder's face was a glowering mass of red blotches.

"He said a bunch of stuff, I don't know. He said Ma was having second thoughts, like she didn't want to come back to Pop, but she wanted to see us."

"Are you kidding me? A month after she left, she called Pop about coming back?"

"Kind of. Like I said, she wasn't definite about anything; as far as I could make out from Pop, she was just thinking out loud."

"And?"

"Pop told her he wasn't sure it was a good idea."

"Not a good idea?" Grinder walked across the room to the cage where he sat on the arm of the adjoining chair. He rubbed his hands on his pant legs. "Is that what he said, 'Millie, I'm not sure it's a good idea.' Just casual like."

"Well."

"Tell him, Lucas. He's a grown man," said Martha.

Lucas got up from the bed and sat on the opposite arm of Grinder's chair. He put his hand on his brother's shoulder and then pulled it away when Grinder stiffened.

"What did Pop say?"

"He said that if Ma came back, he'd kill her."

"He said what?"

Lucas tried to temper the effect of what he was saying with an I-just-read-something-interesting-on-my-Twitter-feed tone of voice. "And that he would kill us, too."

"You've got to be shitin' me. That sonofabitch said he would kill us all and you didn't tell me. Or tell, like, the police. You just listened and did nothing. Am I understanding this right? 'cause I wouldn't want to sell you short or make a wrong assumption." He went stone-faced as he waited for Lucas to respond. Lucas swallowed several times.

"Look, the next day he didn't even remember what he said. I asked him about it, and he said I was crazy. I reminded him what he had told me, and he took a swing at me. Called me a damn liar." Lucas got up again and leaned against the wall. He pulled a tissue out of the box and wiped his forehead and nose. "For all I knew, none of it was true. So why tell you. You seem to have forgotten that at that point, you still couldn't get out of bed and go to school in the morning. I brought breakfast to you every day and you never even took a bite. I was the one who made sure you didn't do anything stupid. So what was I supposed to do: 'Hey, Grinder, guess what? Ma said she might want to come back but Pop said he'd kill her; in fact he'd kill us, too, if she tried. Eat your cereal.' You think that would have been the thing to do? Well, then, I am sorry, little brother. But at the end of the day, she was gone and Pop was Pop."

Grinder was numb. Lucas tried to console him. He stood by him clutching the towel with one hand and tousling his brother's hair with the other. "Hey, you okay?"

"I never knew Ma thought about coming back."

"Well, she didn't come back. End of story."

"But she thought about it."

13

"Okay, so Martha and me are gonna go down to the desk," said Lucas, hands in his pocket, a sympathetic look on his face. "Okay?"

Grinder lay on his unmade bed, ankles crossed, hands behind his head. He studied an intricate crack on the ceiling that looked like a tributary of the Ohio River.

"Grinder? Is that okay?"

Paul chattered nervously and rattled his cage. He drew from his water bottle and shelled several walnuts; he dropped a dried apricot onto the floor.

"Eats like a pig," said Martha, tossing the fruit into the wastebasket. "I thought birds were neater. This one's a mess. Look at his nasty feathers, all spikey every which way." She leaned over to take a closer look. Paul blew raspberries at her. "What the hell is that?" Martha looked at Grinder. "Huh?"

"Bee-otch, bee-otch, bee-otch," cried Paul in a sing-song voice.

"Are you listening to this?" Martha nudged Lucas. "I'm gonna smack him, bird or not. I've never been disrespected by an animal before."

Lucas pursed his lips and leaned onto his right leg, increasing the distance between himself and Martha by one blessed inch.

"Grinder, you hearing me? We're going down to the desk to check on Pop's reservation." Grinder turned his head to his brother but said nothing. "Okay then."

"Aren't you gonna say something to that bird?" said Martha.

"No. I am not."

After they left, a soothing quiet blanketed the room. Grinder's chest relaxed and his belly rose and settled with ease.

Paul coughed three times and began to sing— "On top'a ole' Smokey, all covered with snow"—the slightest West Virginia twang in his voice. Grinder didn't move a muscle. Paul coughed again and then snorted and clicked.

Nothing. He swayed back and forth, finding his rhythm. "Rock a bye baby on the treetop, when the wind blows the cradle will rock, caw, caw, caw."

Grinder opened one eye and then closed it.

Paul persisted. "Hey mister, hands up! Don't make me use this thing. Pow, pow, pow."

Grinder reached out with one hand and folded his fingers into the shape of a gun, then cocked and released his thumb once. Paul groaned— "Ohhhhhhhhhh"— and toppled over in his cage. The room went silent again. Grinder sat up and looked at Paul, who lay in a crumpled, motionless pile. "Paul?" Nothing. "Playing possum, huh?" Paul didn't move. One wing stuck awkwardly out from his body. Grinder sat up. "Hey!" When Paul didn't respond, Grinder got off the bed and shook the cage gently. "Yoo-hoo."

"Gotcha, gotcha, gotcha," said Paul, as he stood and shook the cage.

Grinder unlatched the door and Paul hopped out. "Okay, you're free."

Paul circled the room several times and then fell like a rock onto the bed; he righted himself and stood on the headboard.

"Impressive."

"Smooth as silk," said Paul.

Grinder looked at him quizzically. "What did you say?"

"Eeeeeeeek!"

Grinder knelt beside the bed, scrutinizing Paul, who bobbed and weaved like a featherweight boxer.

"Aaaaaaawk!"

"Smooth as silk?"

"Nick-nick-nick."

"No, say smooth as silk."

"Craaaawk."

"Okay. I'm the crazy one." Grinder got up and headed toward the bathroom. "Don't do anything I wouldn't do."

"I won't."

Grinder stopped cold, turned and eyeballed Paul. "What did you say?"

"Say, say, say, say—"

"No, stop. What did you say?"

"I didn't say anything."

Grinder settled into a stare-off with Paul, holding his breath to see what would happen next. Paul didn't blink.

"Where's the cat?" said Paul.

"Huh?"

"The cat that got your tongue."

"We're back," called Lucas as the door flew open, banging against the wall bumper and almost hitting Martha in the face.

"Watch it!" she said.

"Here you go, little brother." He tossed Grinder a two pack of Hostess cupcakes. The package hit the mattress and bounced off the bed and onto the floor. "Good hands." Martha shlumped into the easy chair and clicked on Hoda and Kathy Lee.

"Say it again," whispered Grinder. Paul had jumped onto the desk.

"Why is he out?" said Martha. "He's dangerous. I'm telling you, he doesn't like me and I don't like him."

"Say it again. C'mon buddy." Paul clucked and clicked and shuffled across the desk.

Lucas picked up the cupcakes and laid them on the bed. "Hey, what are you doing?"

Grinder looked up at his brother. "Listen to this." He turned back to Paul and put his hand on the desk beside him. "C'mon, Paul, say it again."

"Grinder? You okay?"

"I'm fine. Sit down and listen to this."

"Be careful, he'll rip your lips off." Martha rifled through her purse, searching for an emery board.

Lucas sat down on the end of the bed. Grinder motioned him to come closer and Lucas leaned forward, his elbows on his knees. Grinder smiled.

"Listen to this." He turned back to Paul who was perched, stiff as a board, on the corner of the desk. "Paul, what's the cat got?"

"There's a cat?" said Lucas, concerned.

"No. It's just a joke." Grinder patted Paul on the head. "Paul, ask Lukie what the cat has?"

"Eck, eck, eck."

Grinder chuckled and glanced at his brother. "He's messing with me now."

Lucas raised his eyebrows at Martha who gave him an eyebrow salute in return. "Look, Grinder, I think—"

"C'mon, boy...what...does...the cat...have?" Grinder snatched his own tongue between his thumb and forefinger and pulled it out. "Wha da tha ca ha?"

"Grinder, really, don't do that." Lucas reached for Grinder's hand, pulling it away from his mouth.

"I'm telling you, he's got a sense of humor. He told a joke. Actually not a joke, more of a clever spin on an old saying."

Martha had stopped filing her inch long purple nails. Lucas looked troubled as he gnawed on his bottom lip and reached for more tissue.

"What?" said Grinder.

"Nothing. Everything's fine," said Lucas.

"You both look like you ate something bad."

"No, not at all."

Grinder stood up and Paul hopped to the top of the cage where he roosted.

"Your brother and I think you've lost your mind," said Martha.

"Martha, goddammit."

"Whadaya mean?" Grinder's jaw was set. He placed his hand on top of the cage.

"Nuts, nuts, nuts, nuts, nuts…"

"Enough from the damn bird," said Martha, waving the back of her hand at Paul. "Grinder, honey, look, this is not natural, this bird thing. I mean, I get that he belonged to your mother and all, and he's like a little buddy, but, really, why are you hanging on to him?"

"I'm not *hanging* onto him." Paul scuttled over to Grinder's hand. "Look at him." Paul hopped onto Grinder's wrist and then started preening his belly feathers. "Look at him. I've scraped better looking birds off the pavement. He's sick, he's, like, heartsick over Ma. He's got nothin'. The shrink said—"

"My God with the shrink," said Lucas.

"Like I said, the shrink told us Paul is probably grieving. That's why he's a mess. You just don't walk away when someone's fallin' apart." Paul's head poked up from under his wing. "You don't. So, yeah, I'm nuts. Live with it."

"Grinder, I'm telling you, this is not a good thing. This is going to make your life worse," said Martha.

"Worse, how?" Grinder's face was red, and Paul went bug-eyed on Martha.

"C'mon, you two, shut it down." Lucas hiked up his pants and stood between Martha and Grinder. "Look, Grinder, brother of mine, I think Martha is trying to help, she's saying that this bird is, how do I put this, that he's not helping you at all. She's worried about you. Frankly, I am too. This was supposed to be a trip for the two of us, see Ma's old place, go through some of her stuff and get rid of it, look around town a little bit, and go home. But not this. This here is getting way out of hand."

"What do you mean, 'out of hand'?"

"I mean it's stirring everything up."

"What's wrong with that? What's wrong with things getting stirred up?" Grinder put Paul back in the cage but left the door open. Paul burped and then cawed and then buried his head under his left wing. "Tell me something. When was the last time you and I talked about Ma?"

"Jesus, I don't know."

"I do. It was the Christmas after she left. Remember? When we hung the stockings? Ma's was still in the box. Pop had thrown everything out, all her clothes, her books, everything. But her stocking was right there, exactly where she put it when we'd taken everything down the year before. We didn't want to leave it in the box so we put it on the mantle just like always. Remember?"

Lucas turned his head away from his brother. "Yeah."

"We didn't know what else to do." Grinder swallowed hard. "We got the masking tape and stuck it up with the rest. We didn't tell Pop."

Martha's face grew cloudy. She took a step toward Grinder, but there was nothing in his face to encourage her, so she stopped. Lucas wiped perspiration from his forehead and looked at his hand.

"It was up there for days until Pop noticed. Remember? He tore it down; and he held it in his fist and shook it at me. He said, 'You did this, didn't you?'"

"He was drunk."

"Then he said, what was it? He said, 'You two listen to me. Mildred is dead to us. You better get used to it.' I remember 'cause he didn't call her Ma; he called her Mildred. No one called her that."

"I don't think he even remembered what he did."

"*I* remember!" Grinder's left cheek quivered. He turned to Martha. "You know what he did next, Martha?" She stepped back. "He threw the stocking at me and told me to take it out to the garbage can and throw it away. When I didn't jump right up, he grabbed my shoulders, stood me up and pushed me through the back door. He pointed at the garbage can in the far corner of the back yard, and then he watched to make sure I dropped it in."

"I'm sorry," said Martha.

Grinder slumped into the chair beside the birdcage. Paul stuck his head through the cage wire, trying to reach him. Grinder looked up at his brother.

"Things have been stirred up for years, Lucas; we got so used to it, we didn't even notice after a while."

14

"Here he comes." Lucas tried to breathe evenly as he forced a smile. Grinder's lips were taut as he stood behind his brother, not wanting to be in the initial line of fire.

Calvin Ingersoll, Pop to his sons, Bottleneck to his drinking buddies, got out of the cab, stretched his back and leaned side to side. He squinted and nodded expectantly at Lucas and Grinder as if trying to verify who they were. They tipped their heads slightly and Pop howled like a wolf— "Ooo-oo-ooo!"

"What the hell," said Lucas.

"Do you not remember our father?"

Around his neck Pop wore a wooden cross on a strip of cowhide. A large brass buckle with WWJD in block lettering adorned his wide leather belt. His ample gut flopped over the curled waist of his torn jeans. He had a grey goatee, and a tanned leathery face hidden behind blue tinted aviator glasses. He wore a paneled Hawaiian shirt with exotic flowers and bright green leaves, a charcoal grey brick cowboy hat, a pink and yellow feather in the hat band, and sandals on his feet. He took a satchel from the back seat of the taxi as well as a walking stick with "John 3:16" carved into the handle.

"My sons!" he called as he loped toward them on pencil thin legs.

Lucas leaned over and whispered in his brother's ear. "Before I forget, Dr. Vettman said he'd be glad to take the bird."

Grinder's head jerked back. "What?"

Pop was on them now, grabbing both sons and holding on for dear life. He snorted and swayed and rocked and wouldn't let go. "Praise the Lord!" He started crying. Lucas looked at Martha, like a tag-team wrestler desperate to tap out to his partner. Martha shrugged and then went forward, fingering Pop's shoulder.

"Hi, I'm Martha. We talked the other day. Remember?" Pop gripped his sons tighter. "I was the one in white at your son's wedding." Relieved when he didn't respond, she retreated a few feet so she could take in the spectacle.

Pop was blubbering now, his nose running onto Grinder's shoulder.

"I'm so glad we're all together again. This here's a true miracle."

Grinder tensed and pulled away. "Let me get your bag." He yanked its strap with one hand and reached for the walking stick.

"Oh, no, no, son, that's my staff. I'll take it if that's okay." He slapped Grinder on the shoulder and grasped the stick in his gnarly hand.

"Whatever you say."

Pop pulled himself together, blew his nose and looked around, noticing Martha.

"Is that Marla I see?" He bound toward her, throwing his arms around her as she backpedaled, arms limp at her side.

"Okay, okay," said Martha. "For one, it's *Martha*—"

"Oh, I'm so sorry. I'm just so—"

"And for two, nobody hugs me without an invitation."

Pop howled at this, doubling over in hysterics. "Yessir, that's Martha!" He wagged his finger at her playfully. "You are delicious!" Martha lunged at him, but Lucas gripped her arm.

"Okay," said Pop. "You two come over here and stand right in front of me. I gotta take a gander at my sons." He pulled them by their arms until they were standing at attention in front of him. "Look at you." Pop shook his head and waved his hat in the air. "My God, you're grown men. How'd that happen?"

"Lemme tell you how—"

Lucas put his hand on Grinder's shoulder. "Just the way of things, Pop."

"Excuse me, sir," said the taxi driver, his hand out to Pop.

"Of course, of course." He pulled cash from his pocket. "Man's on a mission, aren't you, son."

"Just heading back to the airport."

The cabby closed the window as Pop called out, "God be with…well, I guess he's gone."

Another cab and then another and another wheeled up under the marquee where the foursome was huddled. "Excuse me, gentlemen and lady," said the doorman. "Can I help you?" He waved his hand toward the entrance. "I'm sure you would be more comfortable inside."

"This here's all the comfort I need." Pop raised his staff as if he might part the lobby. He sidled up to registration while Grinder and Lucas stood at a distance. Martha hustled off to the coffee cart.

"My God, our father is a lunatic."

Grinder grabbed Lucas's shirtsleeve. "What do you mean, Vettman'll take Paul?" said Grinder, his long body curled into an 'S'.

Lucas ignored him. "Pop was always different, but this is different in a whole different way, you know what I mean?"

"Lucas. Look at me." Grinder took his brother by the shoulders and turned him around so they were eye to eye. "What did you do?"

"Called him the other day."

"Where was I?"

"I think it's perfect for us and for the bird. Vettman will find some place for him. It's a win for everyone."

Grinder gripped Lucas by the Buffalo on his Bills T-shirt. "What the hell did you do?"

"Just thinking smart. One of us has too."

"This isn't up to you."

"C'mon." Lucas tried to pull away, but Grinder wouldn't let go.

"I'm telling you, stay out of this."

"Let go of me."

Grinder's grip was tight as a snapping turtle. Lucas struggled to free himself, but to no avail.

"Okay boys." Pop adjusted his cowboy hat and seized his staff. "One a you wanna get my bag?"

Lucas and Grinder continued their stare-off.

"What's with them?" said Pop.

"They're your sons, you tell me," said Martha.

"I don't know." Pop studied his boys. Lucas's trousers bagged over his round-toed shoes. His faced glistened and his balding dome looked like a hairy cantaloupe from behind. Grinder, his patchy three-day beard trying to catch up to his drooping mustache, leaned hard on his stringy legs. They looked a little like Laurel and Hardy but not nearly as funny. Pop scratched his left temple with his thumb. "I don't hardly know anything about them."

"Bingo," said Martha.

"What?"

"B-I-N-G-O, Bingo!" Martha stood right under Pop's chin, her face nearly shrieking. "Tell me, why did you come here?"

"Well, I..."

"I mean, you never gave a good crap about your sons. And now, here you are in this crazy assed get-up, all happy and full of Jesus. Tell me, what's up? Huh? What do you want? Because, I gotta tell you, look at 'em." Pop turned his head. Grinder's finger was in his brother's face, and Lucas's eyes were rolling like a gyroscope. "They got nothin' to give you. Hear me?" Martha reached up and straightened Pop's hat and then tipped it slightly on an angle. "They may not be much, but everything they are, they are *in spite of* you." Martha clapped his cheeks with the palms of her hands. She turned on her heels and headed for the elevator.

It was then that Grinder took a swing at Lucas. Lucas ducked and assumed a pugilistic stance, his arms cocked, his fists at the ready. They circled each other with wind-milling arms, heavy breathing and confusion on their faces.

"Cease!" Pop held his staff high in the air and then thrust it between them. "What's the meaning of this?" Grinder swung his fist for just the second time in over thirty years, this time connecting with his father's chin. The lobby went silent as Pop sunk to the floor with all the grace of a folding metal chair collapsing on its rusty hinges.

Pop stood over the bathroom sink running cold water onto a washcloth. He twisted it in his hands and then held it to his left eye. Grinder stood at the door behind him, rubbing his knuckles.

"Look, Pop, I didn't mean—"

"Ouch." Pop winced as he lifted the cloth from his face. He dunked it back into the sink, now full almost to the brim, and pressed the cloth to his face again.

"Like I said, I wasn't *trying* to hit you, per se."

"Per se?"

"Yeah, per se."

"Sure felt like you were tryin' to hit me." Pop turned to face Grinder, the cloth pressed onto his eye socket, water running down his forearm. "Per se."

Grinder shuffled and looked down at his shoes. "Well…"

Pop guffawed. "It ain't the first time you tried to pop me one."

Grinder raised his eyes. Pop walked past him into the bedroom. Lucas and Martha sat quietly in adjoining easy chairs, a floor lamp between them.

"You musta been nine, maybe ten, who knows. Whatever it was, you were full of the devil about somethin', and you swung hard as you could at my kisser. But you were just a snot-nosed little thing, so you couldn't even reach my chin; but you clipped me good on the collarbone."

"Hm." Grinder's eyes evaded his father's gaze.

Pop tried to smile but grimaced instead. "You've grown since then. Your mother laughed her ass off." Pop was about to chuckle, but when no one else joined him, he cleared his throat instead. He removed the cloth, his eye now swollen into a purple-ish wink. Grinder's jaw was set tight. Pop slid by him. "Excuse me." He dropped the cloth into the sink once more, let it sop a bit before wringing it out. He waved it in the air to cool it down further, then put it back on his face.

"If I was a bettin' man, I'da bet you always wanted to knock me on my keister."

Grinder's face was granite-like. "I guess you'd have won that bet."

Pop howled at this admission. Grinder unfolded his arms, looked at his father, and gave him a half-way smile.

"What do you want me to say?" Pop's eyebrows went up and he gestured with his palm out. "I never meant nothin', Grinder. I mean a long time ago. Hell, I hardly remember whole years, let alone specific stuff I did."

Grinder didn't blink. It wasn't clear that he was even breathing.

"Gregory?" Pop waved a hand in front of Grinder's face.

"Say Pop, how was your flight?" Lucas got up from the chair and stood by his father. "Rough or smooth? Crying babies? Anyone get sick?"

"What? Oh, smooth as silk. Slept like a baby. Lady beside me didn't think so. She kept jabbin' me and complainin' about my snorin'. I told her, 'You buy your ticket, you take your chances.'"

"Let me look at that eye." Pop lowered the cloth and Lucas whistled. "It looks like the swelling's gone down a little." Lucas nodded toward his brother. "Whadaya think?" Grinder didn't look; he didn't answer.

"Your face definitely looks kind of lopsided, though," said Martha. "Grinder, maybe you could punch his other eye to even things out."

Lucas erupted with forced laughter. "Martha, Martha, always with the jokes."

Pop's face opened up to Martha. "Yes, now I remember you very well. Remind me of my first wife, these boys' mother."

"What's that supposed to mean?"

"C'mon, let's just slow down." Lucas reached for a box of tissues. His nose wasn't running, it was galloping and his forehead was dripping like it was the spring thaw. "Can't we just get along, for chrissakes?"

"No, no, it's alright," said Pop. "I get it. I know there's a long trail of bad behind us. But let me tell you—your mother, God rest her soul, she's dead and gone, and I come here to make things right after all these years. I'm workin' my step program and I've got a Higher Power kickin' my old ass. This here's the fullness of time, for me. I'm a new man!" His arms were raised over his head in triumph.

"Lucas, help me here. What's he talking about?" asked Martha. Lucas held a hand up for her to stop.

Grinder's heart was drumming as Pop started up again. "I been takin' inventory on myself for five years, six months and twelve days. I've prayed; I've sought the guidance of Brother Oswald Tatterbaum."

"Excuse me?" said Martha.

"Martha," said Lucas, frowning.

"Brother O, I call him. He's a man of God. He was a low-down stinkin' drunk, but he's been lifted up and he's liftin' me up with 'im."

"Brother Oswald Tatterbaum." Grinder sat on the bed, balled a pillow and leaned back on the faux headboard. "I gotta hear more about Brother O. What church is he?"

"Church?"

"Yeah, does he have a church or something?"

"Not exactly. He is otherwise employed at this point in his journey."

"Doing what?"

Pop cleared his throat again. "He is in the employ of a respected local automobile dealer."

"Car salesman?"

"No. He's in service."

"Service manager?"

"No."

"Mechanic?"

"I guess you could call him that. He prefers Pastor of Auto Parts and Services. He is a jack of all trades, but his Master is Jesus." Pop bowed his head as he said this.

Grinder grinned and shook his head, a sneer at the corner of his mouth.

"Let me get this straight." Martha pulled at the elastic of her yoga pants. She placed a finger on her lips as she gathered her thoughts.

"Martha." Lucas wiped his face yet again.

"You are a recovering alcoholic now thanks to Brother O, the car mechanic and his ministry of auto parts and tools."

"I am walking the path with Brother O," Pop corrected, "but we are being led, actually carried by Jesus, hisself."

"Big strapping guy, this Jesus?"

"Jesus Christ, Martha, c'mon." Lucas was beside her now. "Pop, that's great news. It's gotta be hard. I mean the whole twelve step thing."

"Good for you, Pop." Lucas startled at the sound of Grinder's voice. Pop squared his shoulders and stood a little straighter.

"Thank you, son, I appreciate that coming from you. I know—"

"Tell me something."

"Anything."

"What number is this?"

"Number?"

"Number of times you've stopped." Grinder air-quoted 'stopped'.

"Well, I don't know…"

"I mean, it seems to me you've said this before. And before and before and before." Grinder stood up again. He went over to Pop and patted him on the chest. "I could be wrong, but didn't you say this to Ma all the time. In fact, they mighta been the first words I ever heard you say. Of course, they were usually kinda slurred back then." Grinder turned from his father.

Pop's face got all sheepish and sincere. "Look, Grinder, this is for real, I'm tellin' you. The Lord—"

Grinder reached the door and turned. "How long have you been gone?" He looked at his brother. "When did he leave with Consuela, or whatever her name was, for Mexico, Lukie?" Lucas shrugged. "Well, a long goddam time ago. And you've never made any effort to be a part of my life, never told me you were sorry for all the bullshit you pulled. And now you're back all of what, an hour? And I'm supposed to believe all this crap?" He turned to his brother. "Maybe you can, Lukie, but not me."

With that, Grinder opened the door and left.

Pop turned, a quizzical look on his face. "Time's supposed to heal all wounds, ain't it?"

"Not so much," said Martha.

15

Grinder stood at the motel room window watching scores of Pirate fans scurrying across Clemente Bridge. Leisure crafts were tying up on nearby docks and fans in lesser boats were huddling in the river, hoping that sometime during the game a homerun would reach them. The lights at PNC Park were already on and the stands were bustling, like popcorn popping in a bowl. Grinder reached up to Paul, who was perched on Grinder's head, to offer him some green grapes. "Yuuuuum!" cried Paul as he scarfed them up one after another.

Grinder caressed Paul's back, hunting for fresh pinfeathers. "Getting you appetite back, are you? Good boy."

Paul hopped up and down on Grinder's head and whistled. Then he jumped down onto Grinder's shoulder and pecked his left ear gently. "What the…" Then he launched into the air, but immediately smacked into the sliding glass door and skidded down its moistened surface.

"God, Paul, are you okay?" Grinder tried to pick him up, but Paul, though slightly dazed, was off again. He circled the room a couple of times like a wounded drone.

"Stay away from the glass." Grinder reached, but Paul eluded him. "C'mon, Paul. Stay away from the glass." Grinder stumbled around the room, hands over his head. "C'mon, Paul, I'm tellin' you." But Paul, apparently convinced that blue sky awaited him, bounced off the glass again.

"Calm down now, buddy, calm down." Grinder spoke low and steady, much as he did when he discovered a road kill that wasn't quite dead. He would kneel by the animal and if it allowed him, he would pet it. If it was agitated or afraid, he would sit close and speak softly until it didn't move. Paul leaned against the dresser, stunned. "You're okay." Paul threw his head back and forth as he wobbled to and fro. "Okay, okay, take your time." His beak was wide open like he was sucking air after a marathon. "That's it, breathe deep. Shhhh."

Grinder reached out with one finger and ran it down Paul's head and back. "There you go." Grinder moved closer. He ran his hand down Paul's cherry-red tail and then tapped him gently on his jet-black beak. Paul was quiet and nearly still. He turned his head to Grinder and then nodded.

Grinder scratched his neck as if he were a dog. "Do you like that?" Paul nodded again. Grinder tossed a grape into the air and caught it in his own mouth. Then he tossed one to Paul who caught it effortlessly. Grinder high-fived him on the beak. Then they were both quiet for a long while.

"Twenty years, you and Ma. That's a long time." Grinder gazed at Paul expectantly, but Paul was busy with another grape. "I had eleven." Bits of skin and tiny seeds were falling from Paul's mouth. He reached for another and another. "But I've missed her longer than you have."

Paul began to cough and gag. "Are you okay?" Paul's stubby black tongue hung out, his feathers went flat as a cheap toupee. His eyes bulged and he shook all over. Then suddenly his grey feathers puffed like a soufflé about to explode. "Paul?" Grinder got on his knees in front of him. Paul's head was tipped downward in an exaggerated bow. Grinder put his ear close to Paul's beak. "My God, you're not breathing." Paul fluttered his wings. Grinder picked him up and shook him. Paul's stared, dazed. "Sorry, sorry!" He made a raspy guttural hawking noise. Grinder held Paul in the traditional Heimlich position against his chest. "I'm not trying to kill you; I'm not trying to kill you." Paul's pupils were big as saucers now. Grinder squeezed his chest and Paul gasped. "Oh my God, I'm killing him, I'm killing him."

Lucas opened the door and walked in, then dropped his jacket on the floor. Grinder was standing near one of the beds, Paul crushed against his chest. Lucas took two steps forward and then stopped. "Grinder?" But Grinder didn't answer. His hair was stuck to his face and his eyes were bulging. "Why are you killing the bird?"

Grinder pleaded with Paul. "Cough it up, cough it up!" Paul's claws sank deep into Grinder's belly. "Ouch!" Grinder closed his eyes, raised his open palm and smacked Paul's back repeatedly. This time Paul yowled and out flew a stem, and then another and another. Grinder collapsed onto the floor and lay motionless, except for his heaving chest. Paul de-puffed and started breathing normally. He coughed once more and then, noticing a stray grape on Grinder's pant leg, took it in his beak and hopped away.

"Well." Lucas sat on the bed and crossed his legs. "That was special."

"I saved his damn life."

Grinder sat up, his hands still quivering, and his shirt clinging to his chest.

"I can see that," said Lucas. "I just don't understand why." Lucas shook his head tiredly. He took a few tissues from the ample supply in his pocket and handed them to Grinder. "Are you okay?"

"Yeah." Grinder was on his feet now. He opened the mini-bar and reached for an RC cola, then sat back down on the floor beside Paul who was skinning another grape. He reached for Paul, scratching his tail feathers with his fingertip.

"Grinder, my baby; Grinder, my baby, eeeeeek."

Lucas stood up and leaned over Paul. "What did he say?"

Grinder looked over his shoulder at Lucas. "He said, 'Grinder, my baby.'"

"Grinder, my baby?"

"Yeah."

"What is that? Grinder my baby."

"Ma used to call me that. Remember?"

"Grinder, my baby. No, I don't."

"Well, she did. Until I must have been ten. Finally told her to cut it out when my friends started calling me baby."

Paul leaned forward, feathers flat again, and stuck out his tongue. He wiped his beak on the back of the chair, pulled his leg up under his wing and stood, statue-like, listening.

"Why would you teach him to say that?"

"I didn't." Grinder got up and sat on the bed.

"Whadaya mean, you didn't?"

"I didn't."

Lucas's hands were on his hips. He inhaled through his nose and let the breath out slowly through his mouth, then dropped his shoulders, trying to calm down. "Look, Grinder—"

"I didn't teach him anything. He came like this. He's been saying things."

"What do you mean, saying things?"

"I don't know, little things. Things Ma would say. I'm telling you, sometimes he even sounds like her."

Lucas opened the minibar and took another Toblerone. "Listen to yourself. You're not making any sense. You're getting as crazy as the old man." Lucas sat on the bed beside his brother. "I know this trip has brought up all this stuff that we buried a long time ago. Maybe we shoulda never come here. Maybe I shoulda just hung up on Janice when she called me in the first place. Because it's messing you up all over again and I can't stand it."

Grinder's shoulders slumped and his head tilted to one side as he glanced at his brother. "Didn't you ever miss her?"

"Not really." Lucas's tone was apologetic but his face was stern. "Look, when she left us I got up the next day and went to school. I cooked the meals. I got a job and I did what needed to be done." He was standing now, pacing. "And then, before I knew what hit me, I was twenty. And then I was thirty. And then forty. Miss her? Who had the time?"

Grinder looked up at his brother, his face rainy. Lucas reached out with one hand and laid it on his brother's shoulder.

"Look, man, I'm sorry, I'm sorry, I'm sorry." Lucas removed his hand and straightened his back. "But Ma is gone gone. And Pop is it. He's all the family we got. And he came here to make things better, as crazy as that sounds. And even though you punched him in the face, I think you should give him a chance."

Grinder breathed heavy through his nostrils, opened his mouth, then shook his head.

"And why in the hell should I do that?"

Lucas walked to the door and as he opened it, turned to his brother.

"Because."

He closed the door quietly behind him.

16

Grinder sat on a ledge at the tip of Point State Park as the Monongahela and Allegheny sloshed mindlessly into each other, birthing the Ohio. From there the Ohio, that great brown serpent, lazed off to the west, a statue of Mr. Rogers looking on from its banks. It wended its way past Weirton and Huntington and then Cincinnati, slithered along the edge of Kentucky and Indiana, then emptied into the great Mississippi near Cairo, Illinois. St Louis followed. And New Orleans. And the Gulf of Mexico. And the rest of the world.

Despite the great escape route right in front of him, when Pop sidled up the Grinder, there was nowhere for him to go.

"Sure is something to behold, ain't it." Pop squinted into the sunset. "Shoulda brought my shades." He tipped his cowboy hat low, looking like a would-be gunslinger.

Grinder turned to face the fountain, its heavy spray filling the air. A toddler soaked his feet. A dog lapped at the water's edge. The outline of an ancient fort was drawn in cement upon the grass and beyond that, glass and steel rising.

"Y'know, son, old George Washington swam across one of those rivers." Grinder turned his head away. "True. He was trying to cross in a small boat and it sunk, so he swam it." Pop chuckled. "Read about it in the motel. Came here seven times, Washington, that is."

Grinder took several steps toward the fountain, picked up a stone and tossed it into the water.

Pop followed. "Musta been quite a baptism for old George, doncha think?"

Grinder put his hands in his pockets and began to walk around the fountain. His face was rock solid. He wiped the mist from his brow. The wind shifted, and the spray soaked the folks on the other side of the fountain. They opened their mouths wide and laughed. Some took off their shirts and danced in the puddles, while dogs barked and leaped. Pop laughed loud; then, when

Grinder didn't, he fell silent.

"Looks like everybody's gettin' a little baptized today, even them dogs." Pop walked with Grinder, except a few feet to the side, like he was with his son but, at the same time, not. "Baptism's a damn good thing, y'know. Everybody could use it once in a while. Cleans things right off. I should know, been baptized more times than I can remember. Had a lot of grime built up."

He looked at Grinder who had stopped again, this time to watch a duck boat slide into the river from a nearby street. The tour guide quacked loudly into the microphone and soon everyone on board was quacking and making duck lips with their hands. Families on the grass nearby quacked in return. One young man in torn jeans and bare feet gave them all the finger. An old man wearing black and gold suspenders swatted at him with his Steelers' cap. The duck boat churned on toward the far shore.

Pop didn't notice. He was studying Grinder's face. Grinder turned suddenly and Pop held his breath.

"What are you up to, really? I mean, what do you want?" Grinder sounded like he was asking a question, but it was more like he was yelling at his father without even raising his voice. "I mean, seriously, what's your angle? If you think there's anything to get from Ma's dying, you came a long way for nothing."

Grinder started walking again. Pop stood stark still then hurried to catch up. He took Grinder's arm and turned him around.

"If I told you why I come, you wouldn't believe me."

Grinder looked at his father's face, hair flaring from his nostrils and earlobes.

"The Lord compelled me."

Grinder started walking away.

"Listen to me. I'm tellin' you, the Lord's taken His place inside a me and I can't do nothin' except what he wants me to do."

Grinder wheeled around, the corner of his mouth crimped in doubt and suspicion.

"I'm tellin' you, he's taken me up and he won't lemme go."

Grinder pointed a crooked finger at his father. "Remember the time you came home from Jilly's? You were all excited 'cause some guy promised he'd make you rich. All he needed was a little more money to perfect his Shaving Razor Bottle Opener. You came home all 'taken up' by him too, and all you got from it was empty pockets and a cut jaw from trying to shave with a goddam bottle opener."

"That was mammon, this is the Lord. I'm tellin' you, this here's different. I seen something I ain't never seen before. Something nobody ever seen before." Grinder's face looked mummified. "I seen Jesus hisself." Grinder grimaced and started to walk again. "No wait. I did. I seen him."

Grinder stopped, turned around, his head cocked, his arms dead at his side.

"It was last Thanksgiving. Lucille had roasted the bird just about perfect. There it was on the kitchen counter, smellin' so good, just waitin' for me to carve her up. So I started in and the meat come off the bone just so, mmm. And I pulled back the skin here and there, because Lucille don't like it; she says it makes her think about the turkey like it was a person or something—"

"Pop."

"Okay, so I was just workin' away when all of a sudden a piece of turkey fell right off the bone. I mean it fell off without me ever touchin' it. At first I didn't think nothin' of it, but when I took a closer look, I called Lucille. And I said, 'Lucille, what's that look like to you?' And she studied it for a while and said it looked like a gall bladder or maybe the state of Rhode Island sideways, but I said, 'You ain't lookin' at it right' and I turned it just so. And she said, 'I don't know what you mean.' And I about jumped outta my skin right then and there. 'Lucille,' I says, 'look hard as you can,' but she still couldn't see what was right before her eyes and she got mad and walked off to the dining room to set the table, but I kept lookin' because I was sure about what I was seein'." Pop slowed down like he was about to start the final ascent of a great mountain. "Listen to me when I tell you this, son. It was a little bit of dark meat and a little bit of white, but when you took it all together, it was the face of Jesus right there in the turkey."

Pop gave Grinder room to exclaim or shout or pray or whatever he needed to do, but he was unmoved, his face as still as a stroke victim's.

"I know this sounds crazy."

Pop's eyes were glazed now. He was breathing hard and his face was burnt orange, like Charlton Heston after he had come down the mountain with the clay tablets in his arms, only Pop didn't need makeup. "I called to Lucille and she came runnin' and I asked her to look again, because it was plain as the nose on her face. But she said all she could see was meat. I pointed out the beard and the longish hair made by the stringy dark meat, and even the tiny piece that stuck out like a nose, and it took forever, but Lucille finally saw it; she saw the light I seen right there in that turkey carcass."

"Pop, you can't be serious."

"Serious as death and taxes." Pop had struck a dramatic pose, his cowboy hat in his hands and his face wrinkled and heartfelt. Grinder gaped.

"Let me show you something, son."

Pop shoved his hand into his fanny pack and pulled out a small, shrink-wrapped baggy. He held it up to the sun as if he were examining a diamond. His mouth widened, his eyes disappeared into a squint, making room for a broad yellow-toothed smile.

"There he is," he said, as if the triumph were obvious. He cradled it in both hands and reached out to Grinder.

"There what is?" Grinder bent at the waist, studying Pop's relic with impatient confusion.

"Well, look at it." Pop extended his hands further so Grinder could see more clearly. Inside the baggy was a brownish, greenish, dried up something-or-other. "Pretty amazing, ain't it?" said Pop, proud as a new father.

Grinder took one step closer and studied the bag. Then he straightened his back and studied Pop. "This is it?"

"Sure enough is."

"You're not messin' with me?"

Pop let out a hearty laugh and shook his head. "Look at it again. You'll see." This time Pop stretched his hand out, intending for Grinder to take the bag. Grinder reached for it and held it close to his face, all the better to see the truth of it.

"It's Jesus, son."

Grinder was quiet as he turned the bag over and over, his face somber and respectful. "Pop, I don't see a thing. Maybe Rhode Island. If I use my imagination." He handed it back to his father.

Pop's face collapsed in disappointment. His eyes went moist.

"I'm tellin' you son, this here Jesus has changed my life."

"Well, then I'm happy for you, but it's still just a piece of turkey, Pop."

"To you, I guess. Not to me." Pop held the bag to his cheek. "If it weren't for this Jesus, I would be an absolute goner. I'd be lost. Forever lost." He gazed lovingly at turkey-head Jesus. "Turkey or not, it's still Jesus. Just as real as anything. Just as real as that Shroud of Turmon or Turmonson or whatever it's called; or that rag with Jesus's sweat stains on it they found somewhere; or the

Holy Gail or whatever her name was. There is more miraculous stuff in the world than we can possibly imagine. Just have to open your eyes." Pop hitched up his pants at the belt buckle and shifted his weight back and forth. He held the bag tight in his hand and pointed it at Grinder, shaking it in a gesture of beckoning. "This here is the grace of God, I'm tellin' you. Some people, like Lucille and Brother O and Sister Gabriella, his wife, and all the faithful folks at his back yard tent ministry, they can see it clear as can be. And they feel it in their hearts."

"Better watch how you grip that bag, Pop, or all you'll have left is turkey-hash Jesus." Pop's arms fell to his side. He opened his hand and examined the bag, flattening it out and re-shaping Jesus's head to compensate for his over-enthusiastic evangelizing.

A man with a brushy looking moustache walked by, a black and white mutt on a leash leading him along. Grinder knelt to pet the mutt. "What's her name?"

"Jill," said the owner, a look of pride on his face. Jill eyed the bag in Pop's hand and sidled up to him, sniffing hard. Then she licked her lips, shifted back and forth, and sat up on her haunches. Pop didn't notice. He was busy reconstructing Jesus's face. He looked up, though, when Grinder and the dog owner started to laugh. Jill was wagging her tail and hoping against hope that Pop would toss her the yummy tidbit he held lovingly in his hands.

"Well, Pop, I think you got yourself a convert."

Pop put turkey-head Jesus back into his fanny pack and zipped it closed. He shooed Jill away, and the dog, disappointed and misunderstood, slunk back to the man with the moustache. Then Pop tried to make the best of it. "That's a good one, son. Truth is, Jesus'll take whoever or whatever he can get. Shoulda brought a collection plate. And a choir." But there wasn't any laughter in his voice. Jill moseyed away, turning every few feet just in case Pop had changed his mind. "C'mon, girl," said her owner, as he tugged on her leash.

"Good luck, Jill," called Grinder.

The duck boat had disappeared into the river again, too far away now to hear the raucous quacking. The two men stood on the walkway, the river breeze filling the trees as young men tossed Frisbees on the lawn behind them.

"C'mon Pop, might as well head back."

Pop didn't move. "You can make fun of me all you want. Maybe I earned it, I don't know. But I'm tellin' you, if you ain't got somethin' to believe in, somethin' to hold onto in this world, then, whether you know it or not, you're just wandering in the goddam wilderness, all alone, nothin' to hope for, pretendin' its okay. Even though it ain't."

Grinder's eyebrows went up. He opened his mouth, then closed it and slid his hands into his pockets. He tried to smile but couldn't. "I'm heading back. You coming?" Pop didn't move. Grinder turned and headed down the sidewalk.

"What do you believe in, boy?" called Pop. "That bird?"

17

Paul stood on the desk chair preening his belly. His head went up from time to time when a bird crossed the window or the wind whistled through the small balcony just beyond the sliding glass doors. He trilled softly and reached for the window with one claw, tapping it gently. When he saw his reflection, his whole body exploded into a puffball, his irises closing and opening in rapid succession as he concentrated on this intruder. Quickly, though, his feathers relaxed when he recognized himself.

"Paul! Paul!"

He danced lightly across the back of the chair and then jumped at the sliding glass door, hitting it and then plummeting to the floor. He shook his head vigorously and then flew around the room, building momentum as he headed for the glass again. At the last moment, though, he flared his wings and landed on the lampshade beside the bed. His head bobbed contentedly as he looked at the world beyond the motel room. He started whistling but stopped when the door opened and Grinder entered.

"Goddam piece of turkey…what's he thinking?" Grinder tossed the room key onto the bed. "What do *I* believe in? I'll tell you what I *don't* believe in. I *don't* believe in a piece of turkey that doesn't even look like Jesus."

Grinder paced back and forth not noticing Paul, who followed him like he was watching a tennis match.

"Anybody with half a brain can tell that."

Paul hopped onto the bed and started to chicken-scratch the pillow. He flapped his wings and flew in place. Grinder startled and turned around.

"Hey, Paul." Grinder sat on the bed and scratched Paul's head. He leaned into Grinder's hand. "Let me tell you something, buddy. Better not having a father at all, than having to deal with all this crap. You know what I mean?"

Paul pulled his head away and sneezed. Then he cocked his head at Grinder and spoke with a strained whisper: "He's no Atticus Finch. He's no Atticus. No Atticus. But who is?"

Grinder blew back against the headboard like his Geiger counter had just hit plutonium. His eyes got buggy and he faced blanched. He cleared his throat, but then realized he had nothing to say. Grinder hit his fifth deep breath before he could speak.

"What did you say?"

Grinder got up from the bed and walked around the room, looking at Paul from every angle, waiting for him to say something more. But Paul was busy with a bag of peanuts he had found on the floor beside the mini-bar. Grinder opened the sliding glass door and went out onto the balcony for some air. All of a sudden, Paul was there beside him standing on the rail.

"No, no, Paul, get down, get down." Grinder reached for him, but Paul scooted further down the railing. He tried to slide step toward Paul, but Paul wasn't fooled and started jumping up and down and cawing wildly. "Paul, no, don't be crazy." Paul flapped his wings and rose off the railing. "No! No, don't do that. Don't jump. Don't jump. Think of Ma. If she weren't dead, it would kill her." Then he flew out from the balcony in a wide arc and back again, lighting at the far end of the railing. "My God. You can fly. Like outside in the air."

"Paul fly, Paul fly." He rose high above the balcony and then soared down past Grinder and out away from the building before perching again on the rail.

Grinder's chest was heaving. He laid one hand on his heart and leaned over again, the other hand on his knee. Paul hopped along the railing to his side. He knocked on Grinder's head with his beak. Grinder looked him square in the eyes.

"Millie didn't forget," said Paul.

The door to the room slammed shut as Lucas blustered in.

"Where the hell are you?"

Grinder's eyes were fixed on Paul. "What did you say?"

Paul tapped him on the head with his beak then darted back into the room barely missing Lucas's head.

"Goddammit." Lucas waved his arms and ducked as Paul zoomed past his ear. "I'm tellin' you, stay away from me." Paul buzzed him again and then disappeared into the bathroom. "And don't you come out. Hear me." Lucas wiped his head with a tissue and swiped the hair back along his temple with his wrist. "Damn bird." He spied his brother on the balcony. "Damn brother."

Lucas went out and stood by Grinder, hands on his hips. "What happened between you and Pop?" Grinder was gliding his hand back and forth against the breeze. "I mean, he's in his room clutching a Ziploc bag and refusing to speak." Grinder glanced at his brother, raising his eyebrows indifferently. "You didn't hit him again, did you?" Grinder bent over the railing. Lucas came closer and poked his brother in the arm. "Hey."

"No."

"No, what?"

"No, I didn't hit Pop again."

"Well, what the hell did you do?"

"Nothing. I don't know."

Lucas shook his head, then stepped back and let his hands fall to his side. "Like I said, Pop's all we got."

"Yeah." Grinder shrugged, then twirled a tiny feather between his thumb and pointer and let it fly. His voice was flat as he spoke. "You want to know what's in Pop's bag?" Lucas didn't answer. "A piece of turkey."

"A piece of turkey? You mean, like, meat?"

"I mean, like, poultry."

"Poultry."

"From last Thanksgiving."

"What's—"

"He says it's Jesus." Grinder shook his head at his brother.

"Jesus who?"

"Jesus Jesus, that's who."

"Wait a minute…"

"He says it looks like the head of Jesus."

"For chrissake."

"Exactly." Grinder pointed at a chair and Lucas sat. Grinder eased back onto the chaise lounge.

"I looked at it."

"You did."

"Yeah."

"And?"

"And it's not Jesus."

"It's not."

"No. It's poultry."

Lucas swallowed a belch and then grimaced. He sat up straight, trying to make it easier to breathe. Grinder got up again and leaned against the railing, then folded his arms.

"Anyway, it's poultry to you and me."

"Uh huh."

"But it's Jesus to Pop." Grinder rubbed his temples with the tips of his fingers.

Lucas pressed his eyes with both pointers and held them closed for a long while. When he opened them, all that was left was sadness. "My God, Pop's crazy as a shit house rat."

Grinder shrugged and sucked in a chest full of air. "Maybe, maybe not."

"Whada you mean?"

"Somehow that piece of turkey changed his life. Hard to argue with that." Grinder wiped his nose on his sleeve.

"C'mon."

"Who knows?" He hitched his thumbs into his belt loops and pulled his jeans up. "You hear this kind of thing all the time."

"Hear what? People seeing Jesus in their Thanksgiving turkey?"

"Not just that. Different stuff. You know, like someone sees the Virgin Mary in a piece of toast and then they cough up a tumor."

"A tumor?"

"Yes, usually it's a tumor." Grinder's face got all thoughtful. "Or someone who's paralyzed sees Jesus or the Virgin or maybe both of them in his tapioca pudding and all of a sudden he can walk."

Lucas scratched his ear and then pressed his hand over his lips as he considered what his brother was saying. He uncovered his mouth and held his hand in front of his face. "There was that guy, you remember, down on the southern tier?"

Grinder shook his head no.

"Well, he was just this guy, except he couldn't talk, like at all, and one day he was chopping some wood and Jesus's face showed up in one of the shavings and all of a sudden the guy could speak, like, a bunch of languages all at once, whata they call it, tongue-talking or something."

"Well, there you go."

"I guess." Lucas frowned. "I don't know."

"One man's crazy is another man's miracle, you know what I mean?"

Lucas's whole face was furrowed with consternation. "I'm not so sure…"

"Sometimes the crazier something is, the more chance it has of being true;

like if a dog started talking to you, or a goat or a horse, or something. Or even a bird. You gotta listen because they might say something that could change everything."

Lucas held up both hands. "Wait a minute."

"What?" Grinder leaned away as if in defense.

"Talking animals? Talking like what, like Jesus? What's Jesus or the Virgin got to do with talking cats or birds?"

"I dunno. Maybe Jesus and his mother don't always have to be in the mix. Think about it. A miracle could come from anywhere, right? Who's to say? That's what makes it a goddam miracle."

"Seeing Jesus's face in stuff is one thing, but talking animals..."

Grinder's face pinched in frustration. "It's just a damn example, that's all."

It was quiet all of a sudden except for the distant sounds of Paul trilling in the bathroom. Grinder cleared his throat and licked his lips.

"Look, Lukie, there's more weird shit going on out there than any of us can imagine; and you can never tell when you might be the next one to cough up a tumor; that's all I'm trying to say."

Lucas's face had a searching look on it. "Maybe it's like Butch said, once you put a coin in the slot, you ain't got a clue what could happen next."

"That's it." Grinder grinned and patted his brother's shoulder. He turned back to the railing and looked out across the city, satisfaction on his face.

Lucas went up to the railing and stood beside him. He looked down at the parking lot below and then up at the Gulf Building nearby. He sniffed once, reached for a tissue and then put it back in his pocket. He looked at Grinder, who was still taking in the urban vista.

"So."

Grinder turned his head slightly, looking sideways at his brother.

"My guess is the bird's been saying stuff to you, right?"

Grinder bent over to look in the mini-bar. He stared at the contents and decided on a Rolling Rock. He tipped it towards Lucas, who declined. Grinder pulled the tab and tossed it at the garbage can, missing it by a foot or more. He put the can to his lips and tilted his head back as far as he could. Then he wiped his mouth and did it again.

"I mean, really?" said Lucas. "I know the bird is smart, but no bird is that smart. I mean most *people* aren't that smart." He forced a laugh, as if doing so would turn the whole thing into a joke. Grinder drank some more. "Hey, go slow."

123

Parrot Talk

"I'm tellin' you, that's what he said. He said the Atticus stuff and the stuff about Ma not forgetting. And it wasn't like he was just popping off. It was like he knew what he was saying and he knew who he was saying it to. He was talking to *me*."

Lucas's laugh collapsed, the corners of his mouth were now pinned to his chin. "Okay, if that's what's he's doing, let's get him out here so he can talk to me, too."

"It doesn't work that way."

Lucas went into the bathroom, returning with Paul in his hands. "Ouch, dammit." Paul pecked him and was on the wing again, this time out over the balcony and back into the room. Grinder held out his arm, but Paul chose to land on the bedside lamp instead.

Lucas had a fit of sneezing. He blew his nose three times, examining the results after each effort. "Damn bird." Paul sneezed, as well, then cleaned a tiny feather from his nostril.

"I'm telling you he won't talk if you try to force him."

Lucas picked up the bag of nuts that lay open on the floor. He put several in the palm of his hand and walked slowly towards Paul. Paul watched indifferently. He wiped his beak on the rim of the lampshade, trilled, cawed and then stood still, studying Lucas's every move.

Lucas spoke in a high-pitched voice, like a kindergarten teacher. "Here you go, birdy bird; here you go. Uncle Lucas is your friend. Want a nut, huh, want a goddam nut; you talk to me and I'll give you one." He was in front of the lamp now, Paul above him. He flapped his wings and then tucked one leg under his breast. "That's a good bird, that's a good bird. Uncle Lucas won't hurt you. Uncle Lucas just wants you to talk to him." Paul bowed to Lucas, who leaned forward and raised his hand. Paul stepped closer, enticed by the nuts. "There you go little buddy. Take one of these yummy nuts." Paul lurched forward and plucked one. "Atta boy."

"Nutty nuts, nutty nuts," said Paul, pieces of shell falling from his mouth.

"Lucas, he's—"

"Shhhh! I'm working here." Lucas held his hand up to Paul again and Paul took more nuts. Lucas leaned in closer. "We're gonna be good friends, you bird." He looked over his shoulder at Grinder, satisfaction on his face. "I've got him eatin' out of my you know what." Lucas chuckled. Grinder's face went slack. "C'mon, Pauly boy, now it's time to talk." Paul chomped the nuts and wiped his beak on the wall behind him. "Grinder says you can say some amazing stuff. Can you say Atticus? Huh? Can you?" Paul preened his wings quietly. "Look at me." Paul was working on his belly. "Atticus? A-tee-cuss." Lucas turned around and frowned at Grinder.

Paul opened his mouth and out dropped a ball of soggy nuts, partly digested, that hit Lucas on top of his shiny dome.

"What the fuck." Lucas looked at his hands, his face curling in disgust. "What did that little effer just do to me?" Lucas tripped backwards onto the bed, gooey nuts and shells sliding down his left temple. "I'm gonna kill 'im."

"Wait a minute."

But Lucas was on his feet, arms outstretched, fingers splayed. Grinder snagged him and held him back. Lucas flailed at the air. Paul ground his beak softly and fluffed his feathers.

"Lemme go."

"Not until you settle down."

"Your bird puked on my head. There's no settling down."

Lucas took another swing at the air as Paul puffed up in defense. Grinder pushed his brother back onto the bed.

Lucas was pointing now. "I'm tellin' you, get out of my way. He's goin' down."

"Relax. I don't think he was trying to piss you off."

"No?" Lucas dabbed his head with one corner of the sheet and held up the results. "Then what's that, huh? I'm tellin' you, nobody yorks all over my head and gets away with it."

"Don't you remember? The vet told us that parrots can show affection by throwing up on you, like they're trying to feed a baby or something, like they care about you."

"Don't give me that psychobabble bullshit. Nobody spews on Lucas. That's a rule." Lucas could not keep himself from looking at what he was wiping off his head.

"I'm telling you, I think he was trying to let you know that even though you hate his guts, he likes you."

Paul leaped from the lamp to the desk. Then to the floor where he buried his head in the bag of nuts. He was chomping hard when he surfaced.

"Don't even think of it," said Lucas, pointing again. "What's he doing?"

"What do you mean, 'What's he doing?'"

Lucas looked hard at Paul who stared back at him, pupils big as saucers.

"He's planning something," said Lucas.

"Planning something, c'mon."

Lucas slid off the bed, his arm wrapped in a towel for protection. He held his other arm in front of his face. Paul bobbed rhythmically back and forth.

"See that?"

"See what?"

Lucas bobbed back and forth. "That. That's the kind of thing I'm talking about. He's shifty."

Paul bobbed and waved his wings with balletic grace. Lucas sat down on his knees. Paul cawed twice and cleared his throat. He tilted his head to one side and spoke in a high raspy whisper: "Lukie, you will always be my big boy."

18

"I never thought I'd see yinz two again." Janice gestured with her hand for them to come in. "Ronald! They're here!"

"Who?" Through the narrow hallway, the brothers could see Ronald, still in the red lounge chair, naked pasty legs up on the footrest, cutoff sweatpants, slippers and black socks, and a torn Steelers T.

Janice leaned over sideways. "Millie's boys, for chrissakes."

"Get 'em a beer." Ronald balanced a beer stein on his belly as he poured another IC. On the TV, John Wayne was kicking some poor Indian's butt.

Janice disappeared into the kitchen while Grinder settled on the couch across from Ronald, who hadn't yet looked at them. "Thought you was going back to wherever you come from." Ronald took a long swig. "Janice, what the hell happened to your hospitality-ness! Boys need a beer."

"Not really," said Lucas, who stood in the entryway. He went forward, tentatively. Then slid in beside Grinder on the couch.

"Janice!"

"I'm comin'!"

Grinder put his hand up to the side of his face and tried to whisper to Lucas, although the sounds of cavalry on the TV were stiff competition. "Just have a beer. Where's *your* hospitality-ness?"

Lucas, his mouth stiff at the corners, nodded at Ronald who had finally glanced away from the TV long enough to make eye contact. "Sure."

"There you go, buddy. Two beers, Janice! I mean three! Four if you're gonna join us. Hell, just bring a sixer."

Janice emerged from the kitchen balancing three beers on a plastic surveying tray. She set the tray on the coffee table and dried her hands on her flowered apron. "There yinz go." Ronald had already opened his as the brothers reached for theirs.

"This is very kind of you," said Grinder.

"Don't think nothin' of it." Janice pulled a chair from the kitchen and sat beside her husband. She glowered at Ronald. "He likes his beer."

"Of course, I like my beer. What kinda thing is'at to say?" Ronald shifted his weight so he wouldn't have to turn his head much to look at the brothers. "She's a complainer, this one. Doesn't like me drinkin' beer. Doesn't like the way I dress. Doesn't like me sittin' here. I worked all my life!" His arms went out in a show of disbelief. "No pleasin' her." Janice's eyes darted uncomfortably, as if she were looking around the room for a place to hide her husband. "Ain't that so, honey?"

She coughed into her fist, regained her composure, sat up straight as could be and grinned at her company. "It might be hard for us to talk, what with the TV and everything."

"Don't like me watchin' TV neither."

"Maybe we could go into the kitchen."

The boys nodded in agreement, leaving their beers behind.

"Fair warning fellas, once you leave this room, them beers are up for grabs," called Ronald.

Grinder picked up Janice's chair and carried it with him to the kitchen where the three of them gathered round the table.

"Would yinz like a cup of coffee? I got some ready." She reached for cups and lined them on the counter. "Sugar's on the stove, if you want some." She then pulled a quart of milk from the refrigerator and put it on the table. Grinder reached for the sugar and opened the drawer for a couple of spoons. Janice carried the steaming pot from the stove and poured coffee into each cup. "How's Paul?"

"I think he's doing better. Eating more, anyway." Grinder looked at Lucas, who rolled his eyes.

"That's good," said Janice, a broad smile crossing her face.

"He's not picking at himself quite as much."

"I'm so glad you took him to the vet. Your mother would be so happy."

Janice put a cup of coffee on each of three plastic placemats and then took a seat. "Your mother would be relieved knowin' Paul's in good hands, I'll tell you that. She loved him more than just about anything." Janice peeked at the brothers, uncomfortable with her choice of words. "Actually, Millie, your mother, I should say, loved a great many things."

"She did?" Grinder sipped hot coffee and then leaned forward on his elbows.

"Oh yes, she had her favorite things. *Judge Judy* and *Wheel* and *Jeopardy*. Loved her TV. Loved playing Hearts and Uno. Loved her Steelers, of course. I put the Franco picture in the box; did you find it?"

"The box?"

"It's in the trunk." Grinder scowled at Lucas. "Haven't looked at it yet."

Janice burst into laughter. "Well, when you do, your gonna find about a gazillion salt and pepper shakers. I'm tellin' you, the woman was crazy for them things." Her laughter stopped as quickly as it had started. "Yeah, Millie. She loved sittin' out on the balcony in the evening watching the sun go down. She'd call out the colors. Pink, she'd say, or orange or purple. Like she'd never seen them before. She sure loved them sunsets."

Lucas got up from the table and stood by the sink, cup in hand.

"Hated cooking. Loved mac and cheese. And going for walks by herself. In the old days when her health was good. She was my best friend. Listened. Didn't judge. Got along with Ronald just fine, if you can imagine." Janice got up, reached for the pot and raised it to the boys. They nodded no. She sat down again. "And, like I said, she loved Paul. He loved her." Janice shrugged as if she had said it all.

"And she smoked pot, I guess." Lucas was still standing.

"How do they say it—for medicinal purposes." Janice raised her eyebrows and put one hand over her mouth in mock embarrassment.

"And she abandoned her family."

"Hey." Grinder raised a hand.

"Don't 'hey' me." Lucas pulled out his handkerchief and was about to blow his nose. But he realized he didn't need to and stuffed it back in his pocket. Grinder looked like he was ready to pounce if Lucas went on.

Janice sat up straighter in her chair. "You boys never got to know your mother."

"And she never got to know us."

"Okay." Grinder might as well have said 'shut up.' "My brother and me, we came here to ask you about Paul."

Janice finally took her eyes off Lucas. "To ask about Paul? What do you wanna know?"

"Well, he's been doing some things, saying some things…"

Ronald stumbled into the kitchen, his nose a vivid crimson. He was carrying three empties. "I warned ya not to leave these unattended. Someone's run off with their contents." He punctuated his comments with a resounding belch. "You'll never know what you missed." Ronald slapped Lucas on the shoulder. "Why don't you sit down?"

"I'm fine."

"You're the older one, right?"

Lucas shuffled back and forth, trying to get some distance from Ronald.

"Yes, I am the older one."

"And that makes you the younger one," he said, pointing in Grinder's direction.

"Ronnie, please." Janice's face was full of weariness.

"Don't 'Ronnie, please' me, woman." Ronald pointed at Janice. He let his arm rest and then spoke to the brothers. "Y'know, I never believed Millie when she said she had two sons. She had that picture, but coulda been anyone. I always thought Paul was her only kid. She had him for, like...what was it, Janice?"

"Twenty—"

"Twenty years. Over twenty years. That's almost...that's a whole child-raising lifetime if you think on it a minute." Ronald took another beer from the frig and yanked the tab, then threw the tab in the sink. "Anyone?" But he didn't wait for an answer. He slammed the frig closed. "Here's something I bet my dear wife ain't told you. Sometimes Paul'd perch right on Millie's bedpost all night. You'd a thought he was a guard watching over his queen. Y'know what I mean? Her little protector." He was quiet for a moment as he studied the can in his hand. "He was right there beside her on the floor that day we found her. Just sittin' there all quiet. Not moving or nothin'. He knew. Didn't say a damn thing for days after. Then one day we heard a voice comin' from the bathroom. Like it was Millie herself. Janice, she went in there and wouldn't you know, it was Paul just sayin' stuff like Millie would say it. 'Time for Judge Judy,' he'd say. Or 'Watch yourself on that balcony, Paul'. Never did that before." Ronald wagged his head, as if staggered with amazement. "You know they can imitate damn near anything. If they have to. I guess he had to." He opened the frig door and took another beer. "Kinda creepy. And sad." Then he headed back into the living room.

"Is that true?" said Grinder.

Janice reached for the box of tissues on the counter, pulled one out and dabbed her eyes. "Scared me to death, what he did. I know this'll sound stupid, but for a moment I thought your mother was back. I got all crazy with hope."

She balled the tissue and held it in her lap. "Stupid of me, I know."

Grinder caught his brother's eye. "No, it's not stupid at all."

Lucas sat down and put one arm on the table. Grinder closed his eyes for a few seconds and then started: "Look, Janice, Paul's been saying things, things that don't make sense for a bird to say. It's like he's not a bird at all sometimes."

"Oh, Jesus, don't say it like that," said Lucas.

"He talks in this voice. A scratchy old voice."

"That's it." Janice pushed her chair back and stood suddenly. "Kinda high pitched like?"

"Uh huh."

"That's Millie, for sure."

Lucas pulled his chair closer to the table and leaned on his folded arms.

Grinder continued: "It's like he knows who we are; like he's saying stuff to us, but it's really her talking."

Lucas yanked his handkerchief and started wiping the sweat from almost everywhere.

"I know this is pretty damn crazy…" said Lucas.

"Not to me, it ain't. I knew your mother and I knew Paul. Nothin's crazy." Janice held her coffee cup with both hands but didn't raise it to her lips.

Grinder's face had a calm, gentle look about it, like all the tension inside him had jumped ship.

"Your mother talked about you boys a lot. I mean she knew your birthdays and she used to cry over you on Christmas and everything. She talked about how you was the little boss, Lucas, and you was the bright light, Grinder." Janice was dabbing her eyes again while Lucas blew his nose.

"Funny way of loving us." Lucas sniffed and his nose was clear. "Here she was living five hours away; and did she ever write us a letter? Send us a card? Call us on the phone? No. But she bought herself a talking bird and raised it like it was her very own child. I don't know what to make of it all."

Janice was crying hard now. Some of the tension found its way back to Grinder's face and neck and shoulders. His heart, as well. He glanced at Janice, a beckoning look in his eyes. Janice grimaced.

"I wish I could explain Millie to you. But I can't. Every time I tried to talk to her about it, about you two, it was like she would go away on me, like she'd disappear and wouldn't come back 'til I stopped asking. So I'd stop. Then I'd try again. Over and over, cuz I could tell there was something. But no. Even when she was sick, I told her to reach out to yinz two, but she wouldn't." Janice began to tear up again. Grinder handed her another tissue. Lucas fiddled with his fingers, his head bowed. "She was a good friend to me but her insides was closed off tight. Like part of her was just locked up or somethin'."

She looked at Grinder, then Lucas, like she wasn't sure she should have said what she said. She wobbled her head a bit and pushed her coffee cup away. "Maybe I'm just talkin' now, I don't know. But that's what it seemed like to me. Part of her wasn't never gonna come out. It was like she up and decided that was the way it should be." All the folds on Janice's face came together. "And yes, that old bird, Paul, he was the only one who had real deep down visiting privileges."

19

By the time Lucas reached the street, Grinder had already popped the trunk and was tearing through the box of their mother's effects. Torn pieces of the Post-Gazette flew into the air, as if shot from a T-shirt cannon at a Pirates' game.

"Hey, hey! Come on!"

But Grinder kept on. Lucas went for his brother's arm, but he shook him off. Lucas tried again, but Grinder was deep into the box now and could not be stopped. "Goddammit. I'm telling you, no matter what you find, there's nothing there." Grinder would not be deterred.

Meanwhile, Giant Eagle grocery inserts cartwheeled down the street while the funny pages spun in the air like whirligigs. Lucas ran after the packing, balling each piece against his chest as he went. An old woman wearing a white raincoat trapped a page under her shoe and dutifully waited for Lucas to retrieve it. Unaccustomed to running or jogging or walking fast or even plain old walking, he was breathless when he finally reached her. After several huffs and puffs, he smiled and said, "Thanks." She looked at him, fault lines creasing her stern face.

"We're not from around here," said Lucas, by way of explanation.

"They throw paper in the street where yinz come from?"

"I'm sorry," he offered, but she had already started to walk away. "I'll make sure we get it all!"

Lucas gathered up as much newspaper as he could. Then he sauntered back to the car where a tall man with bushy sideburns and a black Penguins' skullcap stood on the curb, a bag of groceries in his arms.

"Hi," said Lucas. The man nodded. They stood for a moment in silence watching the man in the box.

"My brother."

"Oh. What's he lookin' for?"

"Our mother."

"Oh." The man shifted the bag from one arm to the other. "How long's he been at it?"

"About ten minutes."

The man raised his knee to the bag so he could rearrange the contents, then shifted the bag back to the first arm. He then pulled his skullcap down closer to his eyes and watched the goings-on for a while longer.

"You'd think he woulda found her by now."

Lucas turned his head and looked at the man, who, noticing the widening tear in his bag, decided to head home.

"Good luck."

"Thanks," said Lucas.

Lucas opened the back door of the car and dumped the scraps of newspaper in. Then he sat on the curb, his legs outstretched. The box was completely still now. Grinder's head popped up first and then the rest of him. He was holding the picture in his hands. He tumbled out of the trunk and sat beside his brother. Two boys sped down the middle of the street on their bicycles, long sticks in hand.

"Well." Lucas put his hand on his brother's back.

Grinder held the picture up in front of them. There they stood, the lake behind them, fishing poles in hand, one brother tall, one small, squinting into the sunlight behind the photographer.

"Ma took this picture."

"I know."

The boys down the street started raising a ruckus, poking at something with their sticks. Lucas and Grinder glanced at them and then turned their attention to the picture again. Grinder brought it up to his face, examining every square inch.

"What are you looking for?"

"I'm trying to see us like Ma saw us. You know, this had to be, like, August before she left in the fall."

Lucas took the picture and held it close. "Yeah, could be."

"Made me wonder if she already knew she was gonna leave. Like when she focused the camera and squared us up in the frame, did she think this was the last shot, the one she wanted to take with her."

Lucas rubbed his chin and pulled his legs up. "No, I don't think so. She hadn't even met your asshole teacher yet."

"Oh."

Lucas handed the picture back to his brother. Grinder laid the picture in his lap and leaned back, his hands on the sidewalk. He watched the boys down the street as they hooted and hollered and laughed. They were trying to pick something up with the ends of their sticks, but couldn't quite pull it off, which only made them laugh harder. Grinder stood.

"What?" Lucas looked up at his brother and then down the street at the boys. Before he knew it, Grinder opened the back door of the car, reached for several pages of newspaper and headed toward the boys.

"Hey!" he called. The boys stopped and watched the long-legged man who was bearing down on them. They were about to drop their sticks and high-tail it out of there when Grinder called again: "Wait a minute! Okay?"

Lucas lumbered after him.

When Grinder reached the boys, their legs were getting fidgety with fear.

"Hi guys." They shielded their eyes as they looked up into this stranger's face. "What's your names?"

"I'm Antonio and this is Laquan."

"Nice to meet you." Grinder shook both boys' limp hands. "Whacha doin'?"

"Nothin'." Antonio looked at his friend and nodded for him to agree.

"Nothin'."

"I mean whacha got there?"

"Dead squirrel," said Laquan.

"Yep. A dead squirrel for sure."

Lucas caught up to his brother, the picture still in his hands. He looked at the boys, but said nothing, which only added to their worry.

"We didn't do nothin'," said Antonio. "I mean we didn't kill it or nothin'. Just playin'."

"Yinz ain't callin' the cops or nothin'?" Laquan backed up a few steps.

"No, no, nothing like that." Grinder knelt beside the squirrel. "Come here a minute." Antonio nudged Laquan and they took a step or two toward Grinder. "Down here, I mean." The boys sunk slowly to their knees. "Let me tell you something. Look at this squirrel. Looks to me like it was alive just a bit ago. Like it got up this morning and was ready to do its squirrely thing all day. Running here and there, getting nuts and stuff, going back to its nest. You know, just living, kinda like us. I bet you got up today and figured you'd get together and just do whatever you wanted all day, never giving any thought to anything. Am

I right?"

The boys stared.

"I think the squirrel did kind of the same thing. Got up and went out to do whatever he wanted to do. But he didn't figure on a car coming by too fast for him to get out of the way. And all of a sudden, SPLAT!" Both boys gulped. "Deader than dead. Just like that." Antonio wiped his eyes with the palm of his hand. Laquan sniffed. "Let me show you boys something."

Grinder opened a sheet of newspaper and laid it on the pavement beside the squirrel. Then he put another layer on top. He smoothed the paper flat with his hands. "Can I borrow your stick?" Laquan nodded. "Thanks, son." Grinder reached with the end of the stick and gently rolled the squirrel onto the paper. "Got some guts there don't we." Then he folded one side of the paper over the squirrel and pulled the other side to meet it. He patted the paper down and then folded the bottom half up and the top half down. He tucked the paper under the tiny body and creased it. "There."

"Whacha gonna do with it?" asked Antonio.

Grinder looked around him. "Well, it's not practical to bury it." He pointed at a trash receptacle across the street. "But at least we can get him off this street. Whadaya think?" Both boys nodded reverently.

"Okay, tell you what; Laquan, you take one end and Antonio, you take the other." The boys did as they were told. Grinder walked slowly ahead of them as they processed to the trash receptacle.

Lucas watched, shaking his head and rolling his eyes. "My God."

Grinder raised the lid on the receptacle. "Go ahead boys." They lifted the paper coffin and dropped it in. Grinder let the lid fall with a resounding thud. "Maybe one of you should say something."

Laquan and Antonio looked at each other. Laquan nudged his friend. Antonio glanced at Grinder, then cleared his throat. "Goodbye, squirrel."

"Perfect," said Grinder. "Good job, boys. You know what you just did?"

"Put a dead squirrel in the garbage can?" said Antonio.

"Yeah. You sure did. But more than that, you respected that squirrel. You know why that's important?"

"Huh uh," said Laquan.

"Cause it was a living thing once." Grinder grinned at their blank faces. "Try to remember that, if you can." With that, Antonio and Laquan took a few steps backward, then turned and ran off down the street.

"You are a piece of work," said Lucas. "A dead squirrel is a dead squirrel."

"A life is a life," said Grinder.

Lucas wiped perspiration from the top of his head and handed the picture to his brother. Grinder held the photo at arm's length, studying it. "You know, she was younger than we are now. I mean, she was a young woman."

"Yeah?"

Grinder squinted and leaned his head forward. "I guess she was pretty, too. She had blonde hair and she was thin-ish and she had blue eyes."

Lucas shrugged. "What are you trying to do?"

"Just trying to see her."

"What does it matter?"

"I don't know, it just does." Grinder pulled the picture closer to his face.

"Look, I don't think this—"

"I wonder what we looked like to her."

"Whadaya mean?"

Grinder held the picture an inch from his face as if his eyes were microscopes.

"You know, what she thought of us? What she wanted for us?"

Lucas took the picture from his brother and scanned it. He gave it back to Grinder without comment.

Grinder tapped his brother's arm. "So?"

"I don't think you're gonna find any answers in this picture. My bet is, it was a hot day and Pop was home drunk and Ma had to get out of the house, so she took us fishing. That's about it."

"Why do you think she took a picture at all? And she kept it. Why this one?"

Lucas sighed and put his hands in his pocket.

"And somewhere along the way she got it framed," said Grinder.

"I don't know. Maybe she was in a hurry when she left and she just took it without thinking. Maybe later she knew she wasn't gonna see us again, so she framed it. Who knows? Maybe it was the last one."

Grinder walked over to the car and dropped the picture into the box. He packed newspapers on top again and closed the flaps. He reached for the trunk hatch and pulled it closed.

"Does it really matter at this point?"

"If I close my eyes and think hard, I can still see her face the way it was the day she left, the day she said she was going to the mall and she'd bring me back some socks. I can just about freeze frame her looking over her shoulder at me, and when I do that, her face doesn't give any hint at all of what was coming."

Lucas took the back of Grinder's neck in his hand and squeezed it firmly but gently.

"You can ask all the questions you want, but it doesn't mean you're gonna get any answers."

Grinder looked at the sun idling in the southwestern sky.

"Don't you think we deserve better than that?"

"Yes, I suppose we do."

20

Pop pressed his ear to the motel room door. He could hear thumps and screams inside. He knocked. "Hey! Anyone in there?" He listened but no one responded. Then there was yelling and cursing and more thumping. "Open the door!" More screeching. "Let me in!" There was a moment of silence that exploded into yipping and yowling. "Hold on, hold on!" Pop looked around for something to help him pry open the door. Finding nothing, he stood back several feet, rocked back and forth, clenched his arm into a knot, and rushed the door, crashing into it with his shoulder, then slumping to the floor. "Gosh darn it." Pop rubbed his shoulder and stretched his arm, working hard to regain feeling. Meanwhile the noise inside the room was reaching a crescendo. Pop studied the door some more, retreated a few steps and then lunged forward, smashing the door with his foot. Nothing. Again and then again and finally the door burst open as fragments of the frame flew in every direction.

"Where are you?" he cried.

He glimpsed Martha in the bathroom. She had one foot on the toilet and the other on the edge of the bathtub. She clung to the shower curtain. She was waving a towel wildly at Paul, who stood on the sink, then hopped down on the floor, then up on the tub ledge beside Martha's foot. Pop averted his eyes when he realized Martha's sweatpants were huddled around her knees.

With a hand over his eyes, he called, "What can I do?"

"Get the damn bird out of here!"

Pop stumbled forward, eyes covered, and hit the doorjamb head on.

"Open your goddam eyes!"

"I shouldn't be seeing you like this," said Pop.

"Get the damn bird."

Pop opened his eyes, rushed into the bathroom, and picked up Paul, who seemed to welcome the rescue. Once in the other room, Pop turned to face

Martha again: "Coast is clear."

"Stop looking at me!"

"I'm sorry, but—" Martha slammed the door. Pop stood in the middle of the room holding Paul like a newborn. Paul squawked and tried to free his wings. "Okay, okay, little buddy." Pop put him on the desk and Paul dropped to the floor looking for a nut. Then he jumped back onto the desk and then to the top of the floor lamp, where he stared at Pop.

"Cluck, cluck, eeeck, awk, awk."

"So, you're the bird I've heard so much talk about."

"Paul, Paul, awk, awk."

"Yeah, Paul. Millie's Paul."

"Oooooo-eek-eek. Millie, Millie, Millie."

"I'm Pop. Calvin, actually." He rubbed his hands together, looked around the room, then sat on the edge of the bed. "Was married to Millie. I'm Grinder and Lucas's father."

"The boys."

"Yeah, the boys."

"Whose boys?"

"Mine."

"Millie's boys."

"Well…"

"Millie's baby boy and big boy."

"Well…"

"Not your boys." Paul blew raspberries, stuck out his tongue, threw back his head and clucked loudly.

Pop squinted at Paul, then stood. He took one step forward, then stopped cold, not sure what he was dealing with. He circled Paul gradually, as if a more complete view would equal a more complete understanding. Paul turned with him, inch by inch.

"Are you really talking or are you just sayin' stuff?"

"Are *you* really talkin' or are *you* just sayin' stuff?"

Pop slapped his leg and started to cackle. "My good Lord, son, you are a smart little thing."

"Praise Jesus."

Pop stopped mid-knee slap and held his breath. "What did you say?"

"What did *you* say?"

"Don't try to pull that on me again. I'm onto you, son."

"My good Lord, you are a smart little thing," said Paul.

"What in the—"

"Is it safe out there? Can I come out?" called Martha.

Pop didn't seem to hear Martha. He went over to the lamp and stood face-to-face with Paul, inspecting him.

"Hey!" Martha tapped on the bathroom door, waiting for the all clear.

Pop leaned in close, eyes peeled. Paul leaned in closer, beak to nose. Pop leaned back. Paul did, too. Then they both leaned in again. And so it went. Martha was pounding now.

"Are you just a copycat?"

"Are *you* just a copycat?"

Pop backed away and pointed at Paul, but said nothing. Martha was rattling the door knob so hard that the wall shuttered. "Is it okay for me to come out, goddammit?" He opened the door and Martha fumed into the room. "What the hell's going on? What took you so long? What did you do to the damn door?"

"It sounded like someone was getting themselves killed, so I did what I had to do. I busted the door in." Pop took a sideways glance at Paul. "Didn't know it was you and Paul here. Thought you was in danger."

Martha was breathing more evenly now. She waved her hand in Paul's direction. "I *was* in danger." Pop straightened his back and went silent. "So, thank you. I guess."

"You're very welcome, honey." He nodded toward Paul. "He's a smart one, isn't he? I mean, he can talk, like he's makin' it up on his own, just like you and me."

"That's what your son thinks. Trying to convince my Lucas, but I don't think it's gonna work. Lucas is no genius, but he's not stupid either. At least not about this. Grinder, I don't know about him. He acts like that bird is the absolute answer to everything."

Pop puffed up. "Well, I can tell you for sure there's only but one answer to life's big questions—"

"You can stop right there. In case you hadn't noticed, the 'no sale' sign is in the window. No need for you to bother trying to sell me Jesus."

Pop laughed through a tight grimace. He cocked his head and tried to size Martha up. "You don't know me," he said.

"This is true."

"And I don't know you."

"Truer still." Martha licked her pinky and smoothed her eyebrows. She ran her fingers through her hair and shook her head. "Your point?"

"I'd like to get to know you."

"Why?" Martha reached for a pack of gum on the desktop, unwrapped a stick, folded it and popped it into her mouth. She chewed hard. Pop looked on, intently.

"Well, for one, we're family."

"Don't take this the wrong way. You might be blood but you're not family."

Pop's brow furrowed in perplexity. He tugged on his moustache and then glanced at Paul, as if asking for help. Paul cawed and buried his head under one wing.

"You can't just show up out of the blue, all, like, 'I'm workin' my twelve-step program,' and think that makes everything better. I'm sorry, it just doesn't work like that."

"But I never stopped thinkin' of us as family. I was sick all those years, but I was still a father, a father-in-law."

"You were, were you?" Martha pulled at an eyelash. "Let me ask you something. What is *our* son's name, me and Lucas?"

Pop bowed his head in concentration, then scratched his cheek and looked at Martha. "It's Lucas, Jr., ain't it?"

"We don't have a son. We have a daughter. And just so you don't embarrass yourself further, her name's Mandy." Pop's face sunk. He slumped onto the bed.

Martha sat down beside him. "Millie left. Then pretty soon you hooked up with that Consuela person and moved to Mexico, of all places. Lucas and I got married. We were both working two jobs. Bought a house on a shoe string. We were way too young for the whole thing. But we were making a start. Grinder hadn't even graduated high school. But he wanted to go to college." Martha lifted her shoulders and let them drop. "It should have been simple, really. You should have been there. Millie should have been there. Instead, Lucas took out a loan and picked up the freight for Grinder to go to school. I gotta tell you, I was against it. I said to Lucas, 'Let your goddam father pay for this.' He didn't say a thing. He just did it 'cause he wanted Grinder to have a chance. But Grinder was still a freakin' mess. He tried once, he tried twice, but, in the end, he dropped out. Didn't even tell his brother for months. Said he was going to classes, but he wasn't. Broke Lucas's heart. But they were brothers. So, they stuck together and worked it out."

Pop was sniffling now. Martha sat straight up and studied her father-in-law's face. When she spoke again, her voice was soft. She put her hand on his shoulder. "Look, Pop. I hate to put it this way, but you've never been there. Like ever. Like even when you were there, you weren't there. And 'being there' is what makes a family."

21

Pop was holed up in his room, a bag of Jesus in his hand. The edges of Jesus's face were disintegrating, but the shadow of divinity was still there. Pop pressed the bag to his face and then pulled back because of the smell.

"My sweet Lord, what am I supposed to do?"

He closed his eyes, bowed his head and listened, but screeching traffic and blaring horns made it impossible for him to plug into his Higher Power. "Shit." He held his eyes more firmly shut and began to rock back and forth. "Blessed be the tie that binds, our hearts in Christian love," he sang, but those were the only words he could recall. Determined to set the right tone, he hummed on, but the tune quickly devolved into "When Johnny Comes Marching Home Again," so he stopped mid-hum. "My God, my God, why the hell have you forsooked my wretched butt?"

He looked longingly at the mini-bar, but reached for his copy of the AA Big Book instead. He closed his eyes and let the book fall open and then pressed his finger on the page. He opened his eyes, but the words didn't make any sense. So he closed his eyes again and flipped the pages forward, then sunk his pointer into the text once more. He peaked: "We must not shrink from anything," it said.

"I'm not shrinking, I'm not shrinking!" he bellowed.

Then he gave it another whirl. This time his finger fell on, "How dark it is before the dawn."

"Yes, yes, it's darker than hell!"

He flipped again and read, "There is a solution."

"A solution, yes! Show me, Lord!"

Suddenly there was a knock on the door. Pop startled and sat still as could be, his eyes a little delirious with hope. He waited in the silence and then there was another knock. He whispered, "I'm coming, Lord." He stood up straight as a soldier in the army of God, reached for his hat and placed it perfectly on his head. He looked at himself in the mirror, but realized there wasn't enough time to make any improvements, so he walked tentatively to the door, not sure if he was ready for what awaited him. A knock came for a third time. Pop held his breath expectantly and opened the door.

She was a smallish woman with long black hair braided down her back. Her dark eyes were weary, though she smiled and nodded at him respectfully. She wore a plain blue dress with a white apron. A pair of worn Nikes adorned her feet. Pop's face glowed. He took off his hat and then bowed. She grinned nervously and pulled her linen cart closer to her side.

"You are not what I expected." Pop was breathless. "But the Lord moves in the damnedest ways."

The sound of Pop's voice made the woman smile more broadly. "Okay?"

"Okay."

She wavered back and forth on the edges of her Nikes. "Okay?" she said, eyebrows raised as if asking permission. Pop moved back so that she could enter. Wordlessly she turned the bed cover and sheet down.

Pop cleared his throat. "You know, I have been waiting, uh, waiting on the Lord." The woman took each pillow and fluffed it, then placed them against the headboard at interesting angles. "You see, I'm in an awful jam. I can't hardly talk to one of my sons and the other one hates me and I'm just trying to work my program so I don't tumble off the wagon again, but I feel terrible stuck and don't know which way to go and I been prayin' to the Lord." Pop pointed to the ceiling and the woman looked up briefly, and when she saw nothing, went back to her work. "And I been lookin' for revelation in the Big Book." He took it in his hands and held it out to her, as if she might take it, but she didn't. Instead she went to her cart and then returned. "'Cause I need some answers. And I need 'em fast."

"Okay."

Pop's face was all a puzzle. He sat on the edge of the bed. The woman watched him, then took two mints from her pocket, showed them to him and placed one each on his pillows. She returned to her cart. "Are you leaving?" She took a white face towel from the top of the pile and came back to his side. She started folding the towel slowly, carefully, as Pop watched with rapt attention. Her hands moved quietly, gently. When she was done, she held a perfect swan in the palm of her hand. She reached out with it to Pop, who took it in both hands.

"Is this for me?" Pop's eyes fluttered and gleamed.

"Okay?"

"My gosh, it's the most beautiful thing I ever seen in my life." He held it up in front of his eyes, and caressed its slender neck. "You have made a miracle."

Her laugh was breathy as she stood and bowed, her palms on her thighs.

"Like a dove come down from Jesus hisself." He stood and not knowing what else to do, hugged her, not a full-throated, bone-crusher, but a timid, thank-you-for-being-so-kind embrace. She stood stiffly and when he let go, she bowed again.

"Okay? Okay?"

"Very much okay okay." She retreated to her cart and disappeared into the hall. Pop held the swan in his crusty hands, turning it this way and that, trying to take in its enormity, its grace-filled vastness. He walked to the door. "And thanks for the candy," he called, but she had already entered another room.

The elevator at the end of the hall opened, depositing Grinder and Lucas. Pop waved vigorously and Lucas raised his hand, though Grinder, his head bowed, didn't.

As they approached, Lucas pointed. "Whadaya got there?"

Pop held the bird up higher, its neck dipping slightly. "Manna from heaven is what I got here."

Grinder looked at Pop with stale eyes. "Great. I'm starving."

"Always the joker." Pop tested a laugh but it fell flat.

Grinder slid by him into the motel room. Lucas patted his father's shoulder. "Got a minute, Pop?"

22

"Sorry about that door," said Martha as the bellboy stacked the last of the luggage onto the cart. "My father-in-law's to blame. Crazy man, thought I was dying or something and kicked the damn thing in." She paused expecting the bellboy to laugh. He stood beside the cart, ramrod stiff, a faint, service-ready smile on his face. "Anyway." Martha looked around the room as she picked up her purse. "Looks like we got it all." Then the cawing started. "Let's go," said Martha, but the bellboy hesitated.

"Are we forgetting something?"

"Not that I know of."

"Caaaaaaw, eeeeeeeek!"

The bellboy strode to the bathroom and returned with the cage, Paul clutching his perch with every claw he had.

"Oh my, I completely forgot…"

The bellboy beamed. "That woulda been somethin'; the next people comin' in to take a shower and there's this bird in there."

"Yeah, somethin'."

"Guess we won't have to worry about that now." He hung the cage on the luggage cart's crossbar and started out the door to a room down the hall. He searched his pocket for a keycard, swiped it on the sensor and opened the door. "Here you go." Martha walked in ahead of him, leaning away from the cage as far as possible. Paul hissed.

"Maybe this'll work out better," said the bellboy.

Martha shook her head approvingly as she surveyed the living room and dining area, sitting briefly on one of the bar stools, and running her hand across the backs of the sofa and recliner.

"Yinz got flat screens everywhere, even the bathroom. Never could figure why someone would need a TV in the bathroom, but…"

Parrot Talk

She pulled the curtain and slid the door open to the balcony, letting in some fresh air.

"There's that view again," said the bellboy.

Martha continued inspecting the suite. She opened the door to one bedroom, then the other. She went back and forth between them several times, measuring the space with her eyes, checking to see which one had a better bathroom. She decided on the corner room with the king bed.

"You can put the pink bags and that thing that looks like an oversized gym bag in this room."

The bellboy tossed all the straps over his shoulder and waddled into the bedroom, unloading everything on the bed. "What about the other stuff?"

"Oh. You can just leave it anywhere." The bellboy tossed Grinder's two duffel bags onto the floor and looked at Paul. Martha was already hanging tops and sweaters in the closet. "What about him?"

"What's that?"

"What about the bird?"

Martha came out of her room, a jumpsuit flung over her shoulder. "Would you like to keep him?"

"Oh my goodness," said the bellboy, laughing and unsteady on his feet. "I couldn't possibly. I gotta pit bull at home that would eat'm in a minute."

Martha glared at Paul. "Well, everybody's gotta go sometime."

"Oh my, ma'am; I couldn't possibly do that. Anyway, I don't know if Henry—that's his name—I don't know if Henry likes eat'n birds. He throws up the turkey at Thanksgiving and—"

"Well, then, why don't you put the cage in the other bedroom. On the pillow, please."

He picked up the cage and grinned at Paul. "Polly-wally-doodle want a cracker, huh?"

"Jesus," said Paul.

"Oh my gosh! Did ya hear that?"

Martha was wrist deep in her purse. She came out with a five-dollar bill, arm stretched toward the bellboy. He was bent over the cage now. Paul puffed his feathers and flared his wings. "Here you go, honey," said Martha, waving the bill in his direction. The bellboy stood uncertainly, eyes still concentrating on Paul. He reached for the tip, but didn't speak. He stood still a minute more, waiting for something to happen. "So, thank you so much for your help." Martha took his arm and led him toward the door. He pushed his cart a few feet and then stopped.

"You teach him that, ma'am?"

"Teach him what?"

"To say 'Jesus' and stuff."

"No, he came that way."

"My gosh, that's the most—" But Martha had closed the door. She took a bag of Doritos and a Coke from the mini-bar and then went back to her bedroom, where she unpacked. Paul started whistling. She tried to ignore him, but when he persisted, she turned on the TV and upped the volume.

The staccato voice of Judge Judy machine gunned a sorry-looking guy who was standing at the rail, his mouth open wide, his wife shaking a fist at him. "Aw, c'mon, don't give me that," said the judge. "Don't pee on my leg and tell me it's raining. You may be that stupid, but I'm not."

Paul leaped from his perch and clung to the side of the cage, biting and pulling at the latch.

"Aaaaaawwwwk!"

Martha munched her Doritos and laughed at Judge Judy. She laid her underwear aside and sat on the end of the bed. "Don't take any shit, Judy."

"Aaaaaawwwwk!"

Judge Judy took aim at the wife: "Why did you marry an idiot like this?" She scowled at the husband. "I'm tellin' you, I eat morons like you for breakfast. You're gonna be cryin' before this is over."

"Go girl." Martha slid back on the bed and plumped the pillows behind her.

Paul beat his wings as hard as he could. Feathers billowed as the cage shimmied and shuddered back and forth on the pillow, tipping precariously toward the edge of the bed.

Judge Judy had found her groove now. "Look, if it doesn't make sense, it's not true. Simple as that. I am all about the truth, in case you didn't notice. So, you better tell me the truth or by the end of this thing, you're gonna be eating your shoes."

"Oh my God." Waves of glee rippled across Martha's face.

"Millie, Millie, Millie, here come the judge!"

Paul flapped his wings frantically and threw himself against the cage. "Millie, Millie, Millie, my Millie—Caaaaaaaaaaaaaaawwwwww!"

Martha, hunkered down in from of the TV, was oblivious to Paul's cries until she heard a crash bang coming from the other bedroom. She hit mute and listened. At first all she could hear was the faint thumping and bumping of guests in the room upstairs. But then she heard a baby crying. Not "Waa-Waa" crying like adults imitating newborns. Instead it was a deep, raspy, guttural cry of distress, like when Mandy was a baby and had lost her binky in the middle of the night, a cry of desolation and despair. She stood, but then it stopped. She tilted her head forward to listen more closely and it started again, this time with added whimpers of exhaustion.

Martha tiptoed into the living area that separated the bedrooms, still holding the bag of Doritos in one hand and a Coke in the other. "Hello?" When no one answered, she walked gingerly to the bedroom door and pushed it open. "Is anyone in here?" She stuck her head in and saw the cage lying on the floor beside the bed. "Oh my God." Paul lay motionless on his side, his feathers at odd angles and his mouth open wide. "Are you dead?" Paul's tongue moved slowly with each heavy, sluggish breath.

Martha squatted beside the cage. "Please don't die on me. Seriously." Paul's eyes didn't move. She studied the situation as best she could, trying to figure out a way to get both Paul and the cage back to where they belonged. "I'm telling you, you're going to have to stand up." Paul didn't move, didn't speak. "I know you hate me and want to rip my throat out, but please don't be a prick. Can you stand up?" Paul wobbled and scratched but then stopped, as if giving up. He started moaning again. "Ooooooooooohhhhhhhh, Ooooooooooohhhhhhhh." His head went back; his face looked haggard and forlorn.

"My God, what's wrong with you?" She lay on the floor beside him. "Paul?" She reached for him with her fingers and patted his wing. "Paul?"

"Judge Judy, my Millie; Judge Judy, my Millie."

"Judge Judy?" Martha's face screwed up in confusion. "My Millie?" She lay quietly beside him thinking, and finally her face opened wide as a fresh baked pie. "Judge Judy! My Millie!" She got up, took the cage by the handle and righted it while trying to steady Paul with her other hand. He fluttered his wings and was back on his feet. As the cage came fully upright, he leaped to his perch. "Awk, awk!"

"Okay, okay. Awk, awk, Judge Judy and Millie."

Once in her bedroom, Martha put Paul on the bed directly in front of the TV. Paul fell silent, his eyes steady, his mouth half open. "Judge Judy."

"Baloney, Sir!" yelled the Judge. "My grandmother always told me, beauty fades but dumb is forever. Looks like you are going to live for an eternity, but you are not going to last another minute in my courtroom." She gaveled the bedraggled man who tried to argue, but she would have nothing of it. "Be gone!"

"Be gone! Be Gone! Be gone!" Paul was jumping and dancing. He whistled and clucked and cawed. "Here come the judge, here come the judge!"

"Jesus crimony." Martha shook her head and sat down on the bed beside the cage.

When the show went to commercial, Paul started in: "Millie, Millie, Millie, Millie, Millie, Millie, Millie…"

Martha placed her hand on the cage. "That's alright, that's alright." But Paul would not be comforted.

"Millie, Millie, Millie, Millie, Millie, Millie, Millie, Miiiiiilllllie…" He puffed his feathers out until he looked like a pale grey bowling ball with a hooked nose. He shook his head back and forth wildly. "Millie, Millie, Millie, Millie, Millie…"

"C'mon now, c'mon now, c'mon already!" Martha stood in front of the cage screaming consolation at Paul. "You're gonna be alright, goddammit! You're gonna be alright, I'm tellin' you, for God's sake! Millie's not here! She's not here! She's gone! I'm telling you! She just can't come back! If she could, she would, but she can't! She's dead."

Paul stopped.

Martha's face was flaming red. She was huffing now. "Oh shit, I shouldn'ta said that. Look, maybe she's out there somewhere," she said, gesturing toward the window. "We don't know, maybe she's looking down on you right now, but she's not here no matter where she is, and even if she's looking down on you, you can't look back at her, 'cause she's, like, invisible, like the air." Martha paused and then a bulb lit. "She's gone into the light; she's seen the light and has followed it to a nice place where everything's alright; except, I'm sure she misses you; but she can't come back; I know there's people who say they've gone into the light and have come back, but my money says these people are crazy, but even if they aren't, nobody disappears into the light for this long and then returns, I mean, it's been a couple months, so, yeah, she woulda come back by now." Martha stopped mid-babble. "I'm sorry."

Paul stood at the end of his perch, leaning against the side of the cage. Then he buried his head under his wing.

"C'mon, don't do that." Martha scratched at him through the bars. "Hey, c'mon." She tried patting him on the head but she couldn't quite get her finger under his wing. She opened the cage door and peeked in. "Hey you," she said, chirpily. "You're okay, trust me." Paul pulled his head out from under his wing and cawed softly. "I know, I know. This whole thing's a rotten deal." She reluctantly reached in and Paul perched on the back of her hand. "Don't you bite me." She carefully removed her hand from the cage, a triumphant smile on her face. "There you go." With that, Paul took wing, flew around the room once, then out the balcony door and into the Pittsburgh sky.

23

"Sure, boys, come right in." Pop's smile was back as he opened the door wide, the swan still in his hand. "As they say, mi casa is Sue's casa."

"Okay then," said Lucas.

Grinder exhaled heavily as both brothers trooped into their father's room. The three men stood inside the door waiting for someone to give directions.

"Have a seat." Pop pointed with the beak of the swan. Grinder and Lucas sat on the straight backed chairs at the Formica table in the corner.

"What's with the…" Lucas nodded warily at Pop's swan.

"Somethin', ain't it?"

"Yeah. Sure is."

"You ain't gonna believe this but some lady just showed up at my door while I was reading the Big Book and when I opened it, she walked in and she fixed up my bed and she put candy on my pillows and she listened to me talk and no matter what I said, she said it was 'okay' and she made me feel good."

Lucas stared at the swan.

"And before she left, she got this here special cloth and she sat on the bed and quiet as anything made this magical dove. A peace dove, I think it is, like the peace of Jesus that patches all understanding." Pop patted the swan, a cherubic smile crossing his face. "I didn't know there were such people in the world."

Grinder and Lucas looked at each other. "It's a swan, Pop, made out of a washcloth," said Lucas.

Pop stiffened. His face pinched. "A towel, actually. Made out of a beautiful, soft towel."

"Very nice. We have one just like it. Everyone does. Along with the mints." Lucas caught Pop eye-to-eye. "It's what they do here."

Pop laughed nervously. He glanced at Grinder who wasn't looking. "All I know's she came knockin' at my door right when I was lost in a blanket of darkness and she give me this." He lifted the swan to his cheek as its neck began to unravel.

"Look, Pop, Grinder and me, well, we feel like we've gotten off to a bad start here. We weren't prepared for all of this when we left Rochester. I mean, we came to Pittsburgh because of Ma dying when we'd just about forgot we ever had a mother, and then we got this bird that we don't know what to do with, and then Martha came, which only complicated things, if you know what I mean, and finally, out of the absolute blue, you showed up." Lucas pulled out a tissue and dabbed his forehead. "I can't speak for Grinder, but it's been more than I bargained for."

Lucas paused and gestured at Grinder who looked at his brother's hand, but didn't speak. Lucas's heavy breathing turned into heavy huffing. Pop put the dying swan on the bed.

"I know, I know. I shoulda told someone I was coming. But I thought, you know, I thought that if you knew I was coming, you mighta left before I got here." Pop wasn't looking at either of them now. He rolled his shoulders as if acknowledging what they might be thinking.

The sun cast yellow streaks on the wall behind the brothers. Lucas and Grinder shifted in their chairs, their creaking seats the only sound in the room. When the silence got too dense, Grinder stood, pulled his jeans up and headed to the balcony door. He slid it open and then turned back to his father, missing a parrot as it glided by.

"What's this all about, Pop?" Grinder's voice was missing its edge. Whether he intended it or not, his words were plaintive, almost beseeching. "I mean, I don't know what you want from us, from me. It's been so long. When I look at you, it's like I'm looking across a river at some life I used to live, but don't anymore."

Lucas got up and joined his brother by the balcony door, sucking up as much cool air as possible. Grinder opened his mouth but then closed it and raised his eyebrows at Pop.

"Hotter than hell in here." Lucas pulled his Bills jersey out of his pants and let the tail hang low. Pop's eyes were locked onto Grinder, like he was trying to figure out who exactly he was.

"Pop?"

"Like I said, I been taking my own inventory for a long time, and I got a lot of amends to make, fences to patch, apologies and stuff. The Big Book is clear."

Grinder folded over with exhaustion and leaned on his thighs. Then he straightened up again. "I'm telling you, if you start in with the Big Book or Jesus, I will walk right out of here and whatever chance you were hoping for will be gone forever. You gotta talk sense to us."

There was a calm look in Lucas's eyes and a faint smile on his face as he watched his brother.

Pop swallowed hard. He opened the mini-bar, fondled a can of beer, then pushed it to the side and took a Coke in his fist. He snapped the tab and gulped. He held his hand over his mouth for the longest time and then slumped onto the bed, like a man in full surrender. He looked at the wall in front of him.

"I been a nothin' and a nobody for as long as I can remember. That's as true as I can get. I pretended I was a somebody. But I wasn't. Your mother knew it." He glanced at Grinder. "You had me pegged, too, I'm sure. You hated me and I guess I made you pay for it. I didn't know what I was doing or why. Your mother and me, I don't know; we never once said we loved each other; got married when we knew you were coming along." Pop pointed to Lucas.

"What?"

"Don't get me wrong. I wanted to be a father. I wanted to do right by you. But I gotta confess. I loved the bottom of a beer can more than I loved anything."

"How did I not know Ma was pregnant when you got married?"

"How could ya? I mean, we never celebrated our anniversary or nothin'."

Lucas was doing some quick math in his head.

"Your Ma and me, we hardly knew each other. She had broke up with this guy and we met in a bar and went out a couple times. And, you know. I can't even remember when it happened. Them years are lost in a fog."

Grinder leaned forward, his elbows on his knees.

"When she told me, she cried and cried and I felt so sorrowful that I told her not to worry, that I would make an honest woman of her. She looked at me all strange like and went all quiet, and then she said real low, 'Okay'. She told me she was living at home and couldn't bear it no more. So we went to the JP that afternoon. His wife was the witness. I gave your mother an old high school ring, since I didn't have nothin', and that was that. She went back to work at the bank and I went back to the bar." Pop was smiling, his eyes wide with warm recollection. "It was the happiest day of my life. Here I was all of a sudden, a husband and a father. Guys at the bar went nuts when I told 'em. Bought 'em all a round, drank everything in sight, played darts all night and when daylight come, I realized I didn't even know where your mother lived."

Pop hitched his thumbs into his belt loops and stretched his back as if he'd hurt it carrying some heavy load.

"And that's how it all come to be. Not exactly one of them Herman Rockwell pictures, I know."

"So, if Ma hadn't gotten pregnant with Lucas, would you two have gotten married at all?" asked Grinder.

Pop set to howling over this. "Oh my good Lord, no. Absolutely not. Don't get me wrong, I come to fancy your mother. And I thought I could get her to fancy me, but I couldn't. No, we would never have got married. I think she mainly wanted to get away from her parents. She wasn't no kid anymore, that's for sure." Pop tilted his head back. "Oh my God, if she heard you ask that question, she'd just shake her head." Pop was smiling again, but this time it wasn't a happy smile.

"And we wouldn't have had to go through everything." Grinder got up from the chair. He scratched the back of his head and then sat on the mini-bar.

"That is a fact," said Pop. "On the other hand, you two wouldn't be in this world right now. You wouldn't be no place at all."

Grinder stood and opened the mini-bar door and leaned down to examine the contents. He pulled out another RC cola and tossed it to his father. He took a beer for himself and held one out for Lucas, who declined. He pulled the tab and took a slow sip. Then he sat back down on the mini-bar.

"What about me? If you and Ma hated each other so much, how did I come along?"

Pop held his RC up to say thanks. He pulled the tab but didn't take a drink. Instead he put it on the table and sat in the chair beside it.

"You were gonna be our second chance." Pop crossed his legs and fingered his moustache. He wrapped his hand around the can and then wiped the moisture onto his shirt.

"Second chance?"

"Yeah."

Grinder rolled his hand in the air several times, encouraging Pop to go on.

"I'd been workin' steady for a good six, eight months. I totally stopped drinking. Only about a half six-pack a night. Brought my paychecks home. Your brother was about to start school. Your mom was taking, like, a literature class, or something, at the community college. Things were different for a while. We didn't talk about it none, didn't wanna jinx it, I guess. Thought a baby might seal it, you know? Like you would be the glue on this thing we were trying to build."

Pop took the cola can in hand and read the label. "You know, sometimes I just plain miss beer. Like every single minute of my damn life." Then he hoisted the can like it was the real thing.

"So, was I, like, a back seat of the car thing?" asked Lucas.

"Jesus, Lukie, could you be any further out of bounds?" Grinder put his beer on the floor beside the mini-bar. He leaned back against the wall and slipped his hands into his pockets. "So, what happened?"

"What happened?" Pop laughed. "Judas priest, what didn't happen?" Grinder's face was taut and his gaze was steady. "You could probably write the rest of the story. I mean, I started up again and lost my job. Your mother started workin' a second job at Tops. But she was terrible sick during the pregnancy and couldn't work no more, so we had to go on the dole, food stamps, the whole nine yards. That was a damn thing, I'm tellin' you." A look of disgust creeped into the folds of Pop's face. "We weren't happy. None of us. Lucas, you cried every morning before school. Grinder, you never slept. I mean, man." Pop lifted the can to his mouth, his hand shaking. "I think your mom wanted out from the moment we left the JP's office. I never knew what I wanted. I mean, I wasn't thinkin' too clear for a good long time. The days were cans stacked on cans."

Grinder pushed off from the wall and sat heavy on the bed. The muscles along his jaw line rippled.

"Well," said Lucas. "It is what it is."

"Please don't say that," said Grinder.

"You know what I mean. Can't be changed, so whadaya do? I mean, I was…I don't know what I was. And you, you were the glue that didn't stick." Lucas shrugged and raised his eyebrows before reaching for a tissue and blowing his nose. There was cawing in the background, but no one noticed.

"So Pop, one day Ma went to the mall and never came back."

"That is true."

"That is true?"

"Your mother should be the one to tell that story."

"Apparently, she's can't."

Pop waggled his empty can and sat it on the table. Lucas got him another.

"Did you know she was going to leave?"

"It's hard to say."

"Hard to say?"

"Your mother liked to threaten. I just didn't pay no attention after a while."

"What about that time, the last time she threatened?"

Pop's shoulders were slumped. His knees bowed and the soles of his shoes pressed against each other. He twiddled his thumbs.

"I knew about the teacher. Whatever his name was. I knew about him. I blame him, with his long hair and his big ideas. He fed your mother all this crazy stuff about gettin' away and startin' a new life and crap like that. She come to me cryin' and tellin' me I better change or else. And I laughed right in her face. She said if I didn't stop drinkin' she'd walk away. I laughed again. I knew she'd never leave you two and I told her so. She cried. I said, 'Leave then, see how far you get.'"

He swept his hand, with its long slender fingers and greying nails, along the dome of his head. Grinder noticed that Pop's lower eyelids were separated slightly from his eyes, like a longstanding adhesive had gone dry. Lucas sat with his head in his hands, listening but not looking.

"I pulled back some on my drinkin'. Figured that'd calm her down, get her off my back; after a little bit, I thought she'd given up on the whole stupid thing. She was all quiet toward me, but mostly normal otherwise. She was doing stuff with you guys. I didn't give much more thought to it. I figured everything was okay."

Grinder arched his back and pressed his hands hard against his thighs, as if trying to release something. He pursed his lips. "But it wasn't, was it?"

"No. It wasn't. She left." He shrugged and crossed his legs. "And then I found the bags under our bed."

Grinder squinted at Pop and Lucas raised his head.

"Bags of what?" asked Lucas.

"Your clothes. You and your brother's."

"What?" Grinder stood.

Pop leaned back, looking up at his younger son.

"Bags of your clothes. I told you that."

"No, Pop, you didn't," said Lucas as he closed his eyes.

"I meant to, I guess." The room got deadly quiet. "Well. I sent you to school and I didn't go to work. I called your principal, missus whatever her name was, and told her your mother'd run off with the teacher and that she might try to snatch the two of you and not to let nothin' happen to you."

"You what?"

"I stayed home all day, guessin' she'd come for the bags. I seen her and that bastard pass the house slow like three times, but my car was in the driveway so they kept goin' each time. And then they didn't come no more."

Grinder leaned menacingly over Pop, who bowed his head.

"C'mon, man," said Lucas, reaching for his brother.

"You told her you'd kill us all if she came back."

"Yeah, I did. Later."

"Why?"

The corner of Pop's mouth quivered though his voice was steady.

"Because I was a bitter, drunken sonofabitch."

Grinder stepped back, his throat tightening with a gulp. Pop gazed back and forth at his sons. "I think we can all agree on that, can't we?" he said.

Grinder fell back into a chair, his mouth open. Lucas went to his brother's side.

"Hey."

Grinder looked up at his brother and then at Pop, who was staring at the floor. Grinder got up and walked to the balcony and back twice, chewing his thumb nail. Lucas watched, a worried look in his eyes.

"What is it?" asked Lucas.

"I don't know."

"What?"

"Maybe she didn't run off right away, you know? Maybe she came around the house other times, but we didn't know it. Maybe she kept thinking about it, you know, getting us back, but got too afraid."

Lucas sat on the floor beside Grinder, his legs crossed, Indian style. He leaned his elbows on his knees and rested his head in his hands, hoping that something would come to mind, some words that would make things okay, but nothing came. He straightened his back and coughed once into his fist. "It's a black box, Grinder. We don't know anything. Just that she died and left us a parrot."

All three men startled when there was a rapid knock on the door. When Lucas opened it, there stood Martha, a freakishly broad grin on her face.

24

"He what?"

"Well, like I said, Grinder, he just flew off the balcony. I was holding him because he looked, well, so sad…"

"Martha." Lucas's eyes bulged.

"…and he was starting to calm down while he was watching some Judge Judy. And I'm telling you, that lady is something else. She spits fire and truth-"

"Martha."

Grinder was pacing now.

"Yeah, well, he just up and took off. I mean, I couldn't believe it. Didn't say a word. Just went." For emphasis, she waved one hand in the air like a flapping wing. "I'm so sorry. I really am." She paused, a somber look crossing her face. "He's a troubled bird."

"Martha, please." Lucas was reaching for the box of tissue.

"Well, he is."

"You know what the good book says about sparrows. The Father's care is extended to each and every one." Pop stretched his arms out like Moses might have under a similar circumstance. "I know the Father had a particular thing for sparrows, but I'm sure…"

Grinder waved a hand for Pop to stop. "Did you look for him?"

"I went right to the balcony and there he was in the distance, his wings flappin' like crazy, then soaring down, down, just above the treetops, and then I couldn't see him."

They trooped through the lobby and exited onto the front walk where they skirted the sprinklers, crossed the street, and lined up on the opposite sidewalk for a clearer view. They craned their necks and shielded their eyes as they searched the sky for the lost bird. Soon half a dozen others were squinting into the sun with them, not knowing what exactly was going on.

"Yinz're lookin' for that thing, aren't you?" said an unshaven man carrying a newspaper under his arm.

"What?" said Grinder.

"That thing, you know, the thing people been seein'." He nudged the guy beside him. "Hey, you know what I'm talkin' bout, don't you? That thing we been hearing about on TV."

"The thing?" said a short stocky man wearing a top coat.

"Yeah, the thing."

"You mean the grone."

"The grone? Are you fuckin' crazy? A grone is something a guy pulls when he's slidin' into second base," he said, grabbing the inside of his thigh.

"He means the *drone*," said a young woman with pierced lips as she put on her shades.

"Yeah, the drone. Fuckin' drones. What's that about? They gonna deliver the mail with drones? Drop shit on your head or something. Knock planes right out of the goddam sky. What the hell?"

Grinder watched several pigeons glide across his line of sight, then some crows and not much else. "See anything?" he said to Lucas.

"Just a grone and a drone."

Grinder focused on the canopy over the motel entrance, thinking the bright orange color might attract Paul. But after another fifteen minutes, he gave up. The four of them went back across the street, leaving behind a dozen others staring at the sky. The quartet drifted silently into the motel lobby. Martha pressed the elevator button. Pop sighed. The door opened and they entered. The elevator jumped and the music hummed. The fourth-floor light went on and the bell dinged.

"This is me." Pop exited the elevator and turned to face them. "Sorry about Paul." Lucas pressed the hold button as Pop struggled for more words, but said nothing. Lucas released the button, and Grinder caught his father eye-to-eye as the door closed.

Once in their new suite, Lucas and Martha retreated to their bedroom and closed the door. Grinder headed for the balcony where he looked indifferently at the traffic below. He gazed at the trees tops, not expecting to see anything. When he came back into the living room, he picked up the TV channel guide and the remote, then tossed them onto the couch. He went into his bedroom, instead. He looked at the floral accent wall and the prints of Pittsburgh scenes, then headed to the bathroom.

He glanced at the mirror and was startled by what appeared to be his father's face looking back at him. He had never noticed the similarity, the way his face, its lines and contours, were an only slightly less exhausted version of Pop. When he turned from the sink, he noticed something else. He leaned toward the bathtub to get a better look and, sure enough, there was Paul lying on his back staring at the faucet. Grinder sighed with relief.

"Paul?" Grinder sat beside the tub, but Paul didn't seem to notice he was there. In fact, Paul didn't move. He didn't blink. But when a drip fell from the faucet, he made what could only be called a laughing sound. "Hee eee eee eee aww." Then he fell silent again, watching and waiting.

"Paul? Buddy?" Grinder reached for Paul but another drip was about to fall. Paul opened his mouth in delight and squealed.

"Wow." Paul's lids were at half-mast. The corners of his mouth were drawn up in a goofy grin. Another drip. Paul's stomach shuddered with a deep guffaw. He blinked slowly.

Grinder reached for Paul and patted his belly. "Hey."

Paul startled when he recognized Grinder. "Hey, man." He stood up and then slipped and fell on his side. He laughed. "Do that thing again," he said to the faucet.

"Paul, are you okay?" But Paul was pecking affectionately at his reflection in the chrome fixture. "Paul?" He put his hand on Paul's back, steadying him because he was about to fall again.

"Paul hungry, Paul hungry. Dorito time, Millie. Dorito time. Millie, Millie." Paul waddled to the back slope of the bathtub, dropped down on the porcelain and slid on his belly toward the faucet. "Ooooooooooooo-eeeee!"

"What the hell."

Paul rolled over and looked at Grinder through blood shot eyes. "Dorito time, Millie; Dorito time."

Grinder scurried to the mini-bar and retrieved a bag of Doritos. He tore them open and held one out to Paul who seized the bag instead and ripped it apart. He munched furiously while watching for another drip.

When Grinder slipped out of the room to get a bag of nuts, he noticed his duffel bag, which lay open on the floor. Beside it was a Ziploc baggie, a hole gnawed through it and marijuana buds scattered on the carpet. "Shit." He picked up the remaining pot and flushed it down the toilet while Paul stood in the bathtub, mesmerized by his shiny new chrome friend.

Grinder leafed through the phone book and found a number for the

Greater Pittsburgh Animal Urgent Care Center.

"Hello…yes, it's an emergency…uh huh, my bird…a parrot…okay, yeah, well, I think he's ODed on some weed…yes, marijuana…no, I didn't give it to him…no, he doesn't smoke…ate it, uh huh…okay, okay."

Grinder went back into the bathroom where Paul had just discovered the shower head.

"Look!" he said.

"C'mon, buddy." Grinder took a face towel and wrapped it around Paul and cradled him in his arms, Doritos falling from Paul's mouth.

"More crunchy, more crunchy."

Grinder opened the mini-bar again and snatched another bag. He reached for the car keys on the counter and tiptoed past Lucas and Martha's room.

"Weeeeeeeeeee," said Paul.

When they arrived at the Urgent Care Center, they were immediately ushered into an exam room where they waited for another fifteen minutes. Paul's mood had changed. He was singin' the blues.

"Nobody knows the trouble…"

Grinder tried to perch him on the back of a chair, hoping it would help Paul regain his balance. Wobbly at first, soon Paul was able to stand steady with barely a wing shuffle. Minutes later, he was ambulating without any visible sign of difficulty. His mood, though, hadn't improved.

"Millie gone."

"I know, buddy." Grinder pulled him closer. Paul noticed the bag of Doritos and dove in.

When the exam room door opened, Grinder watched as a tall, waifish, middle-agey woman entered the room, her stringy brown bangs covering her ample forehead unevenly. She pushed her horn-rimmed glasses up her beak-like nose and clutched a medical chart to her chest. She wore a beige shell, an indifferent knee-length dress and New Balance sneakers. Her hair was pulled back on both sides with yellow barrettes. And her eyes were large a saucers and brown as Hershey's kisses. She smiled, her teeth as bright as piano keys, her face as welcoming as a summer sunrise. Grinder's mouth fell open at the sight of her.

"Hello, I'm Dr. Napolitano, one of the vets. You can call me Grace."

Grinder held his breath. His brain went all monosyllabic on him. "Uh. Wha. Ha." She extended her hand and it hung out there for an inordinately long time. Grinder knew what it was but didn't appear to know what to do with it. Instead, he grinned a big toothy grin, his first breath coming out as a snort.

He reached for her hand just as she withdrew it. But she kindly reached out again and he took hold of her thumb. To his credit he let go almost immediately.

"Oh. I'm sorry." Grinder was still grinning.

She laughed, a sweet, lilting laugh. "Let's try that again."

This time Grinder was on his game. He took her hand gently in his and shook it an appropriate number of times before letting go. Success. He slumped into his chair again, then quickly straightened his back. He combed his hair with his fingers and cleared his throat. Her hand had been soft, her palm silky and warm to the touch. She reached for Paul, scratched his head and caressed his back. "Hello there, you must be Paul," she said in a near whisper. "You've been through a lot." She caught Grinder's eye and tilted her head to one side knowingly. "Both of you have, I guess."

Grinder watched her intently as she crossed the room and sat on her rolly chair. She looked at both of them, tenderness in her eyes, and Grinder could feel his cheeks burn. He tried to smile but only raised his eyebrows and cheeks, his mouth lost in a sudden quiver.

Grace placed the chart on her lap and clicked her pen. She pushed her glasses back up again and then asked, "So, what happened?"

For a second, Grinder sat, mouth open, unsure of where to begin. Grace tilted her head to one side. "Trust me, I've heard it all."

With that, the flood gates opened. "Well, our mother left us when we were kids, my brother and me…" And on he went. "I was a mess. Pop was a mean alcoholic…" Then some more. "…and it was just my brother and me, really…" Thirty minutes later, Grinder finally made his way to the present as Grace listened, her demeanor unhurried, her brow furrowed with concern. "…and a week ago we found out our mother…" Paul leaped from the back of the chair and roosted on Grinder's right leg. He pressed his head against Grinder's belly. "Millie," said Paul, sadly. With this, Grace took her glasses off and placed them on the table; she also stopped writing and put her pen down. "…and then there was Paul…" Grinder was sniffling now. "He must have flown back in through the balcony 'cause the door was wide open. When I found him, he was lying in the bathtub staring at the faucet like it was a long lost friend."

Grinder chuckled at this. So did Grace. Grinder took a tissue from his pocket and wiped his eyes. He looked at Paul, who had stopped eating the Doritos and seemed normalish again.

"Wow," said Grinder. "I guess the only thing you wanted to know was how

Paul got stoned."

"No, that's okay. You've gone through a lot. I'm sorry." Grace's face was plain and clean and simple, like a porcelain pie plate. An awkward silence ensued, followed by mutual polite laughter. "So. Paul."

"Yes, Paul."

She got down on her knees and examined him.

"His eyes look fine. His respiration is good. Looks like he's been ill, but from what you've said, it's grief more than anything else. Some signs of new growth on his belly. That's good."

"So, he'll live."

"Yes, he'll live."

"Phew."

"Trust me, I've seen worse. Had a parrot come in that had ingested some cocaine. He was belligerent and he thought he was the Steelers' quarterback. He kept demanding, 'Put me back in coach'. His owner wasn't in any better shape. Let's just say it didn't end well."

"That's unbelievable," said Grinder, hoping Grace would continue talking.

"Grace, Grace, awwwk," said Paul, nuzzling her arm.

"This one's a sweetheart. Lucky he's got you."

"I guess." Sensing that the visit was coming to an end, Grinder stumbled on, trying to stretch things out as far as he could. "So, he's okay?"

"Yes, like I said, he checks out fine. Just have to keep him away from the marijuana."

"Oh, I already flushed it."

"Good." Grace rocked back and forth. She didn't seem to be in a hurry to leave.

"Uh, is there anything else I should know? I mean, I'm not exactly experienced with parrots," said Grinder, expectantly.

Grace talked about food and toys and exercise and play and everything that Grinder already knew. It didn't matter, though. He wasn't listening. He was watching her like he had never seen a woman before. "Is that so?" he said, gazing at her, eyes melting. By now, Paul was in Grace's lap.

Grace and Grinder shifted uncomfortably in their seats when there was nothing more to say about Paul or parrots in general. But neither of them got up. Finally, Grace broke yet another silence.

"You know, I shouldn't say this because it's personal, but I think you and I are kind of alike. A smidgeon anyway."

"How so?" Grinder felt bumblebees in his stomach.

"I don't clean road kill off streets or anything, but if you came to my apartment, you'd see that one wall in my bedroom is a giant ant farm."

"Amazing."

"Amazing. Strange. One of those. It's taken me several years and a lot of time convincing my landlord, but I built it and it's, I don't know, it's beautiful."

"Beautiful."

They looked at each other, one red beacon signaling another.

"And I didn't have such a great upbringing either. I mean, no one left me, but maybe they should have. I don't know. I have a brother, too, but he's in California. So it's just me. If it wasn't for this job and the animals and the internet, who knows?" Grace laughed a little too loudly at this.

Grinder was smiling a little too stupidly. "Amazing."

"Amazing, amazing, amazing," agreed Paul.

The receptionist knocked on the door, then opened it.

"You got a schnauzer with an infected toe in two; a bulldog with the runs in three; and a raccoon with crazy eyes in four." She closed the door before Grace could answer.

"Well."

"Okay, then. Paul and me better let you get back to work."

Grace put her glasses back on. There was an inviting look in her eyes as she stood.

"How much longer will you be in town?"

"Not much, I don't think." Grinder raised his shoulders in apology. "I wish I was."

"Yes, that'd be nice. I mean, I could check on Paul and make sure things are moving along. It can take a while."

"That's what I hear." Grinder reached for Paul who was gnawing on a pencil.

"Well, at least he's in good hands." She patted Grinder on the arm.

"Thanks, I appreciate that." Grinder tried to touch her hand as she pulled it away but missed. "Hey, what if, I don't know, if I run into a problem I call you or something, just to get your advice; or maybe you don't do that sort of thing."

Grace let go of the door knob and leaned against the wall, thinking.

"That would be, sure, that would be fine. I'd be glad to be in touch, you know, if Paul has a problem. Or, like, for anything, you know?"

"Yeah, yeah, that would be great." Both of them swayed back and forth.

"Okay, so." Grace took a business card from her desk, turned it over and started writing. "Here's my work email, and my regular one, just in case you need to contact me, like, on a weekend or something. And here's my phone number, you know, in case I'm not here or something."

Grinder held the card in front of his face like he had found the winning Power Ball ticket. Grace handed him another card.

"How about you? You know, if I don't hear anything, maybe I could contact you to check on Paul."

"Sure, sure." Grinder took the card in his moist hands, dropped it on the floor, picked it up and then took Grace's pencil and started writing. "This is good. I mean, it's a good idea." He gave her the card, wiped his hand on his jeans and held it out. Grace took his hand in hers, but, this time, they didn't shake; instead they just held on, saying nothing. Then she was gone.

Grinder looked at Paul. "Amazing."

"Yeah, amazing," said Paul.

25

When Grinder told his brother what had happened to Paul, Lucas started to laugh. At first he tried to control himself, but the laughter kept coming, completely unbidden, and he couldn't stop. Soon he lost his breath completely and a dreadful look crossed his face. He dropped onto the couch, gasping.

"What the..." Martha was taken aback when she entered Grinder's bedroom to see her exish-husband, mouth wide open, face flushed. The only thing that helped Lucas was when he started to sneeze. His nose ran, so he took a fist full of tissues from the box and started blowing, which brought him back to life. By then Grinder had completed the saga for Martha, who abruptly left the room because she was afraid she would pee her pants.

Paul, mostly better but still a little daffy, watched from atop a nearby lamp, amused and entertained. "Haw haw haw." His memory of recent events was fuzzy, but he did recall that after they left the vet's, Grinder didn't stop whistling the whole way back to the motel. He drove as if in a dream, holding her business card in one hand and rubbing the letters gently with his thumb.

There was a knock at the door. When Grinder opened it, there was Pop wearing his cowboy hat and holding his walking stick, his bags in a pile behind him. Pop had a sheepish smile on his face and he nodded hello, his chin moving barely an inch. Grinder opened the door wide.

"What's up?"

Before Pop could answer, he noticed Lucas and Martha in various states of hysteria. Pop raised his eyebrows at Grinder who sighed and gave him the Cliff Notes version of recent events. Pop listened, his face sober, his head not moving, his eyes half-mast. Grinder punctuated the end of his story with a nod of his head and a shrug of his shoulders. Pop was quiet. He put a hand on Grinder's shoulder.

"Must have scared you clear to death and back."

"What's this?" Lucas stood in front of the dresser mirror holding a business card close to his face. "Who is Grace Napolitano?"

Grinder clutched his father's arm and then quickly let go. "Yes, it did."

"Look, Grinder. Son. I been thinking. You and me, I know we never been close and all, but I gotta tell you, I think we got more in common than you might think."

"We do?"

"Might not seem possible, but, yeah, I think we do."

Pop held his breath, as if waiting for an invitation to go on. Grinder glanced at Pop through his spindly eyelashes. He took one step back and leaned all his weight on his left hip.

"Okay, Pop, I'll bite, how are we alike?"

"Well, I been a lost man most all my life. And when I say lost, I mean, like, just out there wandering aimlessly in my own fog. Worse, for a long time I didn't even know it. I mean, I know'd something was wrong, but I didn't know what. Do you know what I'm saying?"

"Maybe."

"*Not knowing* you're lost is almost as bad as *bein'* lost to begin with."

"Hm."

"'Cause if you don't know you're lost, there ain't much you can do about it. You just keep going in the wrong direction and being pissed that it don't get you nowhere."

Pop smiled and put his hands on Grinder's shoulders, squeezing them gently.

"So?"

"Well, I'm here to tell you, son, you are lost as lost can be. Just like your old man was." Pop grinned from ear to ear and wobbled his head back and forth, satisfied with his own wisdom.

Grinder looked into his old man's blood shot eyes, sleep still nestled in the corners.

"That's what you think, is it?"

"No *thinkin'* involved, that's what I *know*."

"That simple, huh?

"Yessir, that simple."

"Okay, then, Pop, what do you recommend?"

Pop raised his arms over his head and then clapped his hands hard. He closed one eye and squinted at Grinder with the other.

"You get yourself found!"

Grinder's face looked all bedraggled. "That's all it takes, huh."

"Yessir! That's all it takes. I been lost and I been found and, trust me, bein' found is better."

Grinder scratched one ear and looked at the floor. He chewed on his thumbnail for a moment and then let it go. He rubbed one eye with his fist and shuffled back and forth, trying to get his feet right. "Tell me, Pop, how do you do that? How do you get yourself found?"

Pop clapped twice more and threw his head back so fast that his hat fell off.

"My God, I love this. We're talkin' to each other!"

"Pop?"

"Yeah, Son."

"I don't even know if I want the answer, but I'll ask again anyway. How do I get found?"

Pop looked far into Grinder's eyes, his own face perspiring with joy. He shook his head and put his hands on his son's shoulders again.

"I ain't got the foggiest notion. You just keep mucking around and you'll get found, trust me."

Lucas was waving the business card at Grinder while Martha attended to her hair and makeup. Paul hadn't moved from the balcony. Everything seemed to stop. Grinder felt unsettled down to the bone, but okay at the same time. Pop's face shown with a big old yellow-toothed smile.

Lucas had joined them.

"Pop."

"Lucas."

Lucas held the card up in front of Grinder, a curious look on his face.

"Who is this Grace Napolitano?" Lucas's faced was goofy with expectation.

"She's the vet lady. The lady that took care of Paul."

Lucas read the card. "'Happy to meet you. Stay in touch.'"

Martha was in the mix now, polished, glossed and sheened. She removed an eye lash from her cheek and leaned in to see the card.

"What's this?"

"You look lovely this morning." Pop bowed. Martha glared.

"It's a very special card from one 'Grace Napolitano,' who it appears was happy to meet Mr. Grinder here and would like him to 'stay in touch.' What exactly does 'stay in touch' mean, brother of mine?" Effortlessly, Lucas re-captured the ethos of middle school. "Woo-hoo."

"Lemme see this." Martha snatched the card and examined it with a jeweler's eye. "Hm. This is her personal email address. And so is the phone number. So. Well. Must have been quite a visit. Sure this was at the vet's and not at some bar?" she said with raised eyebrows.

"She knew I was going back to Rochester and wanted to make sure I could reach someone if Paul got messed up again."

"Uh huh." Lucas nudged Martha.

"She was being helpful."

"Yeah, right, because there aren't any vets in Rochester." Martha rolled her eyes and clucked her tongue.

"Look, it's nothing." Grinder's face pinked and his breathing went all shallow. Paul flew back into the room and skidded to a stop on the table. He watched the action, but held his tongue. "She was nice, that's all. To Paul."

"And you?" Martha bit her lower lip.

"Yes, well, she was nice to me. She was very professional."

"'Professional', ooooo." Lucas had a scoundrelly look on his face.

"Leave your brother alone. It's none of our business." Pop, at his fatherly best, coughed once and straightened his shoulders. Grinder glanced appreciatively at him from the corner of his eye.

"All that matters is Paul's okay." Grinder raised his shoulders and hooked his thumbs on his belt. "Shouldn't be any more problems."

"Don't be so sure. Maybe he needs drug rehab. Pop, you know all about that sorta thing. Whadaya think?"

Pop demurred. He looked at his feet and smiled sheepishly, then gave Grinder a sideways glance.

"Sure, he'd fit in perfect: 'Hi, my name's Paul; I'm a stoner, awk,'" said Lucas as he snorted and pointed at Martha.

"That is so funny, I can hardly contain myself," said Grinder, deadpanned. "Oh wait; it seems I can contain myself."

Lucas jabbed his brother in the ribs. "C'mon, if this isn't funny, what is?"

Grinder left his brother's side and walked to the table where he patted Paul on the head and then scratched his back. Lucas and Martha had run out of material and the frivolity was suddenly on the wane. Silence followed except for Paul's occasional "Eeeek, aaawk."

Taking advantage of a lull in the action, Pop picked up his hat and sauntered into the middle of the room. He cleared his throat and stretched his arms out full length and waited for his posturing to take effect. When everyone's head turned, he spoke. "This here has been a, what should I say, a very important time, a very important occasion, I guess, being here with all of you." He gestured with his right arm, hand stretched, fingers open, a shepherd to his unruly little flock. "It has been so long, y'know." Pop wiped his nose on his sleeve, the buttons on his western shirt scratching his lip. "But all good things end, I suppose, so I think it is time for me to go back where I come from." Pop tried to smile but his lips quivered a bit, so he licked them and went on. "I wasn't sure I shoulda come, but with Jesus in my pocket and the good blessings of Brother Tatterbaum and Lucille and all the good people back at the tent ministry, I took the big leap and made the trip up north. I came with peace in my heart, the Good Book in my soul and the Big Book in my satchel." He looked around but not directly at anyone. "Comin' here, I felt like Daniel goin' into that old lion's den, not knowing what would come or why. But I had to do it, is all." Lucas looked at Grinder with what-the-what plastered all over his face. Grinder pursed his lips at his brother disapprovingly. "I came here to mend old fences, to put a little salve on some old wounds, and to see you all again. I come because Jesus told me this here was the right thing to do." With this he pulled turkey head Jesus from his pocket and held him gently in the palm of his hand. The bag was squishy and to the discerning eye didn't look like much of anything anymore. "I know I seem like a fool to you, but there's no shame in bein' a darn fool for the Big Guy." With these words, he pointed up.

"When's your flight?" asked Martha.

"Martha!" Lucas glared.

"That's okay, that's okay," said Pop, with a wave of his other arm. "I bought a one-way here, not knowin' how long I'd be, so I'm headin' to the airport and hopin' to hitch a ride on a stand-by. Somethin' will come along."

"Pop, you aren't waiting for a stage coach. You have to get a ticket or there's no point going to the airport." Lucas blew his nose and started searching on his smart phone.

Grinder wiped his face with the palm of his hand. He bit the inside of his mouth and then stepped in front of Pop.

"Look, Pop, why don't you stay."

"What?" Lucas's face was a corkscrew. "I mean…"

"Just for another day or so."

"Well…" Pop's face gleamed, though he tried to hide the shine.

"If you're in a hurry, I understand," said Grinder.

Pop shook the happy look off his face and replaced it with a more sober, almost worrisome look, one that vaguely suggested staying might be an imposition. "Hm," he began, scratching his chin and rubbing his jaw.

Martha shook her head. "Jesus."

"Let me think if I got anything to do back home. Any commitments." He pretended to leaf through the date book in his mind.

Martha's eyes bulged and her nostrils flared. "Grinder, you gotta be kiddin' me!"

"Martha, stop it, I'm telling you." Lucas caught his brother's eye, trying to read what Grinder wanted. Grinder turned toward him, his face sober, but hopeful. Lucas looked at Pop, his face determined. "Pop, whadaya say?"

Pop gulped his next breath. The sight of his sons, so little a part of his life for so long, now wanting something from him, was almost too much. He opened his mouth and tried to speak, but the words were stranded in the back of his throat. He tried to smile, but couldn't and coughed instead. "Yes, I can stay. Where the hell else am I going?"

"Am I the only one who doesn't get this? Have both of you forgotten everything?" Martha ripped at her hair with both hands, as if she might scalp herself in protest.

"There's something left to do," said Grinder.

26

"Okay, I got it, I guess. Makes sense." Pop was thinking out loud, struggling to let the idea seep through to his understanding. He kept shaking his head in agreement with Grinder out of a new found loyalty.

Martha's face relaxed and she let go of her hair, which stood high as a silo. She went over to her brother-in-law, the scent of lilac filling the space between them. She put both hands on Grinder's cheeks and pulled him closer, then kissed him hard on the mouth. "I think you are becoming a goddam grown up man."

Lucas was sweating again. He went into the bathroom to get a face towel, wiped his head and neck, threw the towel over his shoulder and came back into the living room as if he was ready for round two. "What are you talking about? We can't afford that."

"I took care of it."

"What do you mean, 'I took care of it'? How's that possible?"

"Don't worry about it. Just do this one thing."

Lucas grumbled and circled the room. Paul leaped from the table to the back of the chair for a better vantage point. "Walk and talk; walk and talk; walk and talk; walk…"

"Shut up." Lucas tugged at the waistband of his sweatpants.

"Look, honey, it makes sense. It really does. I mean, a little closure wouldn't hurt, you know."

"Closure. We've had absolute shut-the-door-and-throw-away-the-key closure for over thirty years." He pointed at Grinder and shook his finger. "I'm not paying for this damn stone."

"Sticks and stones, sticks and stones, awk, awk, awk."

"Stuff a sock in it, Paul!"

"Awk!"

Grinder seemed unfazed. His face was smooth and cool, his hands hung slack at his side, his shoulders were square but relaxed. He was the picture of calm, which surprised even him.

"I think this idea is a good one; your takin' one of life's big leaps, son." Pop had a self-satisfied grin, as if he had won a convert.

"Easy for you to say, old man. You've never been around to pick him up off the pavement after one of these leaps. I'm the one, not you." Lucas looked right through Pop.

Pop took one step back. "You don't have to remind me. Don't you think I know that?" Pop's face was furrowed and achy. He sat on the couch, his gangly legs spread wide, his hands fiddling between them. "But today I'm here. Okay?"

"Pop, pop, pop, pop goes the weasel," cried Paul. "Eeeeeeeeck!"

"I know I owe you everything, Lukie. I've told you that a million times and I've thanked you a million times, but this is different." Grinder walked across the room and sat on the love seat by the kitchenette. He looked at Lucas and Pop and Martha in turn, his face befuddled, as if he had lost something and found something all at the same time.

"Do you still love her after she walked out on us? I mean, do you love her at all?"

"I don't know." Grinder shrugged one shoulder and tilted his head to one side, as if acknowledging a deep truth.

"Milieeeeeeeeeee." Paul bobbed his head back and forth, then scratched at the upholstery on the back of the chair.

"You're okay, buddy," said Grinder. Paul cocked his head puckishly and glided across the room to Grinder's side.

Lucas blew his nose hard, looked at it, rolled the tissue into a ball and tossed it at the wastebasket in the corner. "Maybe it's just me, I don't know, but this doesn't make one bit of sense. You haven't seen our mother in like forever and now you want to buy her a headstone, something that's gonna cost *me* a goddam fortune. And for what? Really? I know you got this idea that Ma tried to come back and just couldn't. But we don't know if that's true. We don't know a damn thing about her. Except she left. And now she's dead."

Lucas's jowly face stiffened, his limp jaws suddenly rock hard. Pop backpedaled to the balcony window, happy that he was not in the line of fire. Martha watched, ready for the bout to continue. Grinder cocked his head and bit his bottom lip. He raised his arm, wagged a finger at Lucas, and then let it fall to his side.

Parrot Talk

"It's like this," said Grinder as he shifted back and forth like he was preparing to lift a great weight. "I've decided that Ma loved us." He arched his eyebrows up and down repeatedly, then curled the corner of his mouth, as if to say 'That's what I've come to'.

Lucas breathed himself into a state of relative calm. His voice reasonable and steady. "How did you come to this conclusion, Grinder? We haven't stood face-to-face with Ma since we were two young boys who didn't know shit about anything. We still don't actually know anything about her. When I close my eyes, I can't even see her. What would make you think that she loved us? Because she kept a picture of us? Because Janice whatever-her-name-was, someone we don't know from a hole in the ground, said Ma loved us? Because Paul knows things and says things that you think came from Ma?"

"Lucas, come on," said Martha.

Grinder puzzled over what Lucas said. He studied Pop's face, hoping to find an answer there. Pop gave him a sad smile. Then Grinder spoke: "Yeah."

"Yeah, what?" said Lucas.

"Everything you said. The picture of us fishing at the lake; everything Janice said about Ma remembering us, how she couldn't talk about stuff; and, yeah, Paul repeating things from the book Ma was reading me when she left; Paul calling me 'my baby' and you 'my big boy'; she must have said that stuff to him a thousand times or more. And why? Why would she do that if it didn't matter? I know she walked away, but she didn't let go and, yeah, that's enough. That's all the proof I need."

"Grinder…"

"Look, Lucas, would you rather believe that our mother didn't love us?"

Grinder's cheek, just below his right eye, twitched and then he blinked twice, like a windshield wiper swiping the mist away. Lucas bowed his head, as if to give his brother a moment's privacy.

"Look, Lucas, I know I'm grabbing for air." Grinder pressed a finger to his lips and looked at the floor, collecting himself. "Sometimes, though, even if we don't know, we gotta grab, we gotta take pieces from here and there and stick them together; and when the pieces don't quite fit, we gotta cut 'em up so they do, and in the end, even though we never find all the pieces, we have something. Not everything, but something. Having something is always better than having nothing. I feel like I've got something now. And that's all I ever wanted."

Grinder folded and unfolded his arms. He let them hang at his side, but his hands seemed too big, so he hitched his thumbs in his belt loops and rested his body on one hip. Everyone, including Paul, was paralyzed with a kind of understanding that didn't accommodate words.

"You know, Lucas, you asked me a million times why I dropped out of college. And what did I always say?"

"You always said, 'I don't know.'"

"Right. I said 'I don't know,' not 'cause I didn't know, but because there were so many reasons that I couldn't pick just one; one that would make sense of what I was doing. I just knew I was going nuts. Was it about Ma? Yes. Was it because I was scared and depressed? Yes. Was it because I was drunk all the time and was gonna flunk out anyway? Yes. Was it because I just wanted to have fun and lay low and stay away from life for a while? Yes. Was it because I'd rather quit than fail? Yes. Were there fifty other reasons. Yes, yes, yes." Grinder looked at Lucas, apology in his eyes. "But, you know, I was never against the whole idea of going to college, getting that sheepskin, the whole deal. That's exactly what *I* wanted, too. It's just that life was so damn messy that it didn't happen." Grinder was out of breath. "Sometimes you think the road ahead will be exactly what you always figured it would be. Simple as that. Like it's your destiny or something. And then it's not. Am I happy it turned out that way? Fuck no. But it did. So you make the best of it."

Martha was sitting now, her hands quiet in her lap. Pop turned to look out the balcony windows, as if some answer was out there on the wind. Lucas turned an ear to Paul, who was whistling low.

"I think that's kinda what happened to Ma. She started down a road that she figured was hers to follow. But after a while she could see that the road wasn't leading anywhere. So she felt she had to get off. And she went away and never found her way back. I guess that's what she had to do." He bowed his head for a moment. "But did she keep loving us? Yes, she did." Grinder's back was straight and his head was steady on his squared shoulders. "So I've decided that she deserves something back, and there's only one thing left to do. I took the rest of my Racino winnings, all the money I won on that stupid slot machine, and I bought a stone. And I am going to the cemetery tomorrow to pay my respects to Ma." He looked at each one in turn. "And if any of you would like to come, you're welcome to."

27

"Lemme see, lemme see, lemme see." Amos Beringer, caretaker of the Meadowlawn Cemetery, pushed his reading glasses up from the tip of his nose as he ran his index finger down the list of names, page after page. "You know, we must have thirty thousand people buried here. I like to say *living* here actually, because in a way they are. I mean their souls have gone elsewhere but the last evidence of who they were in life lives on with us." He glanced up at Grinder and grinned, a look of pride on his face. "You know, Mr. uh…"

"Ingersol."

"Ingersol, yes, death is the great equalizer. We have the high and mighty and we have the low and, well, meek; we have the old and the very young. We have the rich and the poor. We have a Jew here and there. A few colored people in the south lot, I think. No Muslims, of course—"

"Any luck?"

"Oh my, I'm so sorry. Lemme see, lemme see, lemme see. Okay, Inger, Ingerbettin, Ingercrown, Ingerer, Ingerfink, there's a tough one, whew; Ingerlon, lemme see, lemme see, lemme see. Oh, yes, here she is: Mildred Ingersol." He sighed with triumph, adjusted his glasses again and ran his hand across his bald head, feeling for the feathery few strands that had slipped down his forehead.

"Okay, then, she is in section 451, quadrant B, row 8. So, that would be roughly near the corner of Eternity Drive and Heaven's Rest Lane. Would you recognize her stone?"

Grinder explained the situation as the caretaker's mouth formed a sympathetic 'O'.

"I see then; so your headstone, I mean your mother's, is on back order. I'm sure that one of our staff has put a place holder sign by the grave with your mother's name on it." Amos looked this way and that, as if he were about to enter into a conspiracy with Grinder. "Truth be told, we adopted the place holder signs because some headstones got *mis*placed, which is to say, planted on the wrong graves and people were quite upset to discover they were weeping their eyes out over someone they didn't even know! Can you imagine? It was a complete scandal, I assure you."

"Oh my," said Grinder, his face expressionless.

By now Amos was scanning a map of section 451. "Lemme see, lemme see, lemme see, where is your mom? Okay, I got her. She is between Carter Thornhill and Benny McDougal. Mr. Thornhill was a Captain in World War II, family man, owned his own company, died in his sleep at age ninety-five. A happy story. But Benny, poor Benny. You'll see it says 'Keep Giggling' on his stone. Benny was better known as Giggles the Clown." Amos took off his glasses, huffed on the lenses and then wiped them on his shirt sleeve. "His story, though, isn't so happy. He choked to death on a peanut at the last bar mitzvah he ever did. It was just awful."

Grinder cocked his head to one side.

"The kids were very upset. The party stopped and they had to make a decision about what to do. So while they waited for the ambulance, several of the fathers moved Benny to a private place off the dance floor so they could bring out the gifts. Might sound odd, but Benny was a show-must-go-on kind of guy and I'm sure he approved." Amos grimaced and nodded thoughfully. "Well, that's not why you're here, but I thought you would want to know that your dear mother is in good company."

Grinder wasn't sure what to say. "Ma liked clowns. And soldiers."

Amos dipped his head forward and looked at Grinder over the top of his glasses. "Why don't I get Ellwood to show you where your mother is. That seems best to me." He raised his eyebrows and Grinder realized he was supposed to respond.

"That would be great. If it's not a bother."

"Absolutely not," said Amos as he tapped the ornate gold call bell on his desk. The ring tone was still shimmering in the air when Ellwood appeared. Ellwood, somewhere in his seventies, wore black boots with gold buckles, black trousers with grey pinstripes, a silver vest and white shirt, sleeves rolled up to his elbows. His smile was dominated by two gold front teeth.

"At your service, Mr. Beringer."

"Thank you, Ellwood. Could you please escort Mr. Ingersol to his mother's gravesite? 451-B-8."

Parrot Talk

"Certainly, sir. A fine resting place." Ellwood turned to Grinder, his arm bent toward the door. "Right this way, Mr. Ingersol."

When they walked down the peony lined sidewalk, Pop was standing in the shade of an ash tree, Paul's cage beside him. "Grinder, Grinder, Grinder." Martha was checking her makeup in her compact while Lucas sat on the curb, squinting into the sun. Janice smoothed her dress and Ronald folded the brim of his new Steeler cap as they got out of their car.

"And this is your family?" said Ellwood.

Grinder scanned the motley crew assembled at the end of the sidewalk, a hint of bewilderment on their faces. "Yes, it is."

Ellwood shook hands with everyone, repeating five times, "My condolences for your loss," which elicited saddened expressions from each face. Then he pointed down the lane and began to walk. Grinder picked up Paul's cage. He and Lucas followed Ellwood, the others close behind. They turned right at Everlasting Walk and then began to cross the granite studded lawn, soaring oaks and maples and chestnuts watching. Ellwood, ramrod straight and yet graceful for his age, moved slowly but purposefully amongst the stones, making sure not to step directly on anyone. The others followed in his wake. Grinder carried Paul, who cawed whenever a bird chirped or a squirrel chittered. Pop's eyes were at half mast, his lips moving in continuous prayer. Martha struggled in her heels, a vice-like grip on Lucas's arm. Janice and Ronald took up the rear, Ronald balancing a cooler full of beer under one arm.

Ellwood stopped in front of the tiny fresh grave, barely the faintest hint of grass on its mounded surface, and held out his arm as if seating them at a five-star restaurant. At the head of the grave was a small cardboard sign, wrapped in cellophane, which said, "Ingersol, M." Ellwood encouraged everyone to form a semi-circle around the grave. He cleared his throat, looked at each one and then spoke simply. "I will leave you to your grief. If you need anything I will be nearby." With that he walked away as the group watched, their faces as clueless as kindergarteners on the first day of school.

"Right out of the Addams family," said Lucas, as the others laughed nervously.

"Sure is a pretty spot." Martha shook her head approvingly as she looked around. "Can't imagine the upkeep, though."

"Yeah. There must be twenty Ellwoods around here mowing and raking all the time. That's what you're payin' for." Lucas pulled out his handkerchief in time to catch a sneeze. He looked across the way at large monuments bedecked with angels and lambs and obelisks. He noticed the flat stones and modest ornamentation in section 451. "This must be the low rent district." Grinder scowled and shook his head.

Janice came forward. "When Millie, I mean your mom, died, there wasn't much money left, I'm sorry to say, but there was enough for a cremation and for this small plot." She shrugged apologetically. "Your mom was not a showy person. I think she'd be surprised as heck to find out she's here in such a fine place."

"I can't thank you enough for what you did." Grinder patted her shoulder and squeezed her arm. Ronald leaned forward to get a little of the love. Unable to reach him, Grinder gave Ronald a thumbs up instead. "You were the best friend our mother could ever have hoped for."

"Millie was a fine lady. She listened to me when I had troubles." Janice pushed her tongue against the inside of her cheek, pointing toward Ronald. "And she never judged nobody. And she could laugh; my God, she loved to laugh. And she was always there with a helpin' hand. And she never forgot nothin'. I mean that." Janice began to cry.

"Jesus, honey." Ronald bent over and laid his cooler gently on the ground. He took a step toward his wife. "C'mon, Janice, stop it now before everyone starts blubbering."

Lucas reached into his pocket for a tissue, examined it to make sure it hadn't been used, and then gave it to Janice. "There you go."

"Thank you."

The wind rustling through the trees filled the silence that followed. Everyone's eyes gradually found their way to the sign. They stared at it as if it might speak. Grinder picked up Paul's cage and set it down beside the sign. Then he unlatched the door and reached in. Paul lit on his wrist and Grinder pulled him out. "Grinder, my baby," he said, soft and low, then spread his wings and lifted into the air.

"Shit." Grinder's mouth fell open.

"I mean, goddam it, really." Lucas threw his handkerchief on the ground.

There they stood, heads back, hands shielding their eyes once again, this time, though, with Paul in full view, darting and diving, dipping, circling and gliding, a shock of grey and a streak of red, his eyes wide and his black beak proud. Then Paul soared straight up, reaching a peak where he stopped, motionless as a World War I biplane performing at a county fair, before tipping over, drawing his wings back and dropping like a meteor towards the ground.

Parrot Talk

Martha gasped— "Oh, no!"— and covered her eyes. Pop clasped his hands and lifted them up beckoningly. Ronald clutched Janice's arm. Lucas grimaced, one eye closed, while Grinder stepped back to get a better view.

Just when everyone thought they would need to find a spatula to clean Paul's remains off a headstone, he raised his beak and his body sat briefly on the air, his wings catching the wind, and then he fluttered lightly down onto the sign. Almost never at a loss for words or whistles or groans or squeaks or squeals, Paul didn't make a sound. He held his head high, as if filled with the spirit of an eagle, and studied the faces of the dumbfounded little group standing before him.

"What the hell?" said Lucas. He shot a look at Grinder hoping he might be able to explain what had happened, but Grinder shrugged and shook his head.

"Oh, he's a flyer, alright," said Janice admiringly. Ronald chuckled and shared a knowing look with his wife. "Yeah, your mother used to take him out on the balcony and just about throw him off the edge. Remember?" she said, nudging her husband's ribs.

"Sure do," said Ronald, snorting a chuckle.

"'I don't want him to lose his wings,' she'd say. I think he just let her know he hasn't," said Janice. Ronald put his arm around her, as she dug into her pocket for a tissue. Lucas reached out to her, another clean one in hand. "Thank you, Lucas."

Lucas pulled one from his pocket and wiped his eyes. "Damn allergies. Is there a cottonwood around here somewhere? Looks like it's been snowing for a week."

"C'mon, you're okay," said Martha as she rubbed his back.

Grinder crouched beside Paul, patted his head and smoothed the feathers on his back.

Pop raised his arms to the heavens. "Lord Jesus, bless this assemblage—"

"Pop, Pop, please," said Lucas.

"Don't 'Pop, Pop, please' me. Mildred Ingersol was the very first woman I ever married, the first woman I ever made love to..."

"Ah, Geez," said Martha.

"...the mother of the only children I got, my sons. Her sons. And here's the truth; it don't matter no longer what happened way back when. It don't. Because of her, we are all strung together in an unbreakable way, whether we wanna be or not. And that's why we're here in this beautiful sanctuary to remember this good woman. I got the longest view of this whole thing and I'm tellin' you, that's what she was—a good woman. Goddam amen!"

Ronald whispered "Amen" and leaned over to open his cooler. He took an Iron City from the ice and held it up, thinking it might be thirst-quenching time, but Janice waved him off.

"Thanks, Pop," said Grinder. He stood and opened his mouth to speak, but Pop was in the zone now and not about to relinquish center stage. He reached into his jeans pocket and pulled out the Ziploc bag that held turkey-head Jesus. He raised it up above his head for everyone to see. Martha winced at the sight of it. "Pop, I don't know if—"

"You all have poked fun at this relic of my transformation. And I suppose I understand. It is a doggone nasty lookin' thing. But it changed my life, this Jesus here, this miracle." Pop opened the bag and a mushy, rancid Jesus slithered into his open hand. Pop's face screwed up a little as the aroma hit his unsuspecting olfactory receptors. "Jesus," he said, but not in the reverent way. "I can't lie no more. I never gave my wife any of what she shoulda got from a husband. I was under the spell of barley and hops. But I ain't under no spell no more. I'm under the rule of this Savior." He held the greenish glob of turkey up above his head and then pulled a Swiss Army knife from his pocket. He got down on both knees beside Grinder and Paul. He dug a small hole with the knife's spoon fixture.

"I never seen a knife like that," said Ronald.

"Shh," said Janice.

Pop closed his eyes, bowed his head and then dropped Jesus into the hole. He looked at Grinder. "Like you said, son, sometimes life's like droppin' a penny into a slot machine. Just a game of chance. Sometimes you win, but mostly you lose." He spooned dirt over turkey head Jesus and patted it down. "But I prefer to think life's more like plantin' something and watchin' it grow." He beamed at his boys. "No matter how goddam long it takes."

Ronald leaned over Janice's shoulder and whispered, "What the hell is he talkin' about?"

"Don't worry about it," said Janice, her head low, her eyes on the sign.

Grinder put his hand on Pop's shoulder, then took him in his arms. Lucas came close and sneezed. Pop reached out to him. "Come here you." He clutched Lucas who started bawling like a baby.

Martha was sobbing, too. Grinder gave her one of those cautious hugs where you don't quite touch, but look like you do. "You know, if that asshole had ever shown me even half that amount of true emotion, I wouldn't have dumped him."

"I thought *he* divorced *you*," said Grinder gently, as Martha buried her head in his shoulder.

"Six of one, six dozen of another," she said.

"Oh."

Paul remained atop the sign, perched magnificently. He still looked pretty ragged, but also proud, if that can be said of a bird. When Grinder turned again to look at him, he noticed a picture that Janice had taken from her purse and leaned against the sign just below Paul. It was Janice and Ma and Paul on Ma's balcony. Ronald must have taken it. The table in front of them was covered with bags of Doritos and several beer cans and some chew toys. Paul was roosted on the back of Ma's lawn chair. He was looking down at her like she was the love of his life. Both Janice and Ma had their mouths wide open in mid-guffaw. Ma was reaching for Janice, about to slap her on the arm. She looked old, her hair grey and pin-cushiony, her shoulders saggy, her hands wrinkled. At first he couldn't find his mother in this woman. He held the picture closer and traced her face with one finger. And there it was, a crinkle in the corner of one eye and a fold across the bridge of her nose that were so suddenly familiar he covered his mouth as tears collected in his palm. "Ma."

Lucas looked over his brother's shoulder. It took a minute but then he could see. "My God, that's her, isn't it? She got old. She went away and got old."

Grinder stared at the picture. "I remember that you laughed a lot. And you cried a lot. I remember that you were often unhappy, but never with us. I remember that you liked to take us fishing. I remember that you read to me and you changed your voice for all the characters, including Boo Radley, who didn't even have a line. I remember that I was embarrassed when you held my hand, but you didn't care. These are things I remember. And I won't ever forget."

Grinder handed the picture to Janice but she insisted he and Lucas keep it. Everyone was quiet, not like the quiet before a storm but more like the quiet that comes when the storm is long past. Grinder grinned at Paul, who hopped onto his hand, then sidled up his arm, and rested with a sigh on his shoulder. "And there you have it."

Ellwood appeared suddenly, as if he'd arisen from a nearby grave. His hands were folded in front of him as he glided toward them. He bowed but didn't speak. He turned to leave and the five mourners fell in behind him like a troop of scouts returning from an overnight.

The sun was almost down now and lines of shade crisscrossed the cemetery lawn. Granite cooled in the evening air. Flowers were encased in their tiny shrouds, waiting for another dawn. As they approached the parking lot, there was a single figure standing by a car. Tinker-toy-like in stature, wearing manly trousers and practical shoes and a blousy work shirt, hair tousled in every direction, the overall appearance oddly balanced and right.

"Who is that?" asked Lucas, narrowing his eyes to sharpen his vision.

Grinder beamed. "Grace."

28

Lucas rolled his eyes and puffed. He gripped the wheel more tightly and glanced at his brother. Grinder turned around in his seat and moved the cooler away from Paul's cage so that he couldn't peck at it any longer. Grinder tossed some dried fruit into the cage and a piece of heavy rope. "There you go, buddy."

"Shiver me timbers, aaaawwwwk. Aye, aye, Matey, ooooooooo-eeeeee."

Lucas looked out the driver's side window at a pickup with Ontario plates.

"He's got a pirate thing going today."

"Yes, he does," said Grinder, still on his knees, poking a finger into the cage and ruffling the tiny feathers on Paul's belly. "Some new growth, it looks like."

"Uh huh." Lucas steered with his elbows while he wrestled with a tissue. He blew his nose, balled the tissue and tossed it onto the dashboard without ever leaving his lane.

"Amazing how you can do that." Grinder turned around and slid back into place.

"We all have different gifts."

As they started up a hill, an eighteen-wheeler pulled into the passing lane in front of them, trying to overtake another semi.

"Oh my God, really. You're gonna do this, aren't you." Lucas pulled up within a car length of the semi and leaned on his horn for a full ten seconds. The two lumbering dinosaurs were side-by-side, trapped in each other's gravitational pull, neither giving an inch.

"Maybe he didn't understand your meaning," said Grinder. "Maybe hit that thing again."

Lucas scowled at his brother, eased back on the gas and pulled helplessly into the other lane. "There. You happy?"

"Avast, Avast, Avast, Avast!"

"My God, does he have a different channel? I mean, really, we been listening to this for three hours now."

"What can I say? He's smart."

"If I spoke like a pirate for three hours, I bet you wouldn't think I was smart."

Grinder looked at his brother and then looked at the road ahead. "No, I would not."

Once at the top of the hill, the semis parted company and Lucas stormed past them both. He stayed in the passing lane, leveling off at seventy-five. He did some more elbow driving while he put on his sunglasses and then leaned back, stretched his arms and sighed.

"That's better. Watch for state boys."

Grinder searched the radio dial but gave up when they lost the signal from Toronto. They made a quick pit stop at the last rest area on the PA stretch of 79 and soon they saw the sign for the great state of New York. Lucas maneuvered through traffic to get to the best EZ Pass lane and scooted through, barely lifting his foot off the gas.

"Tell me, has the world ever seen a better invention than EZ Pass?"

"I'm thinking."

"Seriously."

"Still thinking."

"C'mon."

"Okay, okay, no, the world has not."

The vineyards were thinning out, giving way to small towns and open fields. Then high tension power lines, like mammoth tinmen, their arms bent low, started to gather along the road's right-of-way. Grinder reached for the cooler and pulled out a Sierra Mist and handed it to his brother. Then he took a Raspberry Snapple for himself. Both men took sips and then placed their bottles in the arm rest between them. They were quiet for a time as Paul continued his tribute to pirate slang. "Hornswoggle, booty, booty, booty-swoggle!" Lucas and Grinder looked at each other, shook their heads and laughed.

Lucas licked his lips and raised his eyebrows. His face was in a tangle about what to say next.

"So…"

Grinder shook his head, acknowledging his brother, waiting for him to continue, but he didn't.

"So, what?"

"So, you know, so…everything." Lucas gave a clarifying shrug. Grinder imitated him.

"Whadaya mean?"

"Whadaya mean, whadaya mean? Ma, Pop, the whole schmear."

"Batten down the hatches!"

"See, even Paul knows what I mean."

Grinder turned and wagged his finger at Paul jokingly. He leaned back in his seat for a moment and then tried the radio again. Finding nothing, he turned it off and adjusted his window down a few inches and then up a few inches. He cleared his throat and looked at the passing road signs.

"What the hell? We just went through a whole big thing and I wanna know how you're doing. I'm your brother."

"I'm thinking, that's all. I mean, I haven't taken it all in quite yet. It's like, 'Did this happen?' you know what I mean? I never thought we'd see Pop again and there he was, like nobody I remembered at all."

"Yeah, well, he was definitely not the Pop I remember either. But ain't that a good thing?"

"Yeah, I guess it is, but it's hard to figure. I mean, I hated his guts for so long it just became a normal way of feeling. And then he comes along, this goofy, kinda crazy, but thoughtful guy trying to fix things after all these years. Well, I don't know, it's hard."

"Gonna go to Florida to see him? He invited us, you know."

"Maybe. I don't know. What about you?"

"Same. I need a big dose of normal before I take Pop on again. But you never know."

"True."

"Yo ho ho; yo ho ho; yo ho ho!"

"Yeah, buddy, yo ho ho to you too." Grinder was on his knees again reaching for Paul. "Whadaya say I let him out. He's restless."

"Good idea. I'll open all the windows."

"Aye, matey, ram your midships stem from stern, eeeeeeeeeee-aw."

"Jesus criminy, how did Ma stand it?"

Grinder struck a serious pose, his eyes furrowed. "Hey, don't forget. She dumped you after fifteen years. She stayed with Paul for over twenty. Just sayin'."

"She could only stand you for eleven. Boom."

They stared at the statues of buffaloes along the interchange at 190. The traffic was thick and slow. It began to rain, bringing everything to a crawl.

"My God. Buffalo has the worst weather in the western hemisphere, so why does everyone forget how to drive as soon as something falls from the sky."

When Grinder didn't reply, Lucas nudged him. "Hey, you still with me?"

"Yeah."

Lucas looked at him several more times as the traffic began to move. He wanted to say something, but he wasn't sure what. He blew his nose again to clear his mind.

"So, do you think you understand her better?"

"Ma?"

"Yeah, like why she left and all?"

"Not so much."

"Me neither."

Grinder pushed the button and his window came the whole way down. He stuck his arm out like it was the wing of a plane and let the wind play with it. After a minute or so, he pulled his arm back and then closed the window.

"Here's the thing. I don't know why Ma did what she did, but I don't care quite as much now. I mean, I care, don't get me wrong, it still hurts and part of me is pissed to beat the band, but going down there and meeting people who knew her, and, like, loved her, and seeing Pop and getting Paul, it made Ma seem more like a real person instead of a bad memory."

Lucas kept his eyes forward but his eyebrows were saying, "I'm listening."

"I guess it doesn't change things, I mean it doesn't change what happened and all. But I feel different. It's like everything is finally okay even though mostly things are still the same." Grinder stole a glance at his brother, who said nothing. "Anyway. It made me want to do something for her 'cause I'm guessing it was a hard life, a messed up life after she left us. Not all the time, but way down inside her somewhere, something was probably never right again. I mean, what was with that picture of us? She packed it when she left and she kept it on the shelf for the rest of her life. When she died, it was still there; I mean we were still there, the two of us." Grinder turned his head and stared at his brother's ear, his eyes half-mast with exhaustion from trying to figure the whole thing out. "Why she didn't do something about it, I don't know, but I gotta believe it ate her up inside. Had to. She was our mother for chrissakes."

Lucas turned, his face like a full moon. "And that's it? I mean, that's enough?"

"Enough? Hell, no. But that's what we got. I mean it's not like we can super-size the whole thing about Ma so we get a bigger helping of her. It doesn't work that way. We got the portion that was given to us. We can piss and moan about it, or we can say, 'Ma was the Ma we got; Take it or leave it.' I guess I'm taking it."

Lucas opened his hands, wiggled his fingers and relaxed his grip on the steering wheel.

Both men ducked to watch a jet liner screaming toward a runway at the Buffalo airport. Lights were blinking and they could almost make out the faces in the windows. A trucker leaned on his horn, encouraging Lucas to return to his own goddam lane. The brothers were quiet for another ten miles or so until the traffic got untangled again and they could breathe more easily.

Lucas shifted in his seat, trying unsuccessfully to rearrange his weight and lighten the load on his sciatic. Despite the discomfort, his face got all puppy-doggish when he spoke again to Grinder.

"You know, you did a good thing."

"What was that?"

"Back there. The whole tombstone thing, it was a good thing. I'm not sure I would have blown my whole wad like you did, but still." Lucas shrugged approvingly.

"Thanks." Grinder took a twenty out of his wallet and waved it at his brother. "I know you always worry about my finances."

"Wow, now you're set for, like, the rest of the day."

"Skuttle me skippers, scuttle me skippers." Paul was bobbing and weaving in his cage. He flapped his wings and puffed his chest. He threw himself against the cage and tipped it onto its side. "Man overboard, man overboard, oooooo-oowwww." Grinder turned around and righted the cage.

"There you go, buddy." Grinder opened the bag of nuts that was on the floor and dumped some in the cage.

"Thank you, mister Grinder, sir."

"Where the hell did he learn that?"

"Me." Grinder grinned from ear to ear. "Look at him." Lucas tilted the rearview mirror. "He's getting his feathers back. His eyes look sharper."

"Still the same old dead stare as far as I can tell."

"He's active; he's happy."

"If you say so. He's all yours. And they live, like, forever."

"I will leave him to you in my will."

"Hoist the mizzen mast, hoist the mizzen mast."

"Arr, Captain Paul."

"My God."

Grinder took a peanut and tossed it at his brother's head. Lucas didn't move so Grinder tossed another and then another.

"And you are doing this why?"

"Because it makes me happy."

Grinder picked up his Snapple and held it high, waiting for Lucas, who then lifted his Sierra Mist from its holder and clinked his brother's bottle.

"There you go." Grinder chugged, while Lucas struggled to put his bottle back in the holder while slowly drifting out of his lane again.

"A little help here, a little help here." Grinder took the Sierra Mist from his brother's hand as a Dodge Caravan, brim full with family and luggage, careened past them, one pigtailed girl so close that Lucas could have reached out and scratched the tip of her nose. "Okay, no more toasts, no more yo ho ho-ing, nothing. Please."

Paul whistled long and loud and then rattled his cage until it almost fell over again.

"You know, when that tombstone comes in, I hope you're not planning on us taking another road trip, 'cause I ain't going anywhere with you and Captain Walnut Brain back there." He gave his brother a fierce look but when Grinder didn't flinch, Lucas's face turned puzzly. "I'll give you some motel money, if you need it. But that's about it."

"Thank you for your generous offer, but I won't be needing your charity."

"Whadaya mean you won't be needing my charity."

"Just what I said—I won't be needing—"

"I heard you the first time." Lucas was pointing at his brother. He shook his finger, then stopped, lowered his hand and squinted at Grinder like someone might squint at a Christmas tree to see if the lights were distributed just so. "I don't know for sure, but I think the twenty in your pocket is about all the money you got in the world. How you gonna go back to Pittsburgh on that?"

Grinder struck a Cheshire pose. "I got it all figured out. Don't you worry."

"What, you gonna sleep in your car in an alley somewhere."

"No, I'm not gonna sleep in my car in an—"

"What's up then?"

Grinder looked out the window, then down at his lap and finally at his brother again.

"I got a place to stay. For as long as I need to."

He didn't look at Lucas, but kept his eyes on the road like it was the most fascinating thing he'd ever seen. Lucas's face was all scrunchy with consternation as he tried to size up his brother while glancing furtively at the road. Then his mouth flopped open and his head started shaking. He reached over and jabbed Grinder in the arm.

"Ouch, what the hell…"

"I know." He was still shaking like a bobble head doll.

"You know what?"

"I know, I know, I know. That's what."

"What are you talking—"

"It's Grace, isn't it?"

Grinder's eyes were on the road, but his face was lit up and his ears were bright red. Lucas grabbed him by the shirt sleeve and shook him silly.

"Goddammit, this is good news! I mean, this is the best news!"

"Wait a minute, c'mon. Don't get all—"

"It's an effing miracle, that's what it is, a damn effing miracle."

"Hold on. Why is it such a miracle that a woman would like me a little?"

"I think that's the answer; the part where you said a woman would like you, that's the miracle part."

Lucas was all over the road, his horn blaring, motorists slowing down beside him to make sure he could see them giving him the finger. But it didn't matter.

"You have found a hole to put your octagon in!"

Grinder put his face in his hands. "Oh my God."

"You know what I mean. A fit. You fit somewhere."

Grinder's shoulder went limp as Lucas shook him back and forth some more.

"That is my boy, I'm telling you. This is a damn good thing." He snatched Grinder's ear and yanked. "It is."

They fell silent from the weariness of being so happy. The road was straight and the traffic was light. Lucas settled into the passing lane with clear sailing ahead. Grinder took two Hostess cupcakes from the cooler, opened one for his brother and balanced it on the dashboard in front of him. He ogled the other one for a minute, then demolished half of it in one bite. He smiled at Lucas, his teeth grimy with chocolate.

"She sure is a lucky woman," said Lucas.

Grinder washed it down with some Snapple and then popped the rest into his mouth.

Lucas turned sheepishly to his brother. "Hey, before I forget, I got you something." He pointed at the glove box. "It's in there."

Grinder opened it and took out a six-pack of white sweat socks.

"Probably a little too late for gym class, but it was the best I could do."

"Wow." Grinder rolled the bag back and forth in his hands, not quite ready to look at his brother. He took his shoes and socks off, tore open the bag and slipped on a pair. He wiggled his toes and grinned. "They fit perfect."

"Yeah, well, one size fits all."

Grinder tilted his head toward Lucas and nodded his appreciation. Lucas nodded in return then took the tissue off the dashboard and wiped his nose. Both brothers cleared their throats. Then Grinder spoke:

"I'm telling you, I don't think I've ever had a brother as good as you."

"Really."

"You know what I mean."

"Yes, I do."

View other Black Rose Writing titles at www.blackrosewriting.com/books and use promo code **PRINT** to receive a **20% discount** when purchasing.

BLACK ROSE
writing™

Made in the USA
Las Vegas, NV
22 March 2022

46133213R00114